A FROZEN HEART

A FROZEN HEART

ELIZABETH RUDNICK

DISNEY PRESS
Los Angeles • New York

To Dad, for teaching me to dream big and always believing in me. And to Caleb, for showing me that some people really are worth melting for.

—E.R.

Printed in the United States of America
First Hardcover Edition, October 2015
1 3 5 7 9 10 8 6 4 2
FAC-020093-15233
ISBN 978-1-4847-3051-5
Library of Congress Control Number: 2015939970

Visit disneybooks.com

SUSTAINABLE FORESTRY INITIATIVE Certified Sourcing
www.sfiprogram.org
SFI-00993

THIS LABEL APPLIES TO TEXT STOCK

Love conquers all.

—Virgil

PROLOGUE

"FIVE!" PRINCESS ELSA SHOUTED, her cheerful voice bouncing off the castle walls. "Four! Three! Two! ONE! Ready or not, here I come!" Uncovering her eyes, she brushed a long strand of blond hair behind her ear and scanned the large ballroom for her sister. "Anna! Are you in here? I know you're here somewhere!"

From behind a large stone pillar, Princess Anna watched as her big sister began tiptoeing around the ballroom. A giggle threatened to escape, and she slapped a hand over her mouth. She couldn't laugh. Not this time! That was how Elsa always found her. Playing with her big sister made her happy. And when Anna was happy, she giggled. *A lot.* But she was determined that today, *she* was going to win the game of hide-and-seek. Forcing the giggle back, Anna distracted herself by watching as the late-afternoon light streamed through the huge stained glass windows, casting wonderful warm shadows over the whole room. She smiled as she watched rays of sunshine dance over the floor, like the couples she saw swaying to music at her parents' royal balls.

Distracted, Anna began to hum softly. At five years old, she didn't get to attend the balls or other official occasions that took place in the palace. But that didn't stop her from sneaking out of her room to watch from the balcony as women in brightly colored gowns entered the room with men in handsome suits. Anna loved the moment right before the music began, when the room grew silent and the men bowed and the women curtsied. Anything could happen. Any song might play. Any dance might begin. It was like the beginning of a brand-new adventure.

But when she had said that to Elsa, her big sister had looked down at her and shaken her head. "An adventure? It's a nice idea, but it doesn't work that way. Every dance is planned out before the party, every song played at exactly the right moment," Elsa had said.

Despite her sister's practical view on balls, Anna remained convinced that she was missing out on all the fun by not being there. She couldn't wait for the day when she and Elsa would be allowed to attend balls. All that noise and color and light. Even if her sister didn't think so, Anna knew that balls were places where amazing things happened. . . .

"GOTCHA!" Elsa shouted, grabbing Anna by the shoulders.

"AHH!" Anna screamed.

"I found you!" her sister shouted, clapping her hands together and then playfully tugging on one of Anna's pigtails. "I always find you."

Anna put her pudgy little hands on her hips and blew her bright copper bangs out of her eyes, trying to look upset. It lasted for all of a minute. Then she smiled.

"Wanna play again?" Anna asked hopefully.

"Sorry, Anna," Elsa said, leaning down and giving her tiny sister a hug. "I can't play again now. I have a lesson with Erlingur. But maybe later?"

Anna pouted and crossed her arms. She wanted to play *now*!

Elsa smiled. "If you let me go to my lesson now, I super sister promise, we can play later tonight. Maybe I'll even do something . . . special." With a wink, Elsa turned and headed out of the ballroom, her footsteps echoing until they finally faded away.

The frown disappeared from Anna's face. Something special? That could only mean one thing. Elsa was going to use her magic!

THE REST of the day seemed to drag by for Anna. At lunch she didn't even protest when Cook gave her *ärtsoppa*. Usually she hated the thick pea soup, but today she barely tasted it. During history with Erlingur, she barely noticed when he made her recite the names of all the Seven Isles. Normally she'd be excited to learn more about neighboring countries, but today all she could think about was playing with Elsa.

By bedtime, Anna was practically crawling out of her skin. She just needed everyone else in the castle to fall asleep, and then she and Elsa could play! Lying in her big canopied bed, Anna tried to slow her rapidly beating heart. No matter how many times she experienced it, she still couldn't quite believe that her sister was capable of something so cool—literally. Elsa, it turned out, had the power to make things freeze! She could make it snow with a flick of her fingers and turn water into ice with a wave of her hand. She could conjure up snowmen out of the thinnest air and make ice crystals dangle from the chandeliers.

Anna's parents knew about Elsa's magic, but Anna liked to pretend it was her and Elsa's secret. She loved sneaking off with her sister to play when the rest of the castle was asleep. Their magical adventures were such fun that Anna was ready for the next time before the last time was even finished!

And now, Anna thought as she lay in bed watching the clock tick painfully slowly, another adventure was about to start. Finally, she couldn't wait any longer.

"Elsa!" Anna whispered, jumping out of her bed and popping up beside her sister's bed. "*Psst!* Elsa!"

Her sister didn't even move. She had clearly forgotten her promise.

Anna jumped up on the bed and began to bounce up and down. "Wake up! Wake up! Wake up!" she chanted until Elsa finally groaned.

"Go back to sleep," Elsa said sleepily.

"I just can't," Anna said, lying down on her back so that all her weight was now on Elsa. "The sky's awake, so I'm awake. So we *have* to play."

"Go play by yourself," Elsa said, shoving her sister off the bed.

Anna landed with a thud on the floor. She let out a sigh. Elsa had promised! How could she have forgotten? And then Anna smiled to herself. She knew just how to make her sister get out of bed. "Do you wanna build a snowman?" she asked mischievously.

Instantly, Elsa's eyes popped open and she smiled.

Anna smiled back at her older sister. She hadn't forgotten after all. It was time to go play in the snow.

Moments later, the sisters were back in the ballroom. But now the entire space was filled with snow. Standing in the middle of it all, Elsa laughed as she waved her hands together. Snowflakes burst forth and danced between her palms as she magically created a snowball. Anna tilted her head back and opened her mouth to catch snowflakes on her tongue.

"This is amazing!" Anna shouted.

"Watch this!" Elsa said, stomping her slippered foot on the floor. Instantly, a layer of ice began to fan out around her, starting at her feet and quickly spreading. Soon the entire floor had become their very own private ice rink.

Anna clapped her hands in glee as she began to slip and slide around the rink. Her laughter bounced off the walls as she windmilled her arms to keep her balance. Across the room, Elsa began to slide across the icy surface, too, a broad smile on her face.

As they reached each other, Anna took Elsa's hand and tried to twirl in a circle. "Wheeee!" With a thud, Anna fell onto her bottom, laughing.

Elsa grinned at Anna. "Ready?" she asked. Raising her hands above her, Elsa wiggled her fingers. In front of Anna's eyes, snow began to form in the air, falling softly to the ground. Elsa rolled some of the snow into a giant ball.

Yes! Snowman time! Anna thought with delight as she began rolling a second ball to serve as the snowman's tummy. Five pieces of coal, a carrot, and two branch arms later, the sisters had finished their masterpiece.

Elsa quickly ran behind their creation.

"Hi," she said in a goofy voice, pretending to be the snowman. "I'm Olaf, and I like warm hugs."

Anna laughed. An Elsa snowman was almost as good as a real live one.

"I love you, Olaf," Anna said, giving the snowman a hug. Then she looked up at her sister, a gleam in her eye. "What else should we do?"

Elsa concentrated hard and reached out toward the ceiling of the ballroom. Anna watched with pure joy as her sister began to turn the entire ballroom into a winter wonderland. Long glittering icicles soon hung from the large chandelier, and Elsa turned the windows into works of art with intricate snowflake-shaped etchings. With every movement of her fingers, it seemed as though Elsa's powers—and her ability to take control of them—were getting stronger and stronger.

Running over to the base of an Elsa-created snowbank, Anna craned her neck to look upward. Then she glanced over her shoulder at Elsa. They had played this game before. Anna would run up the bank and jump, and Elsa would create another bank for her to land on.

Scrambling up the snowbank, Anna took a deep breath and jumped off the edge. "Catch me!" she cried. The forward momentum of her body propelled her until she hovered in midair. Then she began to fall. Just when she thought she was going to hit the ground, Elsa flung out her arms, creating another snowbank. Landing in the soft powder, Anna let out a laugh and then leaped again. Over and over she ran and jumped, and over and over, Elsa caught her. Anna's breath was coming fast in her chest and her little legs and arms ached from the effort, but she didn't want to stop.

"Again! Again!" she shouted.

"Slow down!" she heard Elsa call back.

But Anna didn't want to slow down. She wanted to fly! With another burst of speed, she raced to the edge of the largest snowbank yet and leaped.

Anna flew through the air, convinced that this was the best moment of her life so far. But then she looked down. Elsa was racing to catch up with her. Anna had only a moment to register the fact that Elsa had lost her footing and was falling down before she saw an icy stream of snow headed straight for her.

And then everything went black.

Anna's head hurt. A lot. She opened her eyes slowly, letting them adjust to the light. Anna was surprised to find herself lying in her bed. A thick quilt was tucked up to her chin, and a fire roared in the fireplace. Despite the warmth, Anna couldn't stop shivering. But it wasn't just the chill in her bones that was causing her to shake. It was the confusion. She had no idea how she had gotten back to her bed.

The last thing Anna remembered was sledding down a big hill with Elsa. She remembered the feeling of weightlessness as the sled hit a bump and hovered, suspended in the air, before heading back toward the ground. She remembered laughing and the feeling of her sister's arms around her waist. She remembered how safe Elsa's arms made her feel. And then . . . nothing.

Lifting a hand, Anna gingerly touched her head. A wave of pain flooded her body, momentarily replacing the chill with burning heat. The sled must have crashed. That would explain the bump that Anna felt under her probing fingertips and why she was resting in bed. *I bet Elsa is going to say "I told you so" when she gets up,* Anna thought. *She never likes going fast.*

Smiling ruefully, Anna called to her sister softly. "Elsa?" She waited for the rustle of sheets as her sister turned over. But there was no sound from across the room. "Elsa? Elsa, are you awake?" Still nothing. Glancing out their bedroom window, Anna saw that the moon was now sinking in the sky. The dark blue of night was giving way to the brighter colors of day. Elsa was probably just sleeping.

Gingerly, Anna sat up. Her eyes grew wide as a fresh wave of shivering overtook her small body. Elsa wasn't sleeping—she wasn't there! And she wasn't the only thing missing from their shared bedroom. All of Elsa's things—the dresser full of pretty clothes and shoes, the vanity, with its elegant mirror and matching stool, even Elsa's collection of toys—were gone. In their place was Anna's smaller furniture, rearranged to try to fit the empty spaces. It was as though her sister had never lived there at all.

Worried and confused, Anna pushed off the covers and struggled out of bed. She swayed on her feet for a moment as blood rushed to her head and made her dizzy. When the moment had passed, she pulled open her door and looked into the hall. All the candles were lit, their flames making shadow shapes on the wall. Grateful for the light, Anna took a deep breath and began to tiptoe down the hall. Passing by a series of large doors, she turned the corner that led to the East Wing of the castle. This was where her parents slept and where the larger bedrooms were found. The nursery, which Anna had always shared with her sister, was located between the East and West Wings—the perfect place to sleep when you were between a baby and a grown-up, her mother told her.

Standing in the East Wing now, Anna wanted nothing more than to put her hands on her hips, stomp her feet, and throw an adult-sized tantrum. *Where is Elsa?* she wanted to shout. *Why isn't she in our room, and why is all her stuff gone?* But before she could open her mouth, she saw the door to her parents' room open. A stream of light illuminated the ornate carpet in front of the room, the royal purples and golds bright against the surrounding shadows. A moment later, her mother and father appeared. To Anna's surprise, they were dressed in their riding clothes. Her mother's hair, which was usually styled and smooth, was coming loose from its bun, the wisps of brown catching the light and making it appear as though there were a halo over her head.

"Mama?" Anna said, racing forward. "Mama, where's Elsa? Why are all her things gone?"

The queen didn't respond right away, and Anna felt her chill deepen as she saw her parents exchange serious looks.

Suddenly, Anna's chill was replaced by fear as a new thought entered her mind. "Is . . . is Elsa . . . okay?" Anna asked. "I'm sorry we went sledding. I know we weren't supposed to, but I just love sledding, and I didn't know we were going that fast, and . . ." Her voice trailed off. She had been so focused on how strange it was that her sister was gone that she hadn't even thought about *why* she might be gone.

Kneeling down, Anna's mother gently touched her cheek. "Your sister is fine, dear heart. She's perfectly safe."

"Then why isn't she in our room?" Anna asked, her lower lip trembling. "Is she mad at me? Did I do something wrong?"

"No one did anything wrong," her mother insisted, although now she was looking at the king. Then she turned back to Anna. "It was just time for Elsa to move out of the nursery. She needs her own room now that she's older. Aren't you excited to have the nursery all to yourself?"

Anna shook her head violently. "No! No! NO! I am NOT excited. I want Elsa to come back. Can't she come back? I promise I'll be good. I'll never go sledding again. I don't even need my own dresser if that would help. I just want Elsa back!" As she spoke, her voice got higher and higher and the words came faster and faster. None of this made sense. Why would Elsa move out so suddenly? Unless . . . Another thought popped into her mind.

"Does Elsa not like me anymore?" she asked in a tiny voice. Looking up at her mother through teary eyes, she waited.

There was a long pause, during which Anna's mother and father seemed to carry on a silent conversation over Anna's head. With each passing moment, Anna felt her heart sinking deeper and deeper. She was just about to collapse with sadness when her mother finally spoke.

"Your sister loves you very much, Anna. I promise you," the queen said. "This is just what needs to be done. You must trust me that this is the right thing to do. Someday you'll understand. Now, you should go back to bed. You need your rest."

"But—"

"Bed, Anna," the king said.

Sighing, Anna turned to go. "Please, Anna. Trust us," her mother said behind her.

But as Anna made her way back to her room, she felt anything but trustful. It was as if a piece of herself had been taken away, and her parents' only words of comfort were that she would understand "someday." Anna wanted to understand *now*. If she could just talk to Elsa . . .

Just then, she heard a thud. Looking up, she saw two men carrying Elsa's armoire into the empty bedroom down the hall. Rushing forward, she saw that all the missing furniture from the nursery was, in fact, now in this room. And standing there, in the middle of the big space, was Elsa herself.

"Elsa!" Anna called out hopefully. She took a few steps into the room. "Elsa, why are you in here? Come back to our room! I know Mama and Papa said it's . . ." Her voice trailed off as she caught sight of her sister's expression. It was cold as ice.

"Go to your room, Anna," Elsa said, frowning. "You can't be here."

"But . . ."

"I mean it!" Elsa shouted, her voice cracking. "Go away!" Walking forward, Elsa reached to push Anna out of the room. But just before she touched Anna's trembling shoulder, Elsa recoiled as though she had just remembered something terrible. That hurt Anna more than any of Elsa's words had.

Anna walked slowly into the hallway. As she turned back for one last glimpse at Elsa, her sister slammed the door.

Anna stared at the closed door for several long, sad moments. What had just happened? Why was Elsa suddenly being so cold to her? Why was she leaving the nursery? Sadly, Anna turned and walked back to their—her—bedroom. She had a feeling in the pit of her stomach that something had gone terribly wrong. She just didn't know what. She could only hope that Elsa would warm up and talk to her again . . . soon.

Ten years later

CHAPTER 1

"ELSA? ELSA, I know you're in there. I'm heading to the stables. Do you want to come?" Fifteen-year-old princess Anna stared at the door to her sister's room and waited. She knew it was useless. If Elsa even responded, which happened about once in never, the answer would be no. The answer was *always* no. Why did Anna think that Elsa would suddenly decide to break ten years' worth of silence?

"Elsa?" she called again.

Nothing.

Gently, Anna placed her hand on the door, as though she might feel Elsa's presence that way. Then she pulled it back angrily. What was the point? She had been in this spot countless times. Ever since that night all those years ago when Elsa had slammed the door in her face, it had been just one long series of closed doors and disappointments. Letting out a sigh, she turned and headed back toward her room to put on her riding clothes.

Anna pushed open her own door, kicking aside the stray pieces of clothing that littered her bedroom floor and making her way over to her vanity. Sitting down, Anna began to pull her hair into a loose bun. As she worked, she softly touched the streak of white hair that framed her face. Then she gave it a hard yank. She had lost count of how many times she had sat in this very spot, staring at the white hair. She had had the streak for as long as she could remember, but it always felt out of place, like it wasn't supposed to be there. But trying to figure out why the hair felt so strange was as futile as wishing Elsa would open the door and talk to her.

Anna pulled on the streak again, this time ruining her hastily made bun. She sighed and blew the loose strands of hair out of her eyes. *Well, that won't do,* Anna thought. Even if there wasn't exactly anyone to dress up for, Anna still liked looking her best. It gave her something to do, at least.

Anna glanced out her window, where she could just make out the edge of one of the palace's giant gates. It was closed, as always.

The morning after the sledding accident, Anna had awoken to find the castle much quieter than usual. She hadn't heard the laughter of the maids as they scurried between rooms, dusting the shelves and lighting fires in the many hearths. When she had ventured out of her room, she hadn't heard the clanging of pots from the kitchen as Cook prepared the morning meal for the royal family and the rest of the household. Nor had she heard Kai, the royal handler, issuing his daily instructions to the chamberlain to ensure proper care of the Great Hall. Gerda's voice was oddly absent as well. Anna couldn't hear her instructing the castle staff in what clothes needed to be mended or set out for later.

The whole place had felt abandoned. And, for all intents and purposes, it had been. Her parents had closed the gates to the castle. Almost the entire staff had been dismissed, and any contact with the outside world had been forbidden. And Anna had no idea why. Ten years later, she *still* had no idea why.

Looking at her reflection, Anna gave her white hair one last tug. "Well, at least it's not like I wanted to see the world or anything," she joked, trying to cheer herself up.

Lately, Anna had found herself thinking more and more about life before the gates had been closed. Her memories of that time had started to fade at the edges. Moments were beginning to blur together, and sometimes she couldn't remember if something had actually happened or if she had just made it up during one of her long, lonely playtimes. Glancing over at her bedside table, she smiled ruefully at the sight of a well-worn book.

The book had become her saving grace. It had been a gift from a girl named Rani. The daughter of a dignitary, Rani had met Anna a few months before everything changed. Rani had told her all about her home country—with its large sandy beaches and trees that had big round fruits hanging from their branches. "They get so heavy that when they fall, they make the loudest noise," Rani had told Anna. "And they are hard as rocks, but when you cut them open, they are so sweet. Someday you will have to visit me, and I'll give you the freshest coconut."

"Perhaps Mama and Papa will let me go next year!" Anna had said at the time. But she had never gotten the chance. And she had never seen Rani again. The book, which told a hundred short stories of adventures in Rani's homeland, had arrived along with an invitation to visit just days before the gates had closed. The book had stayed. And so, sadly, had Anna.

Enough! Anna thought, chastising herself. She would have loved nothing more than to get a glimpse of the lands outside the castle, but she knew that wasn't going to happen. There was no point in wishing the morning away. Standing up, she dug her cloak out of a pile of clothes and grabbed the book from her bedside table. It was a beautiful day outside. Even though she wasn't allowed to go beyond the castle gates, there was nothing stopping her from taking Kjekk out of his stall to graze. The horse, at least, never ignored her.

"Maybe I'll see if Mother wants to go with me," she said to herself as she walked out the door. "And then I'll go see if Cook has been baking. A little bit of chocolate will definitely make me feel a lot better."

"Mother?" Anna poked her head into her mother's drawing room. "Mother? Are you in here?"

Walking into the room, Anna glanced around. *Strange,* she thought. Usually her mother spent the early afternoon here, catching up on correspondence or meeting with Gerda to go over the daily list of chores. It was a beautiful room. Floor-to-ceiling windows dominated the far wall, making the space brighter than the rest of the palace no matter the type of day. On especially nice days, such as this one, the room felt warmer, too. A large settee was placed against the windows. Anna often curled up on it as she listened to her mother go about her business. Everything about the space reflected the queen's classic and simple tastes. The walls were covered in ivory wallpaper, the furniture covered in tasteful fabrics of the palest golds and purples. Anna loved it. She loved that as soon as she walked into the room, she felt her mother's warm presence and smelled the faintest hint of her perfume.

But today, her mother was not there.

Popping back into the hall, she spotted Gerda coming out of the king and queen's bedroom. "Gerda," Anna called out. The maid turned, her eyes wide. Anna smiled apologetically. "Sorry to startle you! I was just wondering if you had seen my mother. I was hoping to go riding with her this afternoon."

Gerda shifted nervously on her feet. "She and the king are with your sister, Your Highness," she finally said. "In the solarium. They told me not to disturb them." Then, before Anna could even thank her, Gerda darted away like a rabbit fleeing a fox.

Anna cocked her head. *Interesting.* Running away wasn't like Gerda. And what were her parents doing in the solarium on a day like today—with Elsa? The glass-enclosed porch was stifling in the summer. They usually only used it in the early spring and fall, when the heat was actually a welcome relief. *Well, I won't get any answers standing here with my mouth open like a fish,* Anna thought. Turning, she walked down the hall in the direction of the solarium.

But when she arrived at her destination, she knew immediately that she had been wrong about getting answers. The door to the room was shut. Behind it, Anna could hear muffled voices. She paused, unsure what to do. The solarium door was almost never shut. What could they be doing inside? Curiosity getting the best of her, Anna pushed the door open.

Immediately, she wished she hadn't.

Her father was standing in front of Elsa, his arms crossed. "Try again, Elsa," he said, his usually calm tone laced with frustration. "You *need* to figure this out."

Elsa looked at the ground. Wisps of white-blond hair fell around her face. When she finally glanced back up, Anna was surprised to see tears sliding down her sister's rosy cheeks. "I can't," she said. "Don't you think I would if I could?"

"Be careful. Crying only makes it worse," the king said, the restraint evident in his voice. Anna recognized that tone from times when he and her mother were discussing problems in the kingdom. Something was wrong, and he wasn't sure how to fix it.

Anna took a step back nervously. This was obviously a private moment.

"Agnarr, please." The queen's voice was soothing as she reached out a hand and placed it gently on her husband's arm. "Elsa is exhausted. Let her go. We can try again when we come back."

Elsa shook her head. "I know I failed you. I'll try and do better. I promise. I just . . . I just . . . I don't . . ." She didn't finish. A sob threatened to burst from her chest, but Elsa swallowed it down. She dried her eyes and walked quickly toward the door. Elsa brushed past Anna, barely even giving her sister a glance before bolting into the hallway and disappearing.

From the shadows, Anna watched her parents. She had never seen them so quiet . . . and so sad.

"I just wish we could help her more," Anna heard her mother say softly. "I wish she wouldn't push us away. So many times, Agnarr, I've wanted to hold her in my arms and tell her it will be okay, and so many times, she's just . . . she thinks she needs to handle this on her own."

Anna was beginning to think she should find her mother another time. Something was going on, and she didn't know quite what. Turning, she began to tiptoe toward the hallway. But the floor creaked under her feet. Whipping around, her mother spotted her.

"Oh, darling!" she said. "I didn't see you. Have you been there long?"

"Um, no?" she answered, approaching her parents. "Just got here a moment ago. Is everything . . . all right?"

"Of course, Anna. Of course," her mother said. "Isn't that right, Agnarr? Everything is just fine."

The king, who had been staring after Elsa with a perplexed look on his face, finally looked up. Seeing Anna, he smiled. "Your mother is right, my little one. We were just telling Elsa what she needs to get done while we are away. Nothing to worry about. Thank goodness I have your mother here to remind me to keep my temper."

"But you never lose your temper," Anna pointed out. "Never. Even when I spilled hot chocolate on your white suit, remember? You didn't get upset at all! And when I was four and tripped and fell into your friend, the Dignitary of Somewhere, and he sprained his wrist? You told him not to be mad, that was just my way of saying hello."

Her father laughed and reached out a hand, patting her head. "I guess I'm getting crankier in my old age," he said playfully. "Next thing you know, I'll be talking to myself and yelling at pictures."

Anna smiled, some of the tension in her shoulders disappearing as her father's normal attitude returned. "I'll make sure you don't do anything that silly," she reassured him. "You know, I *could* go with you on your trip next week. Just to make sure you behave." She clasped her palms together and raised them up. "Please?"

"Darling, you know we can't take you with us," her mother said gently. "We would love to. But you need to stay here with your sister."

"Why?" Anna said. "It's not like she's going to talk to me while you're away."

"You must be patient with Elsa," her mother said. "She's going through a difficult time."

Anna rolled her eyes. "If 'difficult time' means wanting nothing to do with me, then I see your point."

Her parents exchanged looks that were hard to read. Then, each putting an arm around Anna, they gave her a squeeze. Anna sank into their embrace. Seeing Elsa had rattled her, and hearing that her mother felt isolated from her, too, made Anna feel even stranger.

"I love you very much, Anna," her mother said, placing a gentle kiss on her head. "I will always love you. And so will Elsa. In her own way."

Anna's father pinched her cheek. "Why don't we plan on doing something special when we get back? All of us, even Elsa. As soon as she starts feeling better."

Anna pulled back. "Really?" she said, clapping her hands together. "That would be amazing!"

"Well, we will talk about it when we return," the king said, squeezing her arm. "Now, I should go meet with Kai and see how preparations are going. I'll leave you lovely ladies to enjoy the day." Leaning over, he kissed his wife gently on the lips. "I'll miss you till I see you next," he said. Then, turning, he left the room.

Anna watched her mother watching him go. The earlier tension in her eyes was gone, and now they were full of love and warmth. "Someday I want to love someone as much as you love Papa," Anna said after a moment.

"I want that for you, too, Anna," her mother said, turning and smiling down at her. "Whoever you love will be so very lucky. Just like I'm so lucky that you love me. Now," she said, changing the subject, "what do you say about grabbing some cookies from the kitchen? I could really use a little something sweet."

Anna nodded eagerly, the idea of a ride forgotten for now. Her mother rarely indulged in treats, and Anna wasn't going to miss the opportunity. She only had a few more days before they left. She would take any time with her mother that she could get. Smiling, she grabbed her mother's hand and began dragging her toward the door. "Let's go!" she said. "I'm pretty sure Cook was baking macaroons today. . . ."

CHAPTER 2

THE SOUTHERN ISLES were not known for being a bastion of quiet. The seven islands that made up the kingdom were, after all, located in the middle of a large expanse of sea. There were no mountains to hold back the howling winds and no sandy beaches to muffle the roaring surf. All the islands but one, where the king and his family made their home, were rocky. And at almost any point in the day, on almost any point of the islands, the air carried with it the strong odor of salt.

The crown jewel of the Southern Isles was, of course, the king's palace. When people who had never been to the Southern Isles first saw the long, low walls stretching across the horizon, they often mistook it for a sea monster. The palace was made from the gleaming black rock that was found only in the Southern Isles. The only breaks in the stony outer walls were four large windows on the northern side, facing the kingdom's nearest neighbor. This made the palace nearly impregnable, but the result was a building that did, in fact, look like a serpent. The people who had been born and raised in the kingdom loved the castle and found it beautiful. They thought there was something empowering about the fact that it had managed to survive—even flourish—in such an inhospitable environment.

But to Prince Hans, the youngest son of the king of the Southern Isles, the castle was ugly. Ugly and awful. He hated it as much as he hated every inch of every island. To him, it did not matter that the sea provided the freshest harvests of fish or that the hard island rock fetched high prices when carved into statues. To him, it didn't matter that his father was, as a result of all this, wealthy beyond imagination. To him, the Southern Isles—and its castle—were a prison, and his father the jailer.

For the past twenty minutes, Hans had been standing outside the door to the castle's Great Hall, unwilling to make his entrance quite yet. The wind had stilled a bit as day turned to night. Usually, nothing could be heard over the whipping wind, and Hans was surprised at how clearly he could now make out the sounds coming from the other side of the door. He could hear his father's voice most clearly. It was impossible not to. The big man's voice was deep, his sentences clipped. The king did not waste words. "To the point, Hans. Always just get to the point," he would say whenever he deemed Hans had stayed too long in his presence.

Beneath his father's boom, Hans could hear the voices of his twelve older brothers. That sound was as familiar to him as the wind in the air or the smell of the salt. And often just as annoying. He had never known life without them. Every memory he had involved one or more of them.

And not many of them were good memories.

Hans took a deep breath. While he would have liked nothing more than to turn and walk away, he knew he had to at least make an appearance. His father had requested his presence, and when the king made a request, you did whatever was asked. In this particular case, that meant attending the last in a long line of dinners being held in honor of his mother's birthday. *I'll just go in, say hello to Father, and give my love to Mother, again, and then I'll be on my way,* Hans thought. *Five minutes, no more. How bad can five minutes be?*

He shuddered. With his brothers, five minutes could be very, *very* bad.

Taking a deep breath, Hans pushed open the door and stepped into the Great Hall. The room was lit by a thousand candles, their flames making the room smoky and the air hard to breathe. At the front of the room his father sat talking to his eldest brother, Caleb. The two men were engrossed in each other, blatantly ignoring the women at their sides. The queen, Hans's mother, didn't seem bothered by it. She was, after all, used to it after nearly thirty years of marriage. She stared out over the room with glazed eyes as one hand stroked the large jewel hanging on her neck and the other held tightly to the stem of her wineglass. Seeing her son, she gave him a weak smile.

Hans returned the smile before turning his attention to Caleb's wife. Unlike the queen, whose tranquility was impressive, the princess could not sit still. Almost nine months pregnant with her second child, she fidgeted in her seat, glancing over at Caleb and then out at the tables before returning her gaze to Caleb. Her hands were in constant motion as well—resting on her belly for a moment before reaching for her wineglass and then thinking better of it. She looked painfully uncomfortable, and for one brief moment, Hans felt sorry for her.

She's as out of place here as I am, he thought. *She might as well be wallpaper the way Caleb is ignoring her.*

Well, at least Father is kind to her, Hans acknowledged, some of his sympathy fading. The woman was carrying the king's future grandchild and would be treated accordingly.

Just then, his father looked up from his conversation. His eyes landed on Hans, betraying no emotion. "Nice of you to join us," he said. In the silence that followed, Hans could feel twelve pairs of eyes on him as his brothers finally took notice of him. "Did you not think your mother's birthday worthy of your presence?"

"I'm sorry, Father," Hans said. Silently he added, *But I don't seem to be missing much of a "celebration."* From what he could see, no one was even talking to his mother. This party was just for the sake of keeping up appearances. Politics. It was always politics with his father.

"It is not me you should be apologizing to," the king said. "You should apologize to your mother. She is, after all, the only one who would have even noticed you were missing."

Hans's face flushed red as the truth of the words hit home. He could hear a few of his brothers chuckle under their breath. Mumbling another apology, Hans quickly turned and made his way to a table at the back of the room. On his dais, the king turned his attention from Hans back to Caleb.

How quickly I'm forgotten, Hans thought, watching the animated way his father talked to the eldest son. Hans wondered if Caleb even appreciated their father's attention. He was probably so used to it that he couldn't even imagine what Hans's life was like. Hans, on the other hand, constantly imagined what it would be like to be Caleb. . . .

The daydream never changed. He was his father's only son. His father adored him, and the two spent hours together. They would go hunting, Hans astride a giant chestnut stallion given to him on his fifteenth birthday. Beside him, his father would call out constant encouragement, and when they slew a wild boar, the king would boast at the feast to follow that only a son as grand and strong as Hans could have taken down such a powerful foe.

When they weren't hunting, Hans would sit at his father's side as the king discussed political turmoil or made plans to invade enemy territory. "Hans," his father would say, "what would you do about the situation? I value your opinion above all." And Hans would answer him eloquently and with forethought, his words booming across the room and encouraging all those who listened. "You are so wise, Hans," his father would say. "What a lucky king I am to have such a perfect heir to the throne."

His daydream would usually end with his father bequeathing

the kingdom to him. "It is time, my son," the king would say. "While you are still just a young man, I know you are ready to take my place as rightful king of the Southern Isles. I am so proud of you, my boy. So very, very proud . . ."

It was always at that moment that Hans would shake his head and the daydream would fade. He knew he was only fooling himself. No matter how many nights he spent watching the sun set over the Southern Isles, the kingdom would never be his. After all, he was the thirteenth son of thirteen sons. He was worthless. A spare. He wasn't even a spare at this point. He was a throwaway. There was no scenario, no chance, no moment that would ever result in his being needed.

As if on cue, he felt a sharp pang as something hit him square on the back of his head. Whipping around, he saw the twins—Rudi and Runo—standing behind him, laughing. Twins only in the sense they had shared the womb and had the same evil sensibilities, they were as physically different as night and day. Rudi was of average height, with reddish hair similar to Hans's. Runo was freakishly tall, with freakishly blond hair that stuck straight up. His pale eyes and paler eyebrows made him look perpetually shocked.

"What's the matter, little brother?" Rudi asked, his tone cruel and just loud enough for their father to hear. Up on the dais, the king turned and looked over at his sons.

"Did you get a boo-boo?" Runo teased cruelly. "Do you need to run to Mommy and have her kiss it and make it all better?"

Hans clenched his fists, the temptation to retort strong. But after a lifetime of being the butt of endless taunting and teasing, he knew it was useless to fight—with words or fists. "I'm fine," he said softly.

"What's that?" Rudi asked, holding up a hand to his ear. "We can't hear you. You really should learn how to speak up. Father abhors mice, don't you, Father?" He looked up at the king for approval.

"The Westergaards are lions, not mice," the king said, nodding. "Hans, you should listen to your brothers. Maybe you could learn a thing or two from them if you stopped acting like you were better than them."

Like sharks smelling blood in the water, a few more of Hans's brothers began to join in the teasing. After each well-placed jab, they would look to their father, eager to gain his approval even at the expense of their youngest brother.

Hans sat silently, his eyes on the table. He noticed the way the wood was worn away in places, smooth to the touch, while in others it was jagged, as though the tree had just been pulled from the ground. He ran his finger over the splinters, grimacing as they caught on his skin but finding the pain oddly pleasant. Physical pain he could handle.

Suddenly, Hans pushed himself to his feet and began to walk toward the door. He didn't care if his father would be mad later. It wasn't worth the torment to sit through any more of this assault. As he passed his twin brothers, he nodded politely but said nothing. Behind him, the twins muttered a few more insults but didn't bother to follow him.

Stepping into the hall, he let out a deep breath. *That could have gone a lot worse,* he thought. At least they had thrown bread, not glassware, this time. Turning, he made his way out of the castle and toward the sea. The dock was one of the farthest points from the Westergaard castle, which was part of its appeal for Hans. His brothers usually couldn't be bothered to walk all the way down there just to tease him, so it gave him the chance for the peace and quiet he craved. It also gave him time to think—something most of his brothers frankly couldn't care less about. All they cared about was their own reflections in the myriad of mirrors that lined the castle walls. It was well known that the Westergaard princes were—minus Runo—a rather handsome bunch. At least in that way, Hans was like his brothers. He was tall, with golden-red hair and big inquisitive eyes. When he had turned seventeen a few months before, he had begun to fill out. His shoulders were now broad and his arms strong from hours of practice with the sword—a prerequisite for a prince, even one who would most likely never see combat.

Over the past few months, it had been growing more and more clear to Hans that despite his intelligence, despite his good looks, and despite his appreciation for the finer things in life, he had become of no consequence to his father. Caleb had married a few years before, and his wife had given birth to their first son soon after, which took a great deal of pressure off the remaining sons to produce heirs. It hadn't stopped some of them, of course. All of Hans's brothers, except the twins, were now married with children. Even the twins were courting, though Hans could not fathom who could possibly like either of those brutish thugs. And while he had heard the royal affairs coordinator discussing potential suitors for his brothers, Hans had not heard a peep about a possible wife for him.

Hans shook his head, trying to rid himself of the negative thoughts that were invading his mind. He knew he was being maudlin for the sake of being maudlin. It wasn't as though he had woken up that morning to find out he was the youngest of thirteen sons, with a distant and careless father. That had been his life—always. And that would be his life—forever. Nothing was going to change that, and the sooner he came to grips with it, the better.

CHAPTER 3

THE KING AND QUEEN of Arendelle had been gone for nearly a week, and despite Anna's hopes, their absence had done nothing to make Elsa more social. If anything, her sister had grown even more reclusive. Elsa had all her meals delivered to her room and took her lessons with Kai privately. If Anna saw her at all, it was as a glimpse of a thin shadow slipping behind a door.

Luckily, Anna's mother had tasked Gerda with reorganizing the palace library while she was gone. Anna immediately volunteered to help—such a big project would help the days move by much more quickly. "I'm not so sure about Anna helping to organize something," the queen had told Gerda, winking at Anna. "You *have* seen her room, haven't you?"

Still, Anna reminded herself now as she made her way along the royal gallery, *I have three weeks to go.* "A lot can happen in three weeks, don't you think?" she asked, looking up at the portrait of her great-great-great-grandfather. He gazed back down at her, his expression stern. Anna smiled and nodded as though the portrait were speaking. "What's that? You lost all your hair in only three weeks?" She took a step back and peered up at the man. His bald head gleamed in the candlelight. "I think it makes you look very dignified, Great-Great-Great-Grandpappy."

Laughing to herself, Anna continued down the hall. The portraits on either side varied in size. Some were small, barely the size of the book Anna carried under her arm. Others were massive, at least twice her size in length and width. Pausing under one of her favorites, Anna looked to her left and then her right. Sure that no one was around, she unceremoniously and rather ungracefully plopped down on the floor. Spreading the skirt of her dress out so that it appeared she was floating in the middle of a pond of blue chiffon, she looked up at the large portrait in front of her.

On the canvas, a handsome man stood beside a beautiful woman. A delicate crown of flowers rested on the woman's head, and her arm was raised so that her fingertips ever so gently brushed the bright petals. Her other hand rested on the arm of the man, who she stared at with unabashed love. The man's expression was harder to read, but he had put his own hand on the woman's shoulder possessively. "You love each other very much, don't you?" Anna said out loud. She had spent hours in this very spot, dreaming up the story behind the painting. Most of the portraits in the royal gallery had known stories. Kai had told Anna all about them.

"It is part of your job as a princess of Arendelle to know your people's history," Kai had told her as he explained what each of the portraits showed. But Kai had never told her about this particular portrait. When Anna had asked him about it, the man's chin rose into the air and the corners of his mouth dropped toward the ground. Taking a well-worn handkerchief out of his finely pressed jacket lapel, he had wiped his hands as if even mentioning the painting made him feel dirty. "All we know of this painting is that the girl is not of royal birth," he had finally said, his tone dripping with judgment. "You don't need to know about them. Just know that the royal artist of Arendelle at that time, Jorgan Bierkman, felt the need to paint them."

Anna, of course, immediately wanted to know everything about them. Kai was so used to seeing the world in shades of black and white that he wouldn't notice the color of a great love story if it jumped in front of him. She imagined the story to be sad but also hopelessly romantic. Who had they been? How had they met? Had it been love at first sight? Had they been forced apart by society? If the girl was not of royal birth, had they stood a chance? No matter how many times Anna stared up at the portrait, she never grew tired of imagining their story. She had given the man and woman names—Sigfrid and Lilli—and made up a variety of stories for them. In some they were star-crossed lovers, torn apart by Sigfrid's mean and heartless parents. Other times it was a marriage of convenience that ended in a great love. In Anna's favorite version, the girl had been a traveler from a faraway kingdom who had adventured over land and sea and finally found herself in Arendelle. There all who met her had fallen under her spell, entranced by her stories of adventure and her tales of danger and excitement. Even the young prince had fallen under her spell, but when he had declared his love for her and asked her to stay in Arendelle with him forever, the girl had told him no. Her great love, she told him, was, and always would be, life. She wouldn't stay stifled behind gates while adventure awaited beyond.

In that particular story, the girl had left the prince behind. But she eventually returned and—together—they left Arendelle to travel the world. That was why, Anna figured, no one dared talk about them. Because that was not how things were done. Or at least that was what Kai would have said.

Turning her head slightly, Anna looked over at her other favorite painting. This one wasn't a portrait but a landscape. In it, the castle gates were thrown open. In the distance, the mountains rose up majestically, the tips covered in snow. In the foreground, a market had been set up in the middle of the village center. Dozens of brightly colored stalls were filled with goods of all kinds. Anna liked to imagine what it would be like to walk through the market, breathing in the scents of spices and freshly baked bread, listening to the old women gossiping and the old men grumbling about the weather.

In one corner, two young girls stood giggling and holding on to each other. Looking at the two girls now, Anna felt a familiar pang of bittersweet sadness wash over her. She and Elsa had been like that once. They had probably even been to a market just like that one . . . back when they could leave the castle. Back when the gates were always open . . .

Usually the painting made Anna happy. She could almost hear the little girls laughing and singing together and would imagine them wandering off to the next adventure, arm in arm. But not today. Today the painting just made her sad. Sighing, Anna lowered her eyes and opened her book. Maybe escaping into the words on the pages would make her forget the way her sister had ignored her again that morning. . . .

Suddenly, she heard someone clear his throat. Looking over, she saw that Kai had come into the gallery, his footsteps nearly silent.

"Kai!" Anna said, startled. "Do you need . . . ?" Her voice trailed off as she took in the expression on his face. All thoughts of her sister and the paintings vanished from her mind. Something wasn't right.

"Princess Anna," Kai said, his voice filled with sadness. "There's been news."

"Yes, Kai?"

"Your parents, Princess . . . they're gone."

CHAPTER 4

WHILE IT WAS TRUE most of his brothers were rather awful, Hans did have one ally in the baker's dozen known as the Westergaard princes. His brother Lars had always been nicer to him than the rest. There had been a stretch of time when it was thought Lars, the third oldest of the princes, would remain the youngest. The queen had been unable to conceive for another five years after Lars had been born. For all intents and purposes, it looked like Lars was going to be the youngest. Although Lars had far from received the same treatment as Hans, perhaps he still recalled the bullying that came with that position, and felt pity for Hans. Or maybe he was just a generally nicer person than the other brothers. Either way, Lars was the one person Hans could talk to.

Searching the castle, Hans found Lars right where he expected to find him—in the library. Lars was an avid historian. He knew everything about the Southern Isles and could name the kings all the way back to the beginning of the kingdom. His knowledge went beyond his own home, too. Lars was the one who kept the rest of the family apprised of information about neighboring kingdoms and the various wars and alliances that had been waged and won over the generations. Often Lars would start talking about a particular moment in the history of the Southern Isles and lose all track of time and place. More than once, Hans had just up and left when Lars was on one of his rants, sure that his brother wouldn't even notice his absence. Lars's passion for history annoyed almost everyone else, but Hans found it rather endearing—as long as he didn't have to listen to it for too long!

Walking into the library, Hans noticed that Lars had laid out several maps and was peering at them intently. "Hello, Brother," Hans called out, trying not to startle the focused Lars. "Plotting an escape, are you?"

Lars looked up, his eyes taking a moment to focus. When he saw that his visitor was Hans, he smiled. "Not quite," Lars said, his tone warm. "I'm just comparing our surveyor's most recent map to one drawn fifty years ago. I'm curious to see if our borders remain in the same place after that most recent 'incident' with Riverland. I swear, sometimes I wonder who is really in charge, the way Father just lets Caleb run amok."

Hans laughed. The king had been giving his eldest son more and more responsibility of late. But instead of taking it seriously, Caleb acted as though he were playing war with his brothers in the stable yard. "Well, at least Father will never ask me for help. Saves me from making errors in judgment that might end in maps being rendered faulty," Hans said with a smile, but there was a hint of sadness to his voice.

Lars didn't miss it. "Were you down at the dock again, little brother?" he asked. "You know that always makes you moody."

"I know," Hans said, nodding in agreement. "I just wanted some peace after yesterday's debacle."

Hans shook his head. He had done enough moping for one day. He needed to focus on the present—no matter how disappointing it might be. "So," he said to Lars, ready to change the subject, "any news on when I might become an uncle again? I am hoping your child might like me at least."

Lars laughed. "If Helga has anything to do with it, the only person that child will like is her." Lars's wife had never really forgiven her own family for shipping her to the Southern Isles. While known to be warm and rich, the isles were distant, and Helga was convinced she would never see her family again.

"Well, I'm sure once Helga has her child, she will feel more a part of the family," Hans said hopefully. *Not that being part of the family has helped me much,* he added silently.

"There is that possibility," Lars agreed. "But how are *you*, Brother? I heard more rumblings about you and the twins having a ball to introduce you to all those eligible maidens."

This time Hans didn't bother keeping the bitterness out of his voice when he laughed and said, "What eligible maidens? You know Father isn't planning on marrying me off. I am just waiting for the moment he orders me to take a vow of silence and join the Brotherhood of the Isles, where I will live my days in the same silence I have lived them here."

WHOOSH!

Behind them, the door to the library flew open, causing a few papers on the nearby table to blow to the floor. The twins stood in the doorway, their faces red and their eyes wide. "Lars!" they cried in unison, completely ignoring Hans. "Lars! Have you heard? The king and queen of Arendelle are dead! Their ship sank to the bottom of the sea."

"The king and queen of Arendelle?" Lars repeated.

"Yes!" Rudi confirmed. "Both dead."

"Father wants you to mark their passing in the royal annals," Runo added. "So . . . do that."

Their news delivered, the twins left the room as quickly as they had come.

For a moment, Lars and Hans were silent, each processing the news in his own way. To Hans, it seemed a tragedy for the kingdom of Arendelle, nothing more. But judging by the intense expression on Lars's face, it meant something more to him.

"Hans," Lars finally said. "This could be your chance."

Hans raised an eyebrow. "My chance for what?"

"To marry!" Lars said. "Don't you know anything about Arendelle?"

When Hans shook his head, Lars sighed. "I really do need to have a talk with the tutors. They are teaching you absolutely nothing of import." Walking to his bookshelf, he pulled out a book and began flipping through its pages. Finding what he was looking for, he walked back over to Hans. He pointed to a map. "This is Arendelle. It is a lovely kingdom known for a decent trade and good port. It is not extremely powerful, nor is it of huge importance to Father. It's just too far away. But it does have a princess. Rumor has it she is beautiful but mysterious. She apparently doesn't leave the castle, and while of marriageable age, she has yet to take a suitor."

Lars paused, his face glowing with excitement. "Hans, don't you see what this could mean? You could be her suitor!"

Hans let out a bitter laugh. "As if Father would ever allow such a thing."

"True, he would probably try to marry one of the twins first. But they are so stupid, I guarantee they don't even know about the eligible princess Elsa. But *you* do. So use that to your advantage. When the time comes for Elsa to take her place on the throne—"

"I can make sure *I* am the one Father sends as the Southern Isles representative," Hans finished.

His mind reeling, Hans turned toward the window. This plan meant getting his father to trust him and then convincing a woman he had never met to marry him. Neither task would be easy. It would probably take years to prepare. He would have to stop spending his days daydreaming and learn how to become more conniving. After all, his brother was implying a political game of sorts. *But,* Hans thought, getting more and more excited as a new fantasy began to form in his head, *what do I have to lose? If I don't try, I'll be stuck here anyway. At least this way, I might have a chance to change my path.*

Turning back to his brother, he smiled. "I think it's time for a history lesson. Tell me everything you know about Arendelle. Starting with this mysterious princess Elsa. And when we're done, I'm going to go have a little chat with Father. . . ."

What was I thinking? Hans thought as he stood outside the door to his father's study. He rocked back and forth, clenching and unclenching his fists nervously. It had seemed like such a good plan when he had been talking to Lars. Learn what he could about Princess Elsa and get his father's permission to go to Arendelle when the time came—without telling him why he wanted to go. One, two, three . . . done.

He had just neglected one big important thing: his father hated him. What were the chances he was going to let his youngest son go sailing off to Arendelle just to attend a stranger's coronation? The answer, Hans thought now, was slim to none. Somehow he would have to earn his father's respect—or at least his tolerance—in the time it took for Elsa to schedule a coronation. That should give him a few years to work with, right?

For one brief moment, he thought about turning around. Walking away and dropping the whole thing. But then he heard his brothers' voices in his head. *Of course you'll turn around,* he could hear Rudi say. *You don't have the guts to do anything.* And then Runo would add something like *Princess Elsa wants a real man, not a boy. Why don't you let us go after her and you can stay here, where you belong?*

With renewed determination, Hans put his hand on the doorknob and turned it. The door swung open silently on well-oiled hinges. The king didn't even look up from the pile of papers he was reading.

Hans cleared his throat. "Father?" he said, wincing when his voice cracked nervously. "May I have a word?"

The king still didn't bother to look up. "What is it, Hans?" he said. He turned over the page he was reading. "As you can see, I'm rather busy. The third isle is behind on its taxes and I still haven't gotten the promised fish from the fifth isle. I don't think people understand that I can't help them if they don't help me. And now our dear neighbors the Blavenians are threatening to stop trading with us. So as you might imagine, I don't have time to listen to you whine about your brothers being bullies again."

A protest formed on his lips, but Hans stopped it. "That sounds tedious. I wonder if perhaps . . . I could help."

His father looked up. "Help?" he repeated, his eyes narrowed suspiciously. "How do *you* propose to help *me*?"

"Any way I can," Hans said, ingratiating himself as much as possible. "I think it is time I made myself useful to you. My brothers are busy with their weddings and babies and other jobs. I have the time. And you have the need for someone with time to travel. Perhaps I can be that someone." Stopping, he held his breath and waited.

For one very long, tense moment, the king said nothing. He just stared at his son as though trying to read his thoughts. Finally, he looked back down at his papers. Shuffling them around, he pulled out a yellowed parchment. "You say you want to help. . . ."

"Yes, sir. Very much," Hans said too quickly.

"And you would be willing to do anything I ask? Anything at all?"

Hans hesitated. There was something in the way his father said "anything" that sent a nervous chill down his spine. Still . . . "Yes," he said with a nod. "Anything."

"Well, then, we might be able to work something out. I have a little issue that needs to be taken care of immediately. There is a villager on the third isle. I've been told he has been saying rather, well, *unsavory* things about me. I can't have my own people talking behind my back. It isn't good politics. I would like you to go and speak to him. Make it clear he is doing himself no favors by getting on my bad side."

"I can do that. But . . ." Hans paused, weighing his next words. "But what if he doesn't listen to me?"

The king raised an eyebrow. "Then I expect you to make him listen. One way or another."

"Make him?" Hans repeated.

"Yes," the king said. "Now, if you have no further questions, I'd like to get back to my work. And I would like you to get going on yours." He dropped his head back to his papers. "You can see yourself out."

"Yes, Father," Hans said, turning to go.

"Oh, and, Hans?"

Hans looked back over his shoulder.

"Don't disappoint me," his father warned, not bothering to look up. "Again."

"I won't . . . sir," Hans replied. Then he walked out of the study, shutting the door behind him. As soon as the door clicked in the lock, Hans sagged back against the wall and let out the breath he had been holding.

What, he thought over the beating of his heart, *have I gotten myself into?*

Three years later

CHAPTER 5

ANNA WAS HAVING the most wonderful dream. She was sitting in the middle of a huge field of the brightest green grass. The sky above her was a picture-perfect blue, and the air was warm, a slight breeze bringing with it the smell of freshly baked pastries from a nearby picnic basket. Hearing a familiar laugh, Anna turned to her right and smiled at her mother and father, who were talking in hushed, happy whispers. Turning to her left, she saw Elsa lying on the ground, blowing at a dandelion. The small puffy white tufts blew slowly into the air, making it look as if it were snowing in the middle of summer.

KNOCK! KNOCK!

Lying in her bed, Anna groaned and squeezed her eyes shut, unwilling to let go of the dream.

KNOCK! KNOCK!

There was another knock, and this time Anna heard Kai call out, "Princess Anna!" The voice sounded distant through the thick door. "Sorry to wake you, ma'am, but . . ."

"No. You didn't," Anna called back. "I've been up for hours."

As soon as the words left her mouth, her eyes drooped closed and she began to drift off. She felt the warmth of the sun and saw her sister and was about to pick another dandelion when . . .

KNOCK! KNOCK!

Anna sat up, startled, the last of her dream fading away. In its place was the reality that her parents were still gone and her sister still wanted nothing to do with her. For the first few months after the king and queen had been lost at sea, Anna had hoped that her sister would reach out to her, offer her comfort during such a terrible time. At least once a day, Anna would go to Elsa's door and knock tentatively, hoping for a reply. But Anna only found silence.

After a while, Anna stopped trying as often. Instead of once a day, she would knock once a week. And sometimes not even then. The months dragged into a year, and then another year, Anna growing older and lonelier. At least when her parents had been alive, they had gone beyond the castle gates and brought news back. Even though Anna never left, she hadn't felt so completely shut in. But since they had died, the gates hadn't been opened. It had been years and years since she had seen the kingdom in anything other than the maps and books that lined the library walls. At times she felt like she was stuck inside a very fancy prison with really good food and a lot of reading material.

Sighing, she rubbed her eyes groggily and tugged at her messy hair. She didn't need to look in a mirror to know she had a serious case of bed head.

"Time to get ready!" Kai called out.

"Ready for what?" Anna said, her thoughts still caught someplace between her dream and her musings.

"Your sister's coronation, ma'am," Kai clarified.

Anna's eyes flew open. Elsa had recently turned twenty-one, and after years of hiding away, it was time for her coronation! Today!

Anna slapped her forehead. *How could I have forgotten?* she thought as she leaped out of bed and ran over to the wardrobe. Her coronation dress sat waiting for her on a dummy, the brilliant green gown bright and spotless—which was not something that could be said for most of Anna's clothing. "I'm just effervescent," she told Gerda whenever the maid good-naturedly grumbled at another stain created by one of Anna's more enthusiastic moments. "It's hard to keep all this . . . this . . . *bubbliness* inside," Anna would tease. Then she would give the little maid a kiss on the top of her head and bounce off, forgiven as she always was.

"You *are* going to be careful with this dress, Your Highness, aren't you?"

With her fingers still clutching the soft, rich fabric, Anna looked back over her shoulder. While she had been ogling her gown, Gerda had slipped into the room. She was now making her way toward Anna, stopping every few feet or so to pick up a stray hair ribbon or a lone shoe.

"Oh, Gerda, of course I'm going to be careful," Anna said. As she spoke, she whipped around and a button on the dress snagged her dressing gown. Anna gasped and froze. "A little help?"

Sighing patiently, Gerda gently untangled Anna from the dress. When the two were at a safe distance, Gerda looked up at Anna and raised an eyebrow.

"I mean starting right *now* I'm going to careful. Just you wait and see. When I get back from the ball today, there won't be a spot on it." Anna smiled sheepishly when Gerda looked at her in disbelief. "Well, a girl can try, right?"

Gerda nodded. "I know you always try your best, Your Highness. But we really should get you ready. We don't want to be wasting this day, after all." As she spoke, she gingerly took the dress from the dummy.

"Oh, Gerda, can you believe it?" Anna asked, clasping her hands to her chest and twirling about. Her dressing gown flared out around her, nearly knocking over a hamper. "I thought this day would never come. It's been forever! Well, almost forever. I didn't think Elsa would *ever* go forward with the coronation! And then *bam*! She asks the bishop to show her the ritual, and she gets you to send out the royal invitations, and here we are! I swear that was the most Elsa has talked to anyone since . . ." Her voice trailed off.

"Since your dear mother and father passed," Gerda finished for Anna. She reached up and gave the princess a gentle squeeze on the shoulder. "They would be proud of you girls today. Very proud. Especially your mother." She smiled, her words easing the darkness that had started to creep in on Anna's mood.

Anna smiled. "Today is all about new adventures, Gerda! I am going to be able to go outside! Beyond the gates! For the next twenty-four hours, the gates will be open, and I'll be able to do whatever I want!" She paused, suddenly overwhelmed by the concept. "What am I going to do first?"

Gerda shrugged as she helped Anna into the dress. "You can do what you want, Princess," she said, guiding Anna's legs through the hoopskirt. Then she straightened the bodice. "You used to love going to the docks when you were young. You always wanted to be the first one to greet the sailors when they arrived in port. Maybe you could go there?"

"Oh! Yes! I do remember that!" Anna said happily. "I want to do that! And I want to go to that candy shop where you always took Elsa and me when Mother and Father were away. I loved the yummy—OOH!" She let out a groan as Gerda tightened her corset. Struggling for air, Anna waited while her rib cage adjusted to its sudden confinement. When she was sure she could breathe again, she narrowed her eyes at Gerda. "A little warning next time?" she teased.

The maid pretended to look contrite, but Anna saw a small smirk tugging at the corner of her mouth. "I'm just trying to make you as beautiful as possible, Princess. After all, you aren't just going to be seeing new things outside the gates. You are going to be seeing new people. New *single* people. New single people who have never seen you before. You're eighteen now. You want to make a good impression." The royal maid waggled her eyebrows teasingly.

Anna blushed. She hadn't even thought of that possibility. But now that Gerda mentioned it . . . Anna smiled. Maybe it would be just like in the stories she made up about the paintings. Anna, for once fetching and put together in her beautiful gown, leaning up against a wall. She would be sophisticated and graceful. Calm and collected. And then, across the room, she would see a handsome stranger. He would be tall, with a quick smile and kind eyes. She would walk over to the stranger and introduce herself, and within moments, they would be laughing, sharing stories, and talking about their future. It would be as though they had known each other forever. The pain and loneliness Anna had felt since her parents' death would fade away, and soon Anna wouldn't be able to remember a time when her life wasn't full of love.

Shaking her head, Anna brought herself crashing back to reality. "That's crazy," she said to Gerda. "I only have twenty-four hours. There is absolutely no way I'm going to fall in love."

"You never know unless you take the chance," Gerda said. "There are many kinds of love out there. You loved your parents. You love your sister. All I'm saying is that you never know where or when love will find you. You only can know that it *is* there—waiting. It will find you one way or another." She paused as though she wanted to say more, but then she shook her head.

"But what if I don't meet anyone?" Anna asked, suddenly worried.

"Living isn't just about loving someone. Living is enjoying what you have as you have it. You still love your parents, do you not?" Gerda asked. Anna nodded. "But their loss hasn't made you stop living, has it?" the royal maid prodded.

"It's made Elsa stop living," Anna said, somewhat sadly. "And loving. At least, she stopped loving me."

"Your sister handles her grief differently, Princess. It doesn't mean she doesn't love you." Gerda gently turned Anna so that she was facing the full-length mirror. "Now go ahead and look at yourself."

As Anna stared at her reflection, her eyes filled with happy tears. She *was* a young lady. And for the first time in forever, she actually *did* feel beautiful and special. The gown fit her perfectly. Gerda had done her hair in a simple updo and she had only the barest touches of makeup. Still, she had to admit, she looked regal.

"Oh, Gerda, thank you!" Anna gushed, throwing her arms around the woman. Then she straightened up and brushed her hands over the skirt of her dress nervously. "Well, guess it's now or never. Real world—here I come!" Taking a step forward, she yelped as the toe of her new shoe caught on the dress. Windmilling her arms, she regained her balance and looked sheepishly over her shoulder at Gerda, who was watching in amusement. "Okay, let's try this again." Taking a deep breath, she opened the door and carefully looked out into the hall. The clock was ticking. She didn't have a moment to lose!

Bursting into the hallway, Anna practically collided with a servant rushing past. In his arms was a pile of clean white linens. Another person flew by, holding a pair of matching silver candlesticks. Anna let out a laugh. The castle was alive! It was the most amazing thing to see. Unable to stop herself, she began to skip down the hallway.

On either side of the long hall, the curtains had been drawn back and the windows thrown open. Outside, puffy white clouds dotted the blue sky. Anna could hear the sounds of people rushing over the cobblestoned courtyard. A horse let out a loud whinny, and Anna could have sworn it sounded like the animal was cheering.

Reaching the end of the hall, Anna turned left and then right and then right again. Every hall she turned down was full of people and every door she passed was open. *I didn't think we had this many rooms,* Anna thought as she passed by another grand chamber. Inside she could make out a maid humming to herself as she dusted a long-neglected piano. Anna laughed. This was all so incredible. It was as though people and rooms had just miraculously appeared.

If only every day could be like this one, Anna thought as she ran down the stairs of the grand entrance. At the bottom she grabbed the railing, narrowly avoiding slamming into a man precariously balancing at least twenty dinner plates. And behind *that* man were dozens more! *Who knew we had, like, eight thousand dinner plates?* Anna thought. *Who knew we knew eight thousand people!* Most days, the only two people Anna saw were Gerda and Kai. But today every room seemed to be filled with people hard at work.

Anna stopped short, a sudden horrible thought coming to her. What if she had to remember the names of all those people? She was horrible at remembering—anything. People's names, countries, historical facts, the name of her favorite flower . . .

No! Anna told herself. *There is no way I will need to remember all those names. That's Elsa's job. One perk of being the younger sister is I just get to meet them and have fun. I can have my cake and eat it, too!*

Before she knew it, Anna was at the castle's main doors. Eagerly, she pushed them open. In front of her, the gates were open, revealing the courtyard beyond. Anna put a hand to her heart. "Beyond those doors lies my future," she whispered. "So what am I waiting for?" Breaking into a run, Anna burst into the sunshine, ready for her adventure to begin.

CHAPTER 6

HANS LOOKED OVER the bow of the ship and smiled. He had made it! In a little over an hour, his ship would dock in Arendelle's port and he, Hans Westergaard, thirteenth and youngest son of the king of the Southern Isles, would finally have a chance to make a name for himself. He would become the next king of Arendelle—or at least that was the plan.

Getting to this point had not been easy. It had taken nearly three years to convince the king that he was responsible enough to be the representative to Arendelle when the time came. And when, at long last, news arrived that Princess Elsa was to be crowned queen of Arendelle, Hans knew his time had come. All the begging, pleading, and generally making himself a lapdog to his father to procure a spot as the representative would pay off. So what if he had never told his father the true reason he wanted to go to Arendelle? He wanted to surprise everyone. He would show his father and his brothers and all of the Southern Isles that they had grossly underestimated him.

For the past three years, Hans had ingratiated himself to his father. Whatever the man needed, Hans did. From the dirtiest of tasks to the most mindless of errands. He had been sent among the isles to deliver wedding invitations for one of the twins, who had met and wooed a young lady in record time. *I still don't know how Runo did it,* Hans thought now. *My new sister-in-law seemed so much smarter than to fall for his smarmy charms.* Hans shrugged. Even now, when he had been given a role of some honor, he couldn't let go of the bitterness of his past. *But never mind that,* he thought. *I'll show them soon enough. . . .*

Hans might have spent much of his time doing only what his father asked, but he was smart. He knew that if he was to get what he wanted, he needed to take initiative. He needed to make himself the most knowledgeable man in the Southern Isles about the kingdom of Arendelle. He needed to be the preeminent authority on the ins and outs of Arendelle's customs and learn the proper ways to pay respect to their queen on her coronation day. He knew none of his brothers would take the time, and his father's current ambassador was old and gassy. Not someone who should be seen as the sole representative of the Southern Isles. So in between his tasks, and with Lars's help, Hans had done hours and hours of research on Arendelle and its soon-to-be queen, Elsa.

There were plenty of old texts that told of Arendelle in general.

Hans had learned that it was a beautiful kingdom with a peaceful history. Nestled at the base of a high range of mountains, it was safe from invasions. The only way into the kingdom was by sea. The ports of Arendelle were known for their fair trade, and the kingdom, while not exceedingly rich, was quite comfortable. The queen would want for nothing. If what Hans had seen in the books was true, the kingdom was a place where darkness and evil were not known.

Elsa, however, Hans thought as the ship sailed closer and closer to port, was still a mystery. There wasn't even a picture of her. For all Hans knew, she could be eight feet tall. Or bald. Or have a fanatical interest in rock collecting. The only thing he had learned for sure was what Lars had told him that long ago day: she never left the castle. Ever.

No matter what sort of queen lay in wait for him inside Arendelle's castle, Hans knew he would find a way to become her king. He had worked too hard for there to be any other outcome.

Hans remembered the day he had received news that Princess Elsa was finally to be crowned queen. He had just returned from a rather unpleasant visit to a village late on paying its taxes. It was time to give the king a full report.

"Father," Hans had greeted the king, bowing his head. "The village has been warned and their punishment completed. I don't think you should have any problems with them in the future."

"And what of their taxes? Were you able to collect?"

Hans suppressed a shudder. "From most of them, yes. The ones who could not provide what they owed . . . paid in other ways." Hans dropped a bag of coins in front of his father. "This is the money. The other . . . payment . . . I disposed of." Bile had risen in his throat as he thought about the "payment." Still, he had done what he had to do.

"Thank you, Hans," the king had replied.

As always, his eyes were distant. But this time, Hans couldn't help noticing that the man's tone wasn't as cold or dismissive. Perhaps this was his chance?

"Father?" Hans had begun, hesitant. The king raised an eyebrow. "I have taken it upon myself to put together a list of potential issues that need to be discussed with the new queen of Arendelle after her coronation. I have spoken to several people recently back from trips to the kingdom, and it is said she will only open the gates for twenty-four hours. Initiating any new agreements and negotiation of terms must be done during that time. I know that you are far too busy to go yourself, what with Prince Runo getting married soon and the arrival of another grandchild. And I know my presence is not required at either of the events. . . ." He paused, hoping his father might actually disagree. But his father didn't say a word. So Hans went on. "I thought it only fitting that I make the trip to Princess Elsa's coronation as the representative of the Southern Isles."

Reaching into his jacket pocket, Hans had pulled out a detailed scroll, complete with talking points and a clear itinerary. He held it out to his father.

Taking the paper in his hand, the king studied it for a moment. Then he looked up at Hans. "I'm surprised by your interest in such a small, distant kingdom."

"Well, Father, as you always say, a kingdom is only as strong as its allies. I thought it best to ensure an alliance with Arendelle."

His father looked thoughtful. "And you feel confident you know what needs to be done?" he asked.

Hans nodded.

"Well, then," the king said, shrugging. "I don't see why it should not be you. You have shown me you can be responsible, and I shouldn't have need for your 'services' in the near future if you have done your job well. Take a small ship and your favorite horse and make your way to Arendelle. Secure a new trade agreement and ensure a strong alliance."

"Yes, Father," Hans said, barely keeping the excitement from his voice.

"When the gates close, return home immediately," the king finished. "I'm sure they'll have need of you in the nursery by that point. Your brothers and their wives have quite the habit of reproducing." Then, without another word of good-bye, the king had turned and left.

For an instant, Hans had been too stunned to do anything. In one moment he had been told he could go after what he wanted, and in the next he had been cut down. It was so typical of his father. But so what if his father thought little of him now? So what if he only had twenty-four hours to accomplish his goal? He would surprise everyone, show his father and his brothers what sort of man he truly was.

Now, as Hans's ship docked next to one of the long piers that jutted into the water surrounding Arendelle, he let out a breath it felt like he had been holding since leaving the Southern Isles. All he had to do now was find Princess Elsa and get her to fall in love with him. How hard could that be?

As it turned out, finding Princess Elsa proved harder than Hans had anticipated. After disembarking the ship and taking a few minutes—well, more than a few minutes if he was honest—to get his land legs back, Hans had mounted his horse and headed into town.

For some reason, Hans had assumed that the town would be quiet in the hours leading up to the big event. He had been wrong. Very, very wrong. It seemed every inhabitant of Arendelle, plus representatives from every kingdom near and far, had packed themselves into the village at the base of the castle. Looking around, Hans saw that the kingdom was as picture-perfect as the books he had read suggested. In the distance, he could see the peak of a snowcapped mountain, but down in the town it was warm. The air smelled of an intoxicating combination of fir trees and sea, the result of the massive forest that lay just behind the kingdom and the water that stretched out in front. Children raced about, their faces glowing, while their parents shopped or gossiped or sold their wares. The streets were clean and the houses well cared for. It was, in a word, lovely. Ruling over this kingdom would not be a terrible job at all.

But as Hans carefully maneuvered his horse, Sitron, between a cart full of eggplants and another cart filled with what looked like bouquets made out of fish, he began to doubt himself. *Did I honestly think I was just going to walk into town and bump right into Princess Elsa? She is probably locked inside getting ready, not out wandering the streets looking for love. . . .*

"Hello, Princess! How wonderful to see you outside the castle gates!"

A woman's voice cut through the crowd and Hans pulled back on his reins, stopping Sitron. *Princess?* Had he heard right?

"It is so wonderful to see you, Princess. It's been too long!"

It seemed he had! Whipping Sitron around, Hans searched the crowd for the source of the comments. Suddenly, he caught sight of a red-and-green flash. A moment later, a young woman bounced into view. She was laughing at something an older fruit peddler had said as she paused to inspect the apples on his cart. Nudging Sitron forward, Hans got a little closer and tried to listen in without being seen.

"This is the prettiest, greenest apple I've ever seen, sir! You must bring some up to the castle so Cook can use them in her pies!"

"Oh, Princess!" the old man said, his wrinkled cheeks flushing as though he were a schoolboy. "You are too kind! I'll go straightaway. And here, take this apple . . . on me! Enjoy!"

THIS is Elsa? Hans thought as he watched the girl take a bite and continue making her way through the town. Everywhere she went she was stopped by one person or another, and each time, she greeted them with a warm smile and a bit of conversation. Following her, Hans couldn't help being impressed. True, she seemed almost like a newborn colt, all legs and a little awkward, but she was actually rather, well, pretty. Her reddish-gold hair was pulled back from her face, and he could just make out a few freckles on her pale skin. Her eyes were lively, and when she laughed, it was contagious. *I wonder why the only thing I could find about Elsa said she was a recluse. She seems anything but.* Hans shrugged. What did it matter? So the book was wrong. And if this was the woman he wanted to woo and wed, well, Hans could imagine much worse options.

But in order for that to happen, Hans had to make an impression. And it seemed now was as good a time as any. He needed to make this good. He needed to seem heroic and poised and powerful all at the same time. *How am I going to do that? It's not like I can ride in and save the day like in all those silly fairy tales. . . . Or can I?*

Noticing that the princess was standing precariously close to the side of a boat that was precariously close to the side of the dock, Hans had an idea. He waited for the princess to turn her back to him. Then, nudging Sitron into place right behind the girl, he waited. From what he had seen so far, the princess was rather . . . effusive . . . in her movements. She was bound to swing around at any moment, and when she did—

As if on cue, the princess whipped around, her mouth open as if she were ready to burst into song. Instead, she burst right into Sitron's chest! Startled, she let out a cry and stepped back. But the boat was in her way and she toppled into it. The weight of the princess was just what the boat, which had already been ready to plummet into the water below, needed. It began to tip—slowly at first, and then faster. Hans heard the princess let out a cry, and then he did exactly what he had planned to do all along. Kicking Sitron forward, he had the horse step right into the front of the boat.

Instantly, the rear of the boat leveled out. Inside, the princess looked up at Hans. Her eyes were wide with amazement, a little bit of shock, and definitely a whole lot of interest.

Hans smiled. *That,* he thought, *could not have gone better.* Princess Elsa of Arendelle was practically his!

CHAPTER 7

WHAT JUST HAPPENED? Anna asked herself. One minute she was turning around to head back to the castle, and the next moment there was a flash of white and then *BOOM*! She had fallen into a boat, and now the only thing keeping her from plummeting into the water appeared to be the hoof of a horse. *I have enough trouble staying on my feet as it is,* Anna thought, rubbing her sore back. *It's not like I need help from a random white beast ridden by who even knows . . .*

Anna looked up, ready to give the rider a piece of her mind. But when she saw the person sitting astride the white horse, who wasn't, to be fair, as beastly as she would have first thought, her mind went blank. All she could think was *eyes*. Beautiful blue eyes that were like deep fjords in the morning sun. Eyes that sparkled. Eyes that mesmerized. Beautiful, beautiful eyes that belonged to what had to be the most handsome man Anna had ever seen.

Great. This is just great. I get out of the castle for the first time in pretty much forever, and the first thing I go and do is embarrass myself in front of this good-looking stranger. Of course I couldn't have been gracefully gliding down the dock, looking all mysterious and thought-provoking like Elsa probably would have been. Nope. Not me. Instead I end up on the floor of a boat. Anna sniffed. *A rather stinky boat,* she added silently. *Good job, Anna. Really good job.*

Anna was so caught up in beating herself up that she didn't even notice that the man was still looking at her. And that he looked rather worried. "I'm so sorry," he said. "Are you hurt?"

Even his voice is wonderful! Anna thought. *I bet he would be a great singer.*

Realizing he was waiting for an answer, she flushed even redder and stammered, "I—uh, no. No. I'm okay." *If by okay you mean totally mortified,* she thought.

"Are you sure?" the rider asked.

"Yeah, I just wasn't looking where I was going," Anna said, waving her hand in the air as though it were no big deal.

As she spoke, the rider hopped down from his horse and stepped into the boat. Up close he was even more handsome. *And tall,* Anna thought. *He's really, really tall. Which is good. I like tall. I think? I mean, I don't actually know, but I'll go with that for now.* "I'm great, actually," Anna added out loud.

Leaning down, the rider offered his hand. "Oh, thank goodness," he said. Tentatively, Anna reached up and accepted his hand. He gently pulled her to her feet until they were standing face-to-face.

For a moment, Anna forgot to breathe. She had never been this close to a man her own age before, let alone one as charming as this. It was just like in all those stories she'd read as a girl. White horse. Handsome. The only thing left was if he happened to be a . . .

"Prince Hans of the Southern Isles," the rider said, introducing himself.

A prince? Anna nearly laughed.

Regaining her composure and remembering her manners, Anna dropped into a curtsy. "Princess Anna of Arendelle," she replied.

"Princess . . . ?" Hans repeated, sounding shocked and maybe even a little embarrassed. Instantly, the prince dropped to his knees and bowed his head. "My lady."

The horse attempted his own version of a bow. Lifting his leg, he curled his hoof under and lowered his head. The problem was it happened to be the hoof that had been holding the boat steady. Instantly the boat began to tip backward. The motion sent Hans tumbling into Anna.

Realizing what he had done, the horse slammed his hoof back down. The boat snapped back, this time sending Hans flying backward and Anna flying forward. They landed on the floor of the boat, Anna lying on top of Hans.

"Well, this is awkward," Anna said, trying not to breathe right into Hans's face, which, at the moment, was mere inches from her own. "Not you're awkward, but just because we're—I'm awkward. *You're* gorgeous. . . ." Anna snapped her mouth shut. Had she just said that out loud? She needed to get it together! She was acting like she had never had a conversation in her entire life.

Gently helping Anna off him, Hans got to his feet and once again held out a hand to Anna. Once she was standing, he said, "I'd like to formally apologize for hitting the princess of Arendelle with my horse . . . and for every moment after."

Aww, Anna thought.

"It's fine," she said. "I'm not *that* princess. I mean, if you'd hit my sister, Elsa, it would be—" She lowered her gaze and began to pat Hans's horse. "But, lucky you, it's . . . it's . . . just me."

"Just you?" Hans repeated.

Anna looked up at him and nodded, ready for him to flee. But to her surprise, he was smiling and looking at her as though her being "just her" wasn't such a bad thing after all. In fact, it was almost as if her being "just her" was fine by him. Anna's heart began to thud loudly in her chest.

DING-DONG! DING-DONG!

"Oh! The bells!" Anna said, snapping back to reality. "The coronation! I better go! I have to . . . I better . . ."

Jumping out of the boat, Anna looked up at the castle and saw the bell ringing wildly in its tower. She could make out people entering through the gate. She really didn't have much time. Turning to look back at Hans, she waved. "Bye," she said, wishing that she didn't have to leave.

Hans lifted a hand and once again flashed his beautiful smile. "See you at the coronation!"

Nodding, Anna turned and raced back toward the castle. She couldn't be late. But that wasn't what made her step so sprightly and fast. She knew that she was going to see Prince Hans of the Southern Isles again. And that made her feel like she could fly.

CHAPTER 8

HANS HAD BEEN at the receiving end of plenty of practical jokes in his life. He had twelve older brothers, after all. It came with the territory. He had fallen for the old "there's a special present for you in that oddly scary room down in the catacombs, Hans. Why don't you go find it and then we'll lock you in there after you go inside" trick. He had woken up with ink all over his face after one of his brothers had dipped his hands in the inkpot while he slept. He had even believed it when he received a "ransom note" from a King Gotya claiming he had taken one of Hans's brothers and would only return him if Hans ran around the castle three times in just his underpants. In his defense, he had only been four at the time.

Still, despite the many, many pranks and practical jokes Hans had lived through, none of them compared to this. This certainly felt like a joke that one of his brothers would play on him. Have him run into a girl and woo her, all the while thinking she was one princess when instead she was another!

Ever since Anna had introduced herself and then dashed off, Hans had been reliving the encounter over and over. Now, as he rode Sitron up to the castle, Hans sighed. He had come to the conclusion that he should look at the situation this way: The two princesses were sisters. Sisters tended to think alike (or so he assumed, having no experience with them). So if they *did* think alike, and Anna thought he was handsome—which he was pretty sure she did—maybe Elsa would be just as easily swept off her feet. So, he figured as his horse trotted into the castle's courtyard, his staged run-in with the wrong princess might not have been entirely wasted.

At least, I really hope it wasn't, Hans added silently. The clock was still ticking.

Hans hopped off Sitron, smoothed out his jacket, and quickly ran a hand through his hair. Then he made his way inside the chapel.

As he walked through the door, Hans felt dozens of eyes on him, sizing him up. He tried not to smile. He was good. No, he wasn't good; he was great. He couldn't have timed his entrance better. Most of the guests had already arrived and were seated in the long pews in front of the dais. When Hans had opened the door, with the sun pouring in from behind him and no one else to steal his thunder, he had to believe he had garnered some interest. To this room full of strangers, he was a mystery. They didn't know who he was, where he was from, or what his intentions were—and he wanted to keep it that way. He would reveal himself when the time was right, and when it was to his advantage.

Keeping his head high, Hans made his way toward the front of the room. Finding a spot close enough to be seen by Princess Elsa but not so close that he seemed overeager, Hans took a seat. Then he began to size up the competition.

Hans had done his homework. After his father had given him permission to attend the coronation, Hans had immediately gotten his hands on a list of potential attendees. "Knowledge is power," Lars had told him once when their father had been forced to wage war on a neighboring kingdom. "It is always better to go into a battle knowing the enemy." And this was going to be the biggest battle of Hans's life. He wanted to know who he was up against. Now, as he looked around, he saw that his homework had paid off.

Across the room he saw a small, thin man with an unfortunate nose. This was the Duke of Weselton, and he was deep in conversation with a dignitary from Blavenia. *The Duke is one to watch out for,* Hans thought. From what he had heard just since getting to Arendelle, the man was intent on forcing the new queen to recognize the importance of their trade relationship and perhaps increase the number of ships going back and forth between the two kingdoms. Hans had overheard someone saying that the Duke was convinced that there was something fishy going on and that Arendelle had been holding out on him and his people. Whether that was true, Hans had no idea. But he did know the little man carried a lot of weight with the people of Weselton and beyond. If he decided to speak out against Hans for whatever reason, it could be damaging.

As he continued to look around the room, he recognized several more people. There were a few other princes, several lords, and at least a dozen other lower dignitaries. But of them all, the only one who really worried Hans was the Duke.

Just then, a pair of men sat down beside Hans. One of them Hans recognized as Prince Freluke. He was extremely tall and skinny, with a sour expression. He nodded politely at Hans and said a quiet hello.

The other man was Freluke's opposite. Whereas Freluke was tall and skinny, this man was short and round. His cheeks were rosy, and his eyes twinkled. Turning, he said something to Freluke that made the serious man laugh. "Well, this is quite the process, isn't it?" the man said, leaning over and semi-whispering into Hans's ear. Then he held out his hand. "The name's Prince Wils, Vakretta's dignitary. How do you do?"

"Prince Hans of the Southern Isles," Hans informed Wils.

"Ah, the Southern Isles! Never been, but I have heard they are beautiful. Quite the trip from there, though, is it not? What made you come all this way? Surely, as prince, you could have sent someone in your stead."

Hans smiled. Clearly this man had no idea that Hans was the "throwaway" prince of the family. Hans was more than happy to keep that charade up. The more people who thought him important, the better. He wanted any rumors of him that reached Elsa to show him in only the most positive of lights. "I would not have trusted such an important task to anyone else," Hans finally answered. "The coronation of Queen Elsa is very important to my family, and"—Hans lowered his voice—"you never know what unsavory characters might show up at these types of things. I wanted to make sure that I was here to build an alliance between the Southern Isles and Arendelle. Plus, I felt it was important to meet the new queen in person and get to know her."

Prince Wils pulled a candy out of his jacket pocket and popped it into his mouth. Then he shrugged. "Good luck with that," he said. "From what I hear, Princess Elsa doesn't let anyone get to know her. Or see her, for that matter."

"She likes her privacy," Prince Freluke said, his voice so soft Hans could barely hear him. "I think that is understandable."

"Sure," Prince Wils said, "if you are just a regular person. But Elsa is about to be queen. You can't rule a kingdom in isolation. People are saying that she has a heart of ice. That kings no longer bother to try to make a match with Arendelle. Every time one has tried, he has been turned away at the door. What kind of future queen turns away a potential suitor? If you ask me, it just doesn't make sense."

"No one asked you," Prince Freluke pointed out, deadpan.

Prince Wils looked taken aback. Then he burst out laughing. "You're right, friend. I shouldn't be saying any of this anyway, I suppose. We are here to celebrate Elsa's coronation, after all. Maybe she'll prove me wrong and be all warm and bubbly . . ." He paused. "But I doubt it. A reindeer doesn't change its antlers, now does it?"

"There is no such thing as a miracle," Freluke said, shaking his head.

As the pair began to discuss whether miracles did exist, Hans tuned them out. It wasn't news to him that Elsa was, well, a bit of a lone wolf. But he hadn't realized just how isolated she was until now. The woman was clearly happier by herself. She didn't like to leave the castle. She was wary of strangers and had already turned down who knew how many suitors. This was going to be tricky. Fortunately, Hans was used to improvising.

Just as his thoughts began to run through a series of alternate plans, he realized a hush had fallen over the crowd. Surprised at the sudden silence, Hans looked up. His breath hitched in his throat. The future queen of Arendelle had taken her spot on the raised platform at the front of the chapel. She stood, staring blankly out at the crowd, her eyes focused on some point only she could see. Anna stood next to her, her gaze jumping from one person to the other as though she couldn't soak up the faces fast enough.

Anna was all energy and light. Her excitement was palpable from his spot in the pews. Her hands fluttered from her neck to her skirt, then up to her hair and back to her skirt while her toes, which just peeked out beneath her dress, tapped wildly. Hans couldn't help smiling as he watched Anna. She reminded him of the colorful fish that swam in the shallows of the water in the Southern Isles. They were always in motion, always shimmering, and with each movement, they seemed to transform. Anna was just like those fish. Alive and vibrant.

Elsa, on the other hand, was anything but.

Turning his attention to the future queen, Hans was struck anew by the contrast between the sisters. Whereas Anna was all barely restrained, excited energy, Elsa hardly moved. She stood there, no expression on her face, her body as still as a statue. Her fingers, which were twitching slightly, were the only things that gave away any hint of emotion.

Hans returned his gaze to Anna. What if he didn't *have* to marry Elsa to get the crown? Clearly, she wanted nothing to do with the crown or her subjects. She was practically throwing the scepter and orb away as everyone looked on. If Hans had learned anything from his manipulative brothers, it was that there was always more than one way to get what you wanted. If Elsa really didn't want the crown, perhaps she would be willing to give it to her younger sister—if said sister was to wed a prince from a good, strong kingdom. Hans's heart beat faster as the idea began to take shape. It was all so obvious now. He would marry Anna and overthrow Elsa. With Anna under his thumb, it would be only a matter of time before he would take control of the kingdom. And then? Then he would rule Arendelle, and he would never have to see his father or his brothers ever again.

He smiled. At that very moment, Anna's wandering gaze landed on him. Raising his hand, he gave her a small wave. Immediately, she ducked her head and her cheeks flushed. *Oh, yes,* he thought, watching her reaction. *This is a much,* much *better plan. . . .*

CHAPTER 9

HE WAVED AT ME. Hans waved. At me.

Anna still couldn't believe it. One minute she had been standing next to her sister, listening as the coronation ceremony unfolded and taking in all the new faces, and the next minute her heart had been racing and her face felt on fire.

Anna stood up straighter, determined to look confident in front of the room full of strangers. And in front of Hans. Of course she had spotted him the moment he walked into the chapel. She had watched as he took a seat, and had been impressed when he seemed to strike up an easy conversation with two men sitting next to him.

Anna had tried not to look at Hans too much. She'd made sure to keep her gaze bouncing around the room, and when the bishop began the ceremony in earnest, she had honestly been too preoccupied watching her sister to give Hans another thought.

Until he had waved at her.

Then her mind had gone blank and her heart had begun to pound, and she wasn't sure if it was the candlelight or Hans's look, but it felt as though she were melting. It had taken all her willpower to rein in her emotions and focus. *Elsa,* she reminded herself. *This is about Elsa. Her coronation. Her moment.*

Anna dragged her eyes away and focused back on her sister—who, she realized with a start, seemed terrified. Elsa's face was pale and she seemed to be shaking. Thoughts of Hans fled Anna's mind and she took a step closer, willing her sister to be calm as the bishop began the part of the ceremony that would make Elsa queen.

If Anna knew her sister—and granted, there was very little she *did* know about her these days—Elsa had probably gone over every part of the ceremony repeatedly to make sure she was ready for her big day. At this moment, Elsa was supposed to remove her gloves and then take the scepter and the orb. That would be the bishop's cue to move on to the final part of the coronation. But Elsa *didn't* remove her gloves. *That's odd,* Anna thought, watching her sister reach out toward the pillow. The bishop seemed to agree and in a stage whisper said, "Your Majesty, the gloves."

Elsa hesitated. Anna could see that Elsa's face had grown even paler and she was trying desperately to keep her breathing steady. Anna took a step forward, nervous that something bad was going to happen. But then her sister took off her gloves and placed them on the pillow. In return, she picked up the orb and scepter.

Anna let out a breath. That had been oddly tense. *Maybe Elsa is even more nervous than I thought.*

And then, just like that, Elsa became queen of Arendelle.

Just like that, her whole world changed.

And my life will probably stay exactly the same, Anna thought, *unless I decide to change it. . . .*

Compared to the somber chapel with its whispered voices and dark corners, the ballroom was awash with light and laughter. Guests had already begun to dance and eat, and the whole room echoed with joyous music. It was a celebration on the grandest scale.

Anna, however, wasn't enjoying the festivities quite yet. Instead, she stood outside, watching the party unfold as she had done so many times as a child. Only, back then Elsa had stood beside her, giggling as they made up stories about each of the dancers. Now Elsa stood quietly—seriously—waiting to be announced.

"I have to do what now?" Anna had asked when Kai had informed the queen and the princess that they must wait to enter the room.

"You must wait until your name is announced and then make your way into the center of the awning we have set up in the ballroom. Then you will stand near your sister and you will wave and you will wait."

"Wait?" Anna had repeated. "For what?"

Kai had smiled then, making Anna oddly nervous. "To be asked to dance, of course."

Of course, he says, Anna thought, peering around her sister. A small platform had been set up in the ballroom, and Kai stood on it. Looking at the leader of the band, he nodded and the music stopped. Instantly, everyone's attention turned toward Kai. With another nod, trumpets blared, and then, in the deepest and most important voice the man could muster, he announced the arrival of "Queen Elsa of Arendelle!"

As the room erupted into applause, Elsa stepped forward. Anna felt a swell of pride as the people cheered for her sister. Despite their differences, Anna knew that Elsa would be a great queen.

Elsa's hands were no longer shaking, and the color had returned to her cheeks. Her new crown rested on her head, glinting in the golden candlelight, and as she waved to the gathered crowd, the intricate stitching on her gown twinkled. *She's so calm,* Anna thought, surprised. *So content. I guess maybe she just needed to get out of that chapel to feel better. I don't blame her. The place was a bit dreary, and that lighting was just—*

"Princess Anna of Arendelle!"

Anna snapped to attention. *Eeks! What do I do? What do I do? Right. I have to walk. But do I walk sort of fast or sort of slow? Do I look straight ahead or do I look out at the crowd? Why didn't I ask Elsa when she was standing right here! Well, here goes nothing.*

Popping through the door, she raced into the room. But she had completely overthought her entrance, and instead of slowly, gracefully entering the room, she practically ran onto the platform. Smiling sheepishly, she stopped a few feet from Elsa. Then she began to wave—awkwardly—until Kai jerked his head to the side.

Does he want me to stand right next to Elsa? Anna wondered.

Apparently, he did.

"Are you sure?" she whispered. Kai was clearly sure. He ushered her over so that they stood shoulder to shoulder, and then he left the two sisters alone.

This was the first time in a very long while that Elsa and Anna had been next to each other for any length of time. Standing beside each other in front of a roomful of people and watching them while they laughed and danced was just weird. And awkward. Very, very awkward.

Anna didn't know what to do. *Should I say something? Congratulations, maybe? Or just "Hey, what's up?" Or do I go with safe weather conversation? Why is this so hard? Elsa is my sister. I shouldn't have to think about what to say. I should just open my mouth and say . . .*

"Hi . . ."

Elsa beat her to it. Eyes wide, Anna looked at her sister. "Hi, me . . . ?" she said, looking down at her feet and then nervously back at her sister. "Oh. Um. Hi!"

"You look beautiful," Elsa said, her voice soft and her tone kind.

"Thank you," Anna said bashfully. "You look beautifuller. I mean, not fuller. You don't look fuller, but more beautiful. . . ." Anna snapped her mouth shut. She couldn't believe that Elsa had been the one to reach out to *her*. Maybe things really *would* be different now. Maybe this was the beginning of something new. If it was, Anna really didn't want to ruin this moment by babbling nonsense.

For a minute, the two sisters just stood there, looking out as couples danced across the floor. There were dresses of every color and shape, and jewels sparkled and twinkled in every color of the rainbow. It was like something in a painting. Only it was happening right here. Anna was entranced.

And, apparently, so was Elsa. "So, this is what a party looks like?" she said.

"It's warmer than I thought," Anna finally said. *And I don't just mean the room,* she added silently. Forcing her arms to stay at her sides even though she wanted to throw them around Elsa, Anna noticed that Elsa's nose was twitching in a rather unqueenly way.

"What is that amazing smell?" Elsa asked.

The two girls closed their eyes and inhaled.

"Chocolate!" they said in unison.

Anna's eyes popped open and she met her sister's gaze. Then they both began to laugh. Chocolate was one thing they most definitely had in common. Before Elsa had gone all silent on her, Anna remembered them sneaking into the kitchen while Cook was baking and dipping their fingers in bowls of warm melted chocolate. Their favorite thing to do had been to dip their fingers first in chocolate and then in powdered sugar. That made for the sweetest treat. Ultimately, Cook would always catch them and scold them, but it had never mattered to Anna and Elsa. To this day, the smell of chocolate always reminded Anna of those stolen moments.

As their laughter faded, Anna found herself wanting to say so much. But how could she begin to talk about all the things she had wondered about for so long? There was no way this was the time or the place to find out if Elsa had missed Anna as much as Anna had missed her.

Anna sighed happily. Her sister was back. She was back and wonderful and funny and there was no way Anna was going to lose her again. She would do whatever it took to keep her warm, loving, happy sister right there by her side . . . forever.

CHAPTER 10

HANS WATCHED AS the two sisters giggled, their heads bent together—one blond, one copper, both beautiful in their own ways. It must be nice to have such a bond, to share each other's ups and downs. He couldn't remember the last time he had laughed with one of his brothers. Lars was far too serious to share a joke with. And the others were more likely to be laughing *at* him.

Hans had been waiting for the right moment to introduce himself to the new queen. He hadn't wanted to seem overeager, nor had he wanted to seem uninterested. The introduction was going to be important if he was going to follow through on his new plan. He was growing more and more confident that marrying Princess Anna was the right way to go. From what he had seen of the new queen at the coronation, it seemed she was as removed and distant as he had heard—at least with everyone but Anna. Let everyone else waste their time trying to woo the queen. He had found a better way to get to her and get what he wanted.

Looking back at the sisters, he saw the Duke of Weselton approaching them. Hans stepped closer, interested to see what would happen next. The little man looked like a weasel, and as he walked across the dance floor, he lifted his nose in the air, giving the appearance that he was sniffing for something.

The Duke stopped in front of Elsa and Anna, did an odd little hitch and kick with his skinny legs, and then bowed, offering his hand for a dance. As he did so, the toupee Hans hadn't realized the man was wearing flipped forward. Hans stifled a laugh. He noticed that Elsa and Anna were struggling not to laugh, as well.

"Thank you," Hans heard Elsa say as she tried to regain her composure. "Only, I don't dance."

The Duke straightened up, clearly offended by the queen's statement. "Oh?" he said, raising an eyebrow, the toupee shifting around again.

"But my sister does," Elsa added, giving Anna a teasing glance.

Anna's eyes grew wide. Hans could practically hear her trying to mentally tell her sister that she did *not* want to dance with the Duke. "What?" she finally squeaked. "I don't think . . ."

But before she could finish protesting, the Duke had grabbed Anna's arm and begun pulling her toward the dance floor. "If you swoon, let me know," he told her. "I'll catch you."

Looking over her shoulder, Anna shot her sister a desperate

"help me" look, but Elsa just giggled and shrugged her shoulders. "Sorry," she mouthed.

As the Duke began to lead Anna in a dance, Hans saw that she was actually a lovely dancer. A little unsteady, but the Duke was not helping that situation. His dancing looked like a cross between a peacock's strutting and a kangaroo's hopping. It was all leaps and head bobs and feet. Feet that kept landing on Anna's toes. Hans winced as he saw the Duke land particularly hard on her shoes after one awkward twirl.

"Ow, ow, ow," Hans heard Anna say. He wondered if he should try to cut in, saving Anna once again.

But Hans could tell the Duke wasn't going to let go of Anna that easily. The little man was using the dance as an opportunity to drill Anna for information about her kingdom.

"So great to have the gates open," the Duke said. "Why did they shut them in the first place? Do you know the reason?" He rose on his tiptoes, trying to get into Anna's face.

Anna shook her head. "No."

The Duke stared up at her, his own face filled with suspicion. Then he shrugged, and as Hans watched in growing horror at the man's awful tactics and even more terrible dance moves, the Duke dipped Anna. Hans saw Anna shoot her sister a look of sheer desperation from her upside-down position.

He couldn't let this go on any longer. But just as he was about to ask Anna to dance, the music stopped and the Duke released his grip on Anna's waist.

It was time for Hans to make his move. Anna had returned to her sister's side, and he could see the two were chatting and giggling. From the way Anna was rubbing her toes, he was fairly positive it was about the Duke and his two left feet. Suddenly, though, Anna's face dropped and Elsa's body stiffened. A moment later, as the music started up again, Anna turned from her sister and began to make her way across the crowded dance floor.

Hans didn't even bother looking back at Elsa. He just took off after Anna. He watched as she tried in vain to avoid the flying arms and moving feet of the dancers. It was nearly impossible on the tightly packed floor. And then, just when it looked like Anna might get out of the ballroom unscathed, a man bowed deeply, his backside bumping into her hard. The motion knocked Anna off her feet and she began to fall. In one smooth motion, Hans stepped across the floor and scooped her into his arms. Looking down at the princess, he smiled. "Glad I caught you."

Bringing Anna back to her feet, Hans bowed. Then he held out his hand, just as the Duke had done. But whereas the Duke had two left feet, Hans was all grace. As they glided across the room, he felt Anna relax in his arms.

"Where were you a few minutes ago?" Anna said after a few moments of silence. "I think my toes are permanently crushed from the Duke's so-called dance moves." She looked up at him.

"What? You didn't enjoy that?" Hans replied, his tone teasing. "I figured that was the highlight of your night."

Anna giggled. "Are you kidding me? I have enough trouble dancing as it is. I don't need help looking less graceful." She paused, as if weighing her next words. Then, in a rush, she said, "You make me look graceful."

Her honesty surprised Hans, and he found himself saying the next words before he could stop himself. "You make me look happy." Instantly, he wished he could take it back.

Anna looked up at him, her eyes questioning. Before she could ask what was on his mind, Hans stopped dancing. He nodded at the balcony doors just a few feet away. "You want to get some fresh air?" he suggested.

Anna nodded. "Fresh air would be nice," she said bashfully.

Anna and Hans were both silent as they looked out over the castle gardens. Hans wasn't sure what to do now. Until his little slipup on the dance floor, he had been in control of the situation. But now he wasn't sure. He knew he needed to keep the evening fun and light and, of course, romantic. He just didn't know how to do that exactly.

"You really are a lovely dancer," Anna said, breaking the silence. "Have you been to many balls?"

Hans shrugged. "I've been to my fair share, I suppose. Isn't that what princesses and princes do?" Catching the eye of a waiter passing by, Hans grabbed two glasses filled with sparkling cider. Then he snagged a small cream puff. "And eat, of course. We royals must eat." He held out the cream puff.

Taking the delicate dessert in her hand, Anna looked at it. "I suppose you're right. That is what we're supposed to do. I just haven't had much opportunity."

Hans smiled. "Well, maybe tonight should be all about new

opportunities," he said softly. "And speaking of new opportunities, I've heard the Arendelle gardens are truly spectacular. Would you be so kind as to give me a tour?"

Together, they made their way down into the gardens. Overhead, the moon hung heavy in the sky, its rays bathing everything in a crystal-bluish light. Hans half listened as Anna babbled on about the various flowers and plants they passed. He couldn't help noticing the way the moonlight made her hair glimmer. "What's this?" he asked, noticing a streak of white hair that had been tucked away. In the moonlight, it was bright white and hard to miss.

Self-consciously, Anna raised a hand to her head and gently touched the white strands. "I was born with it," she explained. "Although I dreamed I was kissed by a troll."

"I like it," Hans said, pleased to see Anna blush at the comment.

The couple toured the garden, laughing and chatting, the comfort between them growing with each passing moment. By the time they made it back to the balcony outside the ballroom, Hans was barely pretending to be having fun and Anna was no longer acting shy or reserved. In fact, she was the complete opposite. She had snagged a *krumkake* from the dessert table and was showing Hans how they ate the dessert in Arendelle.

"Yeah, the whole thing!" she cheered as Hans tried to press the rather large piece of cake into his face. It crumbled everywhere, causing Anna to laugh hysterically.

"You know, you'd fit right in on the Southern Isles," Hans said, wiping his face. "Everything is a competition back home."

Anna, who had been readying another *krumkake*, paused and

looked up. "Okay, wait, wait," she said, clearly eager to learn more about Hans. "So you have how many brothers?"

"Twelve older brothers," Hans replied. "Three of them pretended I was invisible. . . ." Anna laughed. But then Hans went on. "Literally. For two years."

Anna's face fell. "That's horrible," she said.

"It's what brothers do," Hans said, shrugging.

"And sisters," Anna added, her face pained.

Hans was surprised at the look on Anna's face. She and Elsa had seemed so happy together.

"Elsa and I were really close when we were little," Anna explained. "But then, one day, she just shut me out. I never knew why."

Looking down, Hans saw Anna's lower lip quiver.

He reached out and took her hand in his. "I would never shut you out."

CHAPTER 11

IS THIS WHAT LOVE is supposed to feel like? Anna asked herself as she stared into Hans's eyes. *This wonderful? This new?* Her stomach gurgled nervously. *This nerve-racking?*

For years, Anna had felt so alone. Her sister had shut herself off from the world. Her parents were dead. Her only friends were the household staff and the animals in the barn. And then, all of a sudden, Hans had swooped in and turned her life upside down.

Looking down, she saw that Hans's hand was still placed atop hers. She was surprised by the contrast. Hers was pale, the skin smooth and the fingers thin. His was large, and she imagined that under his glove the skin was slightly more sun-kissed. And yet they seemed to fit together so perfectly. . . .

"Can I just say something crazy?" she said, looking back up and into Hans's eyes.

Without hesitation, he answered, "I love crazy."

Anna smiled and opened her mouth, about to tell him that bumping into him was one of the best things that had ever happened to her. But she stopped herself, suddenly nervous and unsure. What if she said that and he didn't feel the same way? What if he ended up thinking she really *was* crazy for saying such a wild and spontaneous thing? So instead, she said the first thing that popped into her mind. "Do you wanna go sock sliding?"

As soon as the words were out of her mouth, she wanted to take them back. Sock sliding? Had she really just said that? Judging by the confused look on his face, she really had.

"Um, yes?" Hans said.

"It's really fun. You'll see." She turned and walked back into the ballroom, gesturing for him to follow her into a smaller parlor next door. Making sure they were alone, she leaned down and kicked off her shoes. She slid one foot forward, then the other. Soon she was gliding across the parlor floor like an ice-skater on ice. Anna kept her head down, worried that when she looked up, she would find Hans staring at her like she had three heads—or worse, she wouldn't find him at all because he would have run away. But when she finally got the courage to raise her eyes, her heart nearly burst out of her chest. Hans wasn't giving her a funny look. He had taken off his own shoes and was moving along the floor beside her! She giggled when he tripped and fell forward, catching himself just before he face-planted on the floor and then, in one smooth move, resuming his glide. *He's a quick learner,* Anna thought as she laughed and tried to keep her balance. Not that she had to worry about falling. Hans was always right there, ready to steady her, his strong hand on her waist making her feel safe.

"This is pretty fun," he said. "I mean, not exactly what I do back home, but I can see how you'd rather do this than dance with Duke Weaselly."

This time Anna didn't just giggle. She threw back her head and laughed. Urging her feet forward, she came to a sliding stop mere inches from Hans. "Like I said, not much opportunity to dance with other people. I often had the whole parlor to myself to slide. . . ." She gestured around the room. Unfortunately, in her excitement, she swung her arm a bit too hard and the momentum sent her flying straight into his chest. She had only a moment to register the thud of his heart against hers and then they were lying on the floor in a heap. "I'm so, so sorry!" she cried. "I keep falling on you and I don't mean to. My feet just seem to have a way of getting away from me. At least that's what Gerda says. She says that if there is something breakable in a room, I'll find it and . . ." Her voice trailed off as she realized Hans hadn't tried to move away from her.

"I'm beginning to realize I like having someone to hold steady," he said, reaching up and tucking a strand of her hair behind her ear.

Anna felt warmth rush through her, and she ducked her head shyly. "Really?" she asked.

"Really," Hans replied, smiling.

"Well, then I guess you must really like me," Anna said, the words popping out of her mouth before she could think better of it.

"I'm beginning to realize that, too," Hans said.

For a moment, they just lay there, the moonlight shining down on them through the balcony door. It was as though they were the only two people who existed in the world. Anna could have sworn she heard music in her head and felt her heart bursting.

Reluctantly, she stood up, breaking the spell. "We should probably get back to the ball," she said softly. "My sister is probably wondering where I am."

She quickly brushed herself off. The last thing in the world she wanted to do was go back into the ball. She felt like if she did, the moment would be over. Hans would waltz out of her life and she would never see him again. Watching as he got up, she suddenly knew she couldn't let that happen. "Or we could wait a little bit longer. Maybe we could go . . ."

"To the lighthouse," Hans suggested, finishing her sentence.

Her mouth dropped open. "I was just about to say that. How did you . . . ?"

"Know?" he asked, once again saying exactly what she was going to. He smiled. "I saw it when we sailed in, and I thought it was beautiful. Would you show me?"

A grin spread over Anna's face. "I would love to," she said happily. "Though I have to warn you, I've never been there myself. Or at least, not in a long time. Not since the gates closed . . ." Her voice trailed off. Despite the happiness flooding her body, the thought of what her life had been like before this night, and what it might be like after this night was over, made her sad.

As if sensing that, Hans grabbed her hand. "Well, what are we waiting for, then?" he asked. "Let's go exploring!"

The next hour felt like a fairy tale come true to Anna. They climbed to the top of the lighthouse and danced to their own tune. When they grew tired, they stopped and sat down, their backs against the lighthouse wall, heads tilted up to the sky. And then they talked. Hans told her more about growing up on the Southern Isles. He described the different islands and the long, low castle that reminded people of a sea serpent. She, in turn, told him what she had done to pass the time behind the closed gates of Arendelle's castle. It seemed as if Hans shared her taste in everything—even sandwiches!

"Only with the crusts cut off," Hans said.

"Oh, absolutely," Anna agreed, laughing. "Crusts are the worst. They're so . . . crusty." Hans burst out laughing. Anna loved making him laugh. And she loved that he made her laugh.

It feels so nice to just let go and enjoy the moment, Anna thought. *Not to worry about gates that never open or people who can never be seen or parents who will never come home.*

With each minute that passed, Anna felt more and more comfortable in Hans's presence. They had so much in common. It was almost as if he were custom made just for her. They just . . . fit. This had to be what love was—having someone who made the pain go away. Someone who filled all the holes in your heart. *Yes, this has to be it,* she had thought as they left the stables and made their way out of the castle gates and toward the hills above Arendelle. This was the big love. The love like she had read about. The love like in the stories she had crafted sitting in the gallery.

So when Hans suggested they make one more stop before going back to the castle, Anna didn't hesitate. She only smiled and nodded. She would go anywhere with Hans. He just had to say where.

Anna and Hans stood looking down at Arendelle. A waterfall rushed in front of them, the sound of the pounding water drowning out the sound of Anna's pounding heart. "I've always wanted to come up here," she said softly, looking up at the full moon. "I would sit in my room and see the water glinting and think it was magical. That the trolls who I dreamed about lived behind the water, and on nights like this they would come down and bestow gifts on the children of Arendelle. Special ones, like my hair. I always thought maybe it meant I was destined for something . . . amazing."

Reaching over, Hans gently pulled the white strand of hair loose and held it in his fingers. "You *are* destined for something, Anna. I can feel it. And I think, maybe, with you, life can be so much . . . more."

Anna smiled. "Do you really think so?" she asked softly.

Hans nodded. "Can I say something crazy?" he asked.

Anna smiled.

"Will you . . . marry me?"

Anna felt her heart skip a beat. She saw Hans looking down at her with hopeful eyes. She listened to the water pouring over the ancient rocks and wondered if this was the first time they had seen someone propose. She felt the cool mist wash over her skin and shivered. It was as though every sense was heightened, every emotion magnified.

True, she had just spent what had to be most amazing night of her life with Hans. And true, it felt like they were in perfect sync. And true, he was funny and handsome. And true, he seemed to be a great listener with a big heart. The part of her that believed in love at first sight wanted to scream yes. But there was a smaller part of her that was whispering, *"Think about what you are doing, Anna! You've just met this boy. Maybe you should take the time to get to know him."*

I don't have time, she argued to the little part of her that was being annoyingly realistic. *The gates will close tomorrow, and then who knows if I will ever see Hans again. And I don't think I can imagine a world without Hans in it. Not now.*

Slowly, Anna looked up at Hans. She knew what she needed to say. She knew what the right thing to do was. All she had to do was open her mouth and say the words. . . .

CHAPTER 12

WHAT WAS I THINKING? Hans thought in the moment after *the* question popped out of his mouth. Proposing to Anna after one evening was what Lars would call impetuous and his father would most likely call idiotic. True, he only had twenty-four hours to win Anna over. But had he moved too fast? Hans shook his head. He was going with his gut, and his gut had told him that this was a good idea. Or was that just all the chocolate fondue gurgling around? It was hard to tell.

Looking down at Anna, Hans waited anxiously. It had only been a second since he'd asked, but as he waited for her answer, it felt like an eternity. He could see Anna's brain working, and he imagined she was weighing the pros and cons. She wasn't stupid. That had become clear over the course of the evening. But she was a romantic and she was spontaneous. That might be all he needed to ensure he never had to go back to the Southern Isles, or his father, or anything else he had fled. Now if only she would give him an answer.

Just then, Anna opened her mouth.

Hans sucked in his breath, ready.

But she closed it again.

Hans's eyes bulged.

Anna took her own deep breath. "Can I say something even crazier?" she asked.

Hans crossed his fingers behind his back and nodded.

"Yes!" she cried, throwing her arms around Hans and squeezing him with all the might she could muster.

Hans let out a sigh of relief as a warm feeling flooded his chest. *Now, now,* he told himself. *Remember why you're here. This is a business transaction, nothing more.*

"Oh, Anna," Hans said, squeezing her hand. "You couldn't have made me happier. This is everything I always wanted and never even knew!" *Which is true,* he added to himself. *I* did *want to marry a princess, I just never thought it would be Anna. Funny how things work out.*

Anna laughed and began jumping up and down. "There is so much we have to do. Of course, we must get married soon! I'll need to talk to the seamstress about my dress—white, of course. Maybe with some lace on the sleeves? And a long train. I've always wanted a . . . Oops!" Unfortunately, the ground Anna had been jumping on was slick from the water, and her feet slid out from under her. Hans grabbed her arm and steadied her.

"Ha! Guess you'll be doing a lot of that for the rest of your life."

"I'm going to live to save you," Hans said, smiling. The right words just seemed to spill from his mouth.

Anna grinned. Gripping his arm tightly, she continued to make her plans. "Anyway, so we'll need to get my dress. And figure out what kind of food we'll have. I'm particularly fond of cheese, so we must have a cheese plate. And fondue, obviously." She winked at Hans.

As Anna continued to rattle off a list of things they had to do, Hans only half listened. *If only Father could see me now,* he thought. *He would have to be proud of me. All his other sons relied on him to make their matches. But not me. I did this all on my own. I can't wait to rub it in his face. And the faces of all my brothers.* Which reminded him . . .

"We will need to have my brothers at the wedding," Hans said, cutting Anna off mid-sentence. "As my groomsmen."

"Yes! Absolutely," Anna said eagerly. "What would a wedding be without family? How soon would they be able to get here? I can't wait to introduce them to Elsa. . . ." Suddenly, Anna's eyes grew wide. "Elsa! We have to get back to the castle and tell her our news right away. She is going to be so happy for us! I just know it. She'll probably want to help with all the planning. She has beautiful penmanship. She can totally help with the invitations. And then . . ."

Hans put a hand on Anna's arm. "My dearest," he said gently.

"Perhaps we should go tell her the news before we start assigning her work, don't you think?"

"Yes, you're probably right," Anna replied. "I'm just so excited."

"I am, too, Anna. I am, too. Now let's go find your sister."

As they walked back toward the castle, Hans began drafting a conversation with Elsa in his mind. If he thought asking Anna to marry him had been nerve-racking, the idea of asking Elsa for her approval was downright terrifying. He was going to have to pull out all the stops to try to impress her. Starting with making sure he looked head over heels in love with her younger sister. He just needed to get her to like him long enough to let him marry Anna. And if she didn't like him after? If he couldn't find an easy way to overthrow her? Well, he had always been a good improviser. Perhaps he would just have to change up his plan a little. Maybe get rid of Elsa altogether. It wouldn't be that hard. Crazy things happened around castles. One never knew when an accident might happen. . . .

He stopped himself. He would deal with that if the need arose. For now, he just needed to make sure he was as charming a prince as possible.

Hans didn't have long to prepare for his introduction to the queen. Anna sprinted back to the castle so fast he was barely able to keep up. Entering the ballroom, Hans was surprised to see that people were still dancing. Time had seemed to fly by while he was with

Anna. He had just assumed it was late and the ball was over. Yet the dance floor was still packed. The band was still playing, and food and drink were still coming out of the kitchen.

He and Anna pushed their way through the crowd. "Oops!" Anna said as she elbowed a young man. "Pardon!" she called as she passed by a waiter so fast that the tray the man was holding almost went flying. "Sorry!" she shouted as her foot caught the train of a woman's dress, ripping it. By the time they made their way to Elsa, Hans felt like he had been through a battle.

Beside him, Anna stood panting as she looked at her older sister. Compared to Anna, Elsa was calm and composed. It seemed as if she hadn't moved since the ball had begun. Her dress was smooth and unwrinkled, and every hair on her head was still in place. Looking over at Anna, Hans smiled. She, on the other hand, was a bit of a mess. Her hair was disheveled and there were water stains on the bottom of her dress. But it was hard to even notice. All anyone could probably see was the happy smile plastered on her face.

Let's hope Elsa sees how happy she is, too, Hans thought as Elsa took in her sister. Then she looked at Hans and raised an eyebrow. Hans gulped.

Quickly, Anna dropped into an awkward curtsy. "Elsa! I mean . . . Queen," Anna corrected herself. "Um, may I present Prince Hans of the Southern Isles."

Hans bowed deeply. Then he stood up straight and smiled his most charming smile. "Your Majesty," he said.

If he had thought Elsa would return his smile, he was wrong.

She merely nodded and gave him the slightest of bows. Okay, so charm might not be the best tactic with Elsa. Hans remembered the advice his father had given him after a particularly unsuccessful attempt to collect some back taxes. If you wanted to get someone to like you, you just had to act like a mirror. People loved their own reflection. He decided to mimic the comradery he had witnessed between the two sisters as best he could.

Anna, however, seemed blissfully unaware of Elsa's lack of interest and was nearly jumping out of her skin in her excitement to share the big news. "We would like . . ." she began.

". . . your blessing . . ." Hans added, trying to look as hopeful and innocent as possible.

". . . of . . ." Anna said. Then she looked over at Hans and smiled.

". . . our marriage!" they finished in unison. Hans reached over and took Anna's hand. That's what couples announcing their intent to marry did, right? Elsa was totally going to soften. She was going to open her mouth and say . . .

"I'm sorry. I'm confused."

That was not what Hans had expected to hear. Maybe an "Excuse me?" Or even an "Oh." But what was she confused about? They wanted to get married. It didn't seem complicated to him.

However, while Hans immediately sensed that this was not taking the turn he had hoped but rather the turn he had feared, Anna seemed to think her sister just needed clarification about the engagement. "Well, we haven't worked out all the details ourselves. We'll need a few days to plan the ceremony. Of course we'll have soup, roast, and ice cream, and then—" She looked over at Hans. "Wait. Would we live here?"

"Here?" Elsa repeated.

"Absolutely!" Hans said at the same time, his tone a little too eager for his liking. Of course they would live in Arendelle. Returning to the Southern Isles wasn't an option. He was done with that place. Finished for good. The only time he would ever even think about returning was when he had managed to pull this all off and he could sail there with his own fleet, trumpets blaring and a crown on his head.

Ignoring the look on Elsa's face, Anna kept going with her plan. "We can invite all twelve of your brothers to stay with us—"

"Wait," Elsa said, cutting off her sister. "Slow down. No one's brothers are staying here. No one is getting married." As she said this, she glared right at Hans.

He could practically hear what she was thinking. Her look said it all. She wasn't fooled by him. All of his smiling and loving glances at Anna hadn't done a thing to win Elsa over. To her, Hans was a stranger. Someone who had just swooped in and messed with her sister's heart. Which was, technically, true. With that one look, he knew Elsa was asking the question Anna *should* have been asking all along: *What are you after?*

Looking down at Anna standing beside him, he saw that the smile had faded from her face. It had been replaced by an expression of confusion, as if she couldn't quite process what her sister had just said. "Wait, what?" she asked Elsa, her voice shaking.

"May I talk to you, please?" Elsa answered. "Alone."

Anna shook her head stubbornly. Then she linked her arm with Hans's. "No," she said, the quaver in her voice gone. "Whatever you have to say you can say to both of us."

Hans tried not to groan. Why did Anna have to go and say that? Pitting the two of them against Elsa would only make the queen angrier. And more intent on separating the pair. *Please don't say what I think you are going to say,* he pleaded silently, looking at the queen's stern expression. *Please don't ruin everything I've worked for. Not now. Please just do not say . . .*

"Fine," Elsa said. "You can't marry a man you just met."

. . . that. Please just do not say that.

Hans let out a sigh. *Well, that went just swimmingly,* he thought. If "swimmingly" meant drowning in an ocean full of sharks while wearing stone shoes.

CHAPTER 13

YOU CAN'T MARRY a man you just met.

Elsa's words echoed in Anna's ears. She wanted to scream. She wanted to throw things and make a scene that would have people all over the kingdom talking for years to come. She wanted to grab her sister by the shoulders and shake her and beg her to be human. Beg her to understand that this was all Anna wanted in the world. But Anna knew she couldn't do any of those things. No matter how much she might want to let loose all the frustration and sadness that had been building for years, she would never do that to Elsa. She would never *really* make a scene and ruin Elsa's coronation. And yet she couldn't help wondering . . . Elsa had spent years denying Anna the love of a sister. Why did she have to deny her this, too?

Maybe that's the problem, Anna thought, suddenly hopeful. *Maybe Elsa just doesn't know what Hans and I have. Maybe I just need to tell her.* "You can if it's true love," she said, trying to keep her voice even despite the emotions raging through her body.

"Anna," Elsa said, "what do *you* know about true love?"

"More than you," Anna snapped, suddenly furious.

Had her sister seriously just questioned what Anna knew about true love? What did *Elsa* know about true love? At least Anna had been among the living since their parents died. She hadn't shut herself away from everyone and everything. Anna could feel her anger at her sister growing. *I was the one who kept trying,* Anna thought. *Every day when we were younger,* I *was the one who went and stood in front of her door and begged her to play with me.* I *was the one who tried to coax her out for silly games and bike rides around the castle. And every time, it was* Elsa *that turned me down cold. It was* Elsa *who offered me nothing. I always wanted my sister back. I always wanted her to love me. She was the one who couldn't have cared less.*

If not for the crowd that had slowly come closer and closer, Anna might have screamed her thoughts at her sister. How dare Elsa tell her what she could and couldn't do? After all these years of ignoring her, why did Elsa even *care* what Anna did with her life?

Staring at her sister's ice-cold expression, she tried to understand how they had gotten to this point. Weren't sisters supposed to be happy for each other at times like this? Did Elsa really not understand how much Anna needed this?

I just want to feel the happiness that comes with trusting someone with your whole heart. I want to know what it feels like to be with someone who wants to be with me, who doesn't turn away from me. Why? she asked Elsa silently, looking into her sister's eyes. *Why is that so hard to understand? Why can't I find out what true love is, even if you don't want to?*

Anna was sure there must be a way to change Elsa's mind. But when her sister finally spoke, her words broke Anna's heart all over again. "You asked for my blessing, but my answer is no." Elsa turned to go. "Now, excuse me."

Anna had been so caught up in her anger at Elsa that she had almost forgotten Hans was still at her side. To her relief, he stepped forward now and tried to support her. "Your Majesty," he said, grabbing on to Elsa's arm. "If I may ease your—"

"No, you may not," Elsa said, cutting Hans off. "And I think you should go." Ripping her arm free, she once again turned to leave. Passing by Kai, she paused only long enough to add, "The party is over. Close the gates."

Close the gates? No! Anna screamed silently. This wasn't over. The party wasn't over. Her time with Hans couldn't be over! If the gates closed, she knew she would never see her prince again. She would be stuck inside the castle with a sister who refused to speak to her. She'd be lonely forever.

"Wait!" Anna shouted. She reached for her sister's hand, but all she managed to do was pull off Elsa's long glove.

Elsa's reaction was swift. She spun around, and Anna saw that her sister's face had grown pale and she had begun to shake. It was as though Anna had chilled her sister to the bone, not just removed a single glove. Elsa reached out desperately. "Give me my glove!" she pleaded.

Anna shook her head as she felt tears well up in her eyes. She didn't want to fight with her sister. Just a few hours earlier, she had truly thought there was hope of salvaging their relationship. It would start with laughing over the Duke of Weselton and then a shared secret, perhaps, and then, *voila*! They would be true sisters again. And now . . . she honestly didn't know what was worse; her sister denying Anna's happiness or the fact that if Elsa didn't change her mind, Anna would never be able to forgive her.

"Elsa, please," Anna begged. "Please. I can't live like this anymore."

Elsa's eyes filled with tears. "Then leave . . ." she said, her voice weak. Turning, she once again began to rush away.

Anna recoiled, the words hitting her like a slap across the face. All of the anger and sadness she had been holding back poured out of her. "What did I ever do to you?" she shouted to her sister's retreating back. Her words echoed over the ballroom, which had gone silent, all eyes on the sisters.

"Enough, Anna," Elsa whispered harshly.

"No!" Anna was done suffering silently, done with the thousand unanswered questions. She wasn't going to let Elsa cut her out of her life without first getting some answers.

"Why do you shut me out? Why do you shut the *world* out? What are you so afraid of?" The questions tumbled out of her mouth, one running into the other.

"I said, *enough*!"

And then, as Anna watched in horror, a stream of ice shot out of Elsa's hand. Within seconds, huge sharp spikes of ice littered the floor. Guests cried out in shock. Some tried to run away, while others clung to one another.

"Sorcery!" Anna heard the Duke of Weselton say as he ducked behind his men. "I *knew* there was something dubious going on here!"

Anna looked over at her sister, all thoughts of a wedding gone. Surely she couldn't have seen what she thought she'd seen. Yet ice was still trailing from the tips of Elsa's fingers. And the look of pain on Elsa's face was almost too much for Anna to bear.

"Elsa?" she said softly.

For one brief moment, the sisters' eyes met, and then Elsa turned and ran.

Anna watched her sister race away. *What have I done?*

How could I have been so blind? Anna thought as she chased after her sister. *Is this why Elsa has always been so scared to be near me? Was she scared I would see her powers? How long has she even had these powers? Did Mama and Papa know? Is that why they kept us hidden behind the castle gates?*

The questions kept coming as Anna ran after her sister. All her anger had faded in the moment Elsa had revealed her powers. It made so much sense now. Her sister's coldness. Her isolation. *And here I was thinking* I *was the lonely one. I can't begin to imagine what life must have been like for Elsa all these years. I'm sure Mama and*

Papa told her never to speak of this, which makes sense. They didn't want people to fear her. Anna grimaced. It had taken the Duke only seconds to label Elsa a sorceress. What else might people be thinking of her? Anna had to go after her sister. Elsa needed her help.

As she made her way out of the castle, Anna could see just how right she was. Everywhere she looked, things had been frozen over. July had turned to December in mere moments. The staircase leading down from the castle was slick, ice covering each step. Below, she saw that the fountain's spray was now solid. Coins glinted at the fountain's bottom under a thick layer of ice. And then, as Anna watched in disbelief, snow began to fall from the sky. In the distance, she could see Elsa running toward the gates of the kingdom.

"Monster! Monster!"

Scanning the crowd below, Anna saw the Duke standing with his men. Anna realized the men were *scared* of Elsa. They were all rubbing their backsides while they shouted curses at her sister's retreating back. *I hope they fell down the stairs,* Anna thought. *No one calls my sister a monster.*

Anna made her way down the staircase as quickly and carefully as she could. She was vaguely aware of Hans's voice calling her name, but she didn't care. She needed to reach her sister. "Elsa!" she called as she ran. "Elsa! Wait!"

Elsa was already down at the fjord's edge. Pausing, she looked back, and Anna felt a flash of hope that this could end right here and now. But then her sister turned back and tentatively stepped onto the fjord. Instantly, the water beneath her feet froze. She took another step and then another, each one faster than the last.

Anna, not as sure-footed, slipped on the ice and fell. She watched in despair as Elsa made it to the far side of the fjord and then disappeared into the trees.

"No," Anna said, looking down at the single glove still clutched in her hand. This was all her fault. If she hadn't pushed Elsa . . .

"Anna!" Hans shouted as he reached her side. Sinking to the ground next to her, he put his arms around her. But Anna barely registered it. All she could see was the frozen fjord. All she could think about was her sister, racing away into the mountains as someone called her a monster.

"Are you all right?" Hans asked again.

He had been asking Anna over and over again since they had left the fjord and made their way back to the safety of the castle. A part of Anna realized it was sweet of him to be worried, but another part, a larger part, could only think about Elsa and wished he would just go away. She needed time to think.

"No," she finally said as they passed through the panicking crowd. She could hear people murmuring, "How can this be?" and "Snow," and "It's July!" Already it was getting colder, the snow beginning to pile up.

"Did you know?" Hans asked, trying to pull Anna out of her shock.

She shook her head. "No." *And what kind of sister does that make me? A horrible one, that's what kind.*

The Duke of Weselton's panicked shouts broke through Anna's

thoughts. "The queen has cursed this land! She must be stopped." He turned to his men. "You have to go after her."

No! No! NO! If the Duke's men went after Elsa, there was no telling what they would do. *I made this happen,* Anna thought as she pulled free of Hans and raced over to the Duke. When he saw her, the little man let out a squeak and ducked behind two of his men.

"You!" he shouted. "Is there sorcery in you, too? Are you a monster, too?"

Anna tried not to roll her eyes. The Duke was an imbecile. "No," she said. "I'm completely ordinary."

"That's right. She is," Hans said, stepping up beside her. "In the best way," he clarified.

For the first time since ice had shot from her sister's fingers, Anna smiled. She had forgotten how this whole thing had started. The marriage. True love. It was nice to have someone in her corner. But now Elsa needed someone in *her* corner.

"My sister's not a monster," Anna announced.

The Duke pointed at the staircase. "She nearly killed me!"

"You slipped on ice!" Hans corrected him.

"It was an accident," Anna said, though she had to admit it made her a little bit happy to know the Duke had indeed taken a tumble. "She was scared. She didn't mean it. She didn't mean any of this. . . ." Anna gestured to the courtyard, which now resembled a skating rink. "Tonight was my fault. So . . . I'm the one that needs to go after her."

"Fine," the Duke retorted. "Do."

Anna didn't bother to respond. She had made up her mind before the words were even out of her mouth. Nothing anyone could have said would have made a difference. But there was one person here she wanted to reassure. Putting a hand gently on Hans's arm, she gave him a squeeze. "Elsa's not dangerous," she said softly. "I'll bring her back . . . and I'll make this right. Until then, I need you here to take care of Arendelle. . . ."

CHAPTER 14

"I NEED YOU HERE to take care of Arendelle."

Hans felt Anna's small hand on his arm and heard her request, but for a few moments, he barely registered either. His head felt fuzzy, as though it, like the kingdom around him, were filling up with snow. Hans still wasn't sure what had happened. One minute he and Anna were getting engaged and telling Elsa, and the next the sisters were airing some major grievances in front of everyone. Then—*BAM!*—Elsa was shooting ice out of her fingers. It was the craziest—and scariest—thing he had ever seen. He had just wanted to turn and run. But then Anna had stepped up and taken charge of the situation. She had stood up to the Duke and now had this great big plan to go after Elsa. It was, he admitted reluctantly, rather impressive. And if Anna could find it within her to be strong in the face of something like this, Hans knew he had to as well. *Who knows,* he thought, some of his discomfort fading as he began to try to think like Anna, *maybe this will work out better for me in the long run. . . .*

"Hans?" With a start, Hans realized Anna was staring up at him, waiting for an answer. She seemed desperate to be on her way. She kept looking over her shoulder at the cold mountains in the distance. He couldn't help wondering if she had any idea of the amount of power she was putting in his hands.

Looking down into Anna's eyes, he finally nodded. "On my honor," he answered. His voice quavered slightly as he said the words, and he hoped Anna would chalk it up to nerves, not excitement.

She didn't even notice. Letting out a visible sigh of relief—after all, the temperature was now well below freezing—she grabbed her cloak from Kai's outstretched hand and then hopped onto her horse. Turning, she addressed the crowd. "I leave Prince Hans in charge!"

Instantly, the gathered crowd began to murmur. He made out a few confused "Prince Hans?" and "Who's Prince Hans?" questions. He could hear others saying things like "The princess shouldn't leave now," and "What will happen to us if she's gone?"

The thought gave Hans pause. He needed Anna if he was going to pull off his plan. What if something happened to her? He reached up a hand and placed it on Anna's knee. "Are you sure you can trust her?" he asked. "I don't want you getting hurt." And it was true. He *didn't* want to see Anna hurt. Elsa he didn't care about. In fact, Elsa's getting hurt or disappearing might just solve all his problems. But Anna . . . everything hinged on Anna now. Everything.

"She's my sister," Anna said. "She would never hurt me."

Then, snapping the reins, she turned her horse and galloped off.

Hans watched as the pair grew smaller. It was foolish of her to go alone. Hans was sure that after years locked in the castle, she knew nothing about tracking people, and surely she had little in the way of negotiating experience. And while Anna might not want to admit it, that was exactly what was going to happen when she finally found her sister—a negotiation. A give-and-take. *I've spent years doing that with my brothers,* Hans mused.

But if Hans had gone, what good would that really have done? They might have both ended up lost in the snowy mountains, and then Arendelle would be left without a leader. Or worse, the people, in their fear and desperation, would turn to someone like the Duke of Weselton. No, staying behind was the thing to do. It was actually a blessing in disguise. With Anna and Elsa gone and Arendelle in crisis, Hans would have a chance to prove himself—to make the people love him.

By the time Anna comes back, he vowed, *I'll have everyone begging her to marry me.*

Composing his features, Hans turned to the crowd. "People of Arendelle!" he shouted into the wind. "Princess Anna has put her faith in me, and now you must as well. I promise, I'll do everything in my power to keep you safe. I don't want anyone to worry needlessly. I'm here for you!" *And for myself,* he added silently. . . .

I might have bitten off more than I can chew, Hans thought a few hours later as he looked out over the courtyard. The situation was dire, to say the least. A layer of solid ice covered everything, and the snow was still falling fast. The sky was a dull slate gray, the sun swallowed up completely. And it was growing darker by the minute. In the port, Hans could hear the wood on the ships' hulls groaning with the growing pressure from the ice in the fjord. He knew it was only a matter of time before the ships would be reduced to little more than wreckage. *And shortly after that, they'll probably become fuel for all these fires,* Hans thought. Desperate for warmth of any kind, Arendelle's visitors were building fires all over the courtyard. The problem was it was July. No one had anticipated bad weather, and kindling was scarce. *It's only a matter of time before people start fighting over it,* Hans thought with worry.

He needed to do something. He had promised Anna. And the people. But every time he made his way off the castle steps and into the crowd, people grabbed at him, begged him to help, and asked him why this was happening. And he really had no answers. His bravado slipped away with each person he passed, and he began to question Anna's decision as well as his own bold words.

Sighing, he turned and made his way back into the castle. Gerda and Kai were rushing about, trying to keep candles lit and fires blazing. But the wind was whipping, and for every fire that stayed lit, two burned out.

"Gerda!" Hans called out. The older woman paused and looked over at him.

"Yes, sir?" she asked, her voice weary.

Hans opened his mouth to bark an order but thought otherwise. He could tell Gerda was scared. It wouldn't do to act like the bully. He needed to show her he was on her side. "Are you okay?" he asked. "Is there anything I can do for you?"

Gerda looked surprised. "I'm fine, sir," she said, giving him a quick, shy smile. "We must carry on. It's what the princess and the queen would want. I just don't know what to do is all."

"You leave that to me," Hans replied. "First things first. We need to make sure people are warm, right?" She nodded, and he felt a surge of confidence. "So I'll need an inventory of all the blankets we have. Both in the castle and in the stables. I don't need them to be clean. I just need them to be in one piece."

"Horse blankets, sir?" Gerda said.

Hans nodded. "At this point, I don't think anyone cares, do you?"

"I'll begin immediately." Gerda turned to go.

"Wait," he called out. "What else do you have to fight the cold? There must be a storeroom of the royal family's winter clothes, no? Send someone to collect everything they can from there, as well. Cloaks, stoles, muffs. Anything." He paused as another idea came to him. "And then let's go check out the Great Hall. We should be able to fit quite a few people in there. We can remove the furniture and then . . ."

Gerda nodded, her eyes wide as the prince continued to rattle off a list of to-dos: setting up cots; getting food from the pantry; providing toys for the young children to keep them distracted. Finally, noticing her look, Hans stopped and smiled sheepishly. "Am I asking too much?" he said.

"No, sir," she replied. "Not at all. I was just thinking . . . well, I was just thinking it is nice to have someone here to support the girls. It's been so long since the king . . ." Her voice trailed off.

Hans walked over and put a hand on her shoulder. "Don't fret, Gerda," he said, giving it a squeeze. "I'm here now."

"Yes, sir. Yes you are." Gerda turned to go and then paused. "I'll get going on the blankets first, Prince Hans. I'll find you as soon as we have some gathered."

As Gerda shuffled down the hallway, Hans let out a breath. This was more like it. He felt in control now. He was going to get the Great Hall set up as a relief station for Arendelle's visitors and get them inside, out of the elements. This day had confirmed what Hans had always believed to be true: he would make an *excellent* king.

It didn't take long for Gerda to gather up a large number of blankets and cloaks. Finding Hans in the library writing lists of what still needed to be done, she gestured for him to join her. When he walked into the hall, he was shocked to see at least a dozen castle staff standing there, arms loaded down with blankets in various colors, sizes, and shapes. A few more held warm cloaks in their hands. It was exactly what Hans had wanted.

"Good job, Gerda," he said. Gerda blushed at his praise. "Now, let's start getting these outside and delivered to our guests. If you see children, be sure to get them the warmest of the blankets, please. Same with the elderly. They will not be able to fight off the cold as well."

As the staff began to head toward the main castle door, Hans looked over at Gerda. "I'm going to go outside now. But I need you to stay here and work with Cook to get the soup and hot glogg into the Great Hall. I'll start sending people in shortly." Turning, he followed the staff out the door. It was time to show everyone the leader he could be—and would be—if they let him.

CHAPTER 15

HOT CHOCOLATE with fluffy marshmallows. Tea in a perfectly warm cup. Bed, right before I get out of it in the morning when it is all cozy and slept-in. Fuzzy slippers and mittens. Logs burning brightly in the big stone fireplace in my room. Warm. I just need to keep thinking warm and maybe I'll actually feel that way, Anna thought as she rode Kjekk through the deepening snow.

Who am I kidding? she thought a moment later as a particularly strong gust of wind sent thick snowflakes flying onto her already numb cheeks. *There is no way I'm going to feel warm.*

As Kjekk continued to trudge along, nickering worriedly every few steps, Anna looked around. It was hard to believe that it was July. Tree branches bowed almost to the ground under the weight of the snow and ice. The smaller shrubs and flowers that should have been blooming in abundance at this time of year were now buried. Every once in a while, Anna caught sight of a bird or a squirrel trying to find morsels of food in the frozen landscape. *Poor things,* Anna thought. *They weren't prepared. None of us were.*

Shivering, Anna pulled up the collar of her cloak, trying unsuccessfully to block the flakes of snow that were making their way down the back of her dress. "Elsa! Elsa!" she called out, hoping her sister hadn't made it too far. "I'm sorry! It's all my fault!"

She was met with silence. Sighing, she urged her horse to move faster. So far away from the lights of Arendelle, it was completely dark. But since Anna had no intention of going home without her sister, she would have to keep looking, light or no light. *I just need to fix this. Then I can go home and see Hans. . . .*

The thought of Hans gave Anna a momentary rush of warmth. Hans. Wonderful, perfect Hans. Thank goodness for him. If he hadn't been there? Anna shuddered to think. She couldn't have left Arendelle without someone in charge, and there was no way she trusted the Duke of Weselton—or any of the other dignitaries, for that matter. The only person she trusted was Hans. She had immediately felt better when he stepped up so gallantly and heroically accepted the reins. It had been like something out of a love story. *I wonder what he's doing now?* she thought, clinging to the warmth that thinking of him brought. *Probably something amazing and adorable, like tucking a young child under warm blankets and reading him a story . . . I'm sure he's already secured the kingdom and ensured everyone's safety.* Anna's heart fluttered. *Thank goodness for*

Hans. Elsa needs me right now, and without him, I never could have gone after her.

As Anna got lost in her thoughts, her hands loosened on the reins and her legs no longer gripped the saddle quite so tightly. So when a branch snapped from the weight of the snow and Anna's horse reared up, she didn't stand a chance of staying on. She felt herself being flung forward and then, with a thud, found herself lying facedown in the snow.

Well, that's just peachy, she thought, sitting up and spitting out a mouthful of snow. Then she caught sight of Kjekk—running back down the mountain. *And that just happened, too. Perfect,* she thought. *Next thing you know, some hungry wild animals are going to show up.*

In the distance, a wolf howled.

Anna scrambled to her feet and brushed the snow off her dress. Taking a deep breath of very cold air, she looked ahead. Then she looked back at her retreating horse. A small part of her wanted to run after him and just go home. Find Hans and have him wrap her in his warm embrace. Maybe have Cook make some of her delicious hot glogg. Put on her slippers . . .

Anna shook her head. She wasn't going to turn her back on Elsa. Even if it meant walking alone, in the dark, in the snow . . .

Another wolf howled.

The long walk back to Arendelle would have to wait.

Anna had come to the conclusion that the three things she hated the most in the world were *ärtsoppa*, people who were mean to animals, and snow. Snow was at the very tip-top of her list. She would actually have made it all three of her least favorite things, but she did remember a time that she had liked playing in the fluffy stuff. So in honor of the memories, she had only listed it once. At number three.

She had been walking for hours, and while she knew she must be making headway, it felt like she had gone nowhere. The landscape looked the same. A mountain. Snow-covered trees. Snow-covered ground. It didn't change. The only difference now was that Anna was colder and her feet were sorer than they had been hours ago.

"Snow. It had to be snow," Anna said, taking another painful step up the mountain. "She couldn't have had tr-tr-tropical magic that covered the f-f-fjords in white sand and . . ." Her voice trailed off as she reached the top of a small rise. In the distance, she saw the most wonderful sight in the whole wide world—smoke! And where there was smoke, there was usually . . . "Fire!" Anna shouted, jumping up and down excitedly.

Unfortunately, Anna's toes were numb and didn't quite comprehend the concept of jumping. With a cry, she fell and began tumbling down the hill. Her roll was only stopped when she landed—*splat*—in an icy stream. Anna fought through the shivers that made her shake all the way to her fingertips. She had seen a fire, which meant there had to be people close by. Maybe people with warm things.

Getting to her feet, Anna double-timed it in the direction of the smoke. By the time she arrived in a clearing in the woods, her dress was frozen stiff and she had to keep reaching up to her face to make sure her nose was still there. In the middle of the clearing was a small log cabin with several outbuildings behind it. A sign that read WANDERING OAKEN'S TRADING POST hung out front. Shuffling over, Anna smiled when she saw the smaller sign underneath that read SAUNA. She had most definitely stumbled upon a good place to stop.

I'll go in, get some supplies, sit in the sauna for a bit, maybe get a snack— Anna stopped herself. This was no time for saunas or snacks. *I need to keep looking for Elsa,* she thought as she made her way up the front steps of the store. *I can get a snack for the road. Elsa may be a little mad at me at the moment, but she wouldn't want me to starve to death. Freeze, maybe, but not starve.*

Cautiously, Anna pulled open the door and stepped through. The door, heavy from the snow, slammed shut, hitting her in the butt and sending her flying into the middle of the store. *That was a quiet entrance,* Anna thought, rubbing her backside. Shrugging, she looked around. It wasn't a very large shop, and what supplies it had all seemed to be for summer. Fishing rods, bathing suits, dresses . . .

"Hoo-hoo!"

Startled, Anna whipped around. A large man with a bright red beard and rosy cheeks sat behind the shop's counter. He was wearing a sweater that appeared a few sizes too small and a hat that barely covered his head. This had to be Oaken of Wandering Oaken's Trading Post. He gave Anna a big salesman's smile. Then he gestured to the shelves she had just been looking at. "Big summer blowout," Oaken said in a singsong. "Half off swimming suits, clogs, and a sun balm of my own invention, yah?" His eyebrows raised hopefully.

"Oh, uh, great," Anna said, trying to be polite. "For now, how about boots? Winter boots . . . and dresses?"

Oaken looked disappointed. "That would be in our winter department." He raised a finger and pointed to another part of the store. A much smaller, less stocked part of the store. The winter section contained exactly one outfit, a pickax, and one lonely pair of boots that Anna prayed were close to her size.

Well, beggars can't be choosers, Anna thought as she went over and picked up the clothes and the boots. "Um, I was just wondering," she said over her shoulder. "Has another young woman, the queen perhaps, I don't know . . . maybe, uh, passed through here?" She brought her new gear up to the counter.

Oaken shook his head. "Only one crazy enough to be out in this storm is you. . . ."

In challenge, the door once again swung open. What might have been a very large man, though it was hard to tell through the thick layer of snow and ice, blew in.

"You and this fellow," Oaken continued with a shrug. Then he looked at the ice man. "Hoo-hoo! Big summer blowout."

The man ignored Oaken and walked right up to Anna. She took a startled step back. *This guy clearly knows nothing about personal space,* Anna thought. She couldn't help noticing, however, that his eyes, which were the only feature visible at the moment, were a deep brown, like the rich mahogany shelves that lined the library walls, and his shoulders were broad and looked strong. She also noticed he smelled a bit like . . . reindeer?

"Carrots," the man said.

Anna raised an eyebrow. "Huh?" she replied.

"Behind you," he explained.

"Oh, right. Excuse me," Anna apologized. Stepping out of the way, she watched as the man grabbed a bunch of carrots and unceremoniously tossed them onto the counter. Then he began to move about the small shop, gathering other supplies.

Well, he's *awfully rude,* Anna thought as the man crashed through the place like a snow-covered bull in a not-so-fancy china shop.

While Anna was bothered by the stranger's behavior, Oaken seemed unfazed. He simply bagged up the supplies as the man threw them. "A real howler in July, yah?" he said, holding up the ice pick. "Wherever could it be coming from?"

"The North Mountain," the other man replied matter-of-factly.

The North Mountain, Anna repeated to herself. The storm was bursting out of the North Mountain. That could only mean one thing. *Elsa has to be there!* Anna grew excited. This was just the kind of clue she needed. Now she had a destination. She looked down at her meager supplies. Just not a way to get there, really. Hearing raised voices, Anna looked over at the two men. Oaken was holding up four fingers.

"Forty?" she heard the snow-covered man say. He shook his head. "No. Ten."

Oaken was having none of it. "Oh, dear," he said in a voice

as sweet as pie. Then he shrugged. "That's no good. See, these are from our winter stock, where supply and demand have a big problem."

Anna could have sworn she saw steam begin to rise off the man when he realized Oaken wasn't going to barter. Then he shook himself like a dog coming out of the water. Snow and ice fell to the ground, revealing a young man probably a few years older than her with rosy cheeks and thick blond hair. He had on a gray fur-lined vest and a thick wool sweater that looked, Anna had to admit, well used but very, very cozy. "You want to talk about a supply and demand problem?" he asked. "I sell *ice* for a living." He pointed out the window. Following his fingertip, Anna saw a sled filled with ice, which was currently being covered in snow. And a reindeer. *That explains the smell,* Anna thought, raising an eyebrow.

"Ooh! That's a rough business to be in right now," Anna said. "I mean, that is really . . ." Her voice trailed off as the young man shot her a look. She coughed. "That's unfortunate." She felt sorry for the stranger.

Oaken, however, did not. "Still forty. But I will throw in a visit to Oaken's sauna." He pointed to a steamed-up glass door on the other side of the store. But it wasn't steamy enough to hide the family sitting inside. Anna waved awkwardly and then looked away. It didn't seem quite the incentive she had first thought.

"Ten's all I got," the man said, holding out his meager money. "Help me out."

Oaken paused, and for a moment, Anna wondered if he was going to change his mind. But then he simply grabbed the carrots and separated them from the rest of the supplies. "Ten will get you this and no more."

While Anna was more than happy to let the pair negotiate until the sun came up, she was eager to get on her way. And to get a few more answers. "Just tell me one thing," she said, tugging on the young man's sleeve. "What was happening on the North Mountain? Did it seem . . . magical?"

"Yes!" the young man said as he rolled up the sleeves of his sweater and raised his fists. Then he glared at Oaken. "Now, back up while I deal with this crook here."

As Anna watched, Oaken stood up, offended by the other man's name-calling, and unceremoniously threw him out the front door. Her mind was racing. She had to figure out what to do next. Elsa was definitely up on the North Mountain somewhere. She just didn't know where *exactly*. But the ice guy seemed to know. . . .

As Oaken turned back and began to wrap up her boots and outfit, Anna looked at the young man's abandoned supplies and smiled. She knew just what to do. Now if only she could get a certain reindeer-scented ice seller to agree.

It didn't take Anna long to find the ice harvester. The first giveaway was the human-shaped indent in the snow outside the store, followed by the footprints leading toward a small outbuilding. The second giveaway was auditory: Anna could hear singing coming from inside the small building.

Anna slowly approached and peeked through the open door.

She saw the man lying back on a big pile of hay, as though he didn't have a care in the world. Next to him was a large reindeer with huge antlers who appeared to be . . . smiling? *Interesting,* Anna thought. Even more interesting was the singing coming from the man. He kept changing his voice, sometimes singing as "Sven," who Anna assumed was the reindeer, and sometimes singing as himself. Not wanting to interrupt, Anna waited for him to finish before she entered the barn.

"Nice duet," Anna said.

The man bolted upright. Then, seeing who it was, he relaxed once more, lying back on the hay. "Oh, it's you," he said, placing his hands behind his head. "What do you want?"

"I want you," Anna said, daring him to challenge her, "to take me up the North Mountain."

"I don't take people places," he replied, not at all daunted by Anna's stare. He closed his eyes.

So he wants to play that *game,* Anna thought as she looked down at the man. *Does he think I've never in my life had to do something like this?* Well, technically she *had* never had to do something like this. But that wasn't the point. The point was that she'd figured this ice harvester character wouldn't be the easiest to deal with and so she had thought ahead.

"Let me rephrase that." As Anna spoke, she picked up a heavy bag of supplies that she had carried from Oaken's shop and tossed it at him. It landed with a thud right on his lap. *Not too shabby,* Anna thought, turning back to the ice gatherer. "Take me up the North Mountain . . . please?" She couldn't help it: the "please" just slipped out. Years of etiquette lessons were ingrained in Anna. Her manners just seemed to come out, whether she wanted them to or not.

When the man still didn't say yes, Anna sighed. "Look, I know how to stop this winter," she explained.

At that, the harvester seemed to perk up. "We leave at dawn," he replied without hesitation. Then he held up the bag. "And you forgot the carrots for Sven."

But Anna hadn't forgotten the carrots. They were right next to her. Grabbing them, she threw them at the man—hard. The orange vegetables hit him square in the face. "Oops! Sorry! I didn't mean—" She caught herself. She *was* sorry, but she wasn't about to let him know that. She needed to look strong and in charge. She put her hands on her hips. "We leave now. Right now."

Turning, she walked back outside. *I really hope that worked,* Anna thought as she waited to see if he would follow her. *Because if it didn't*—she looked up into the darkness of the North Mountain—*I'm in for a very long, lonely walk.*

Anna heard an exaggerated sigh from behind her, followed by the man's thumping footsteps as he gathered his things.

Yes! Anna cheered—silently, of course.

As the man emerged from the barn, he turned to Anna. "Well, if we're going to head up a treacherous mountain into a magical July blizzard, I should probably know your name."

"Oh! I'm Anna. Er, the princess of Arendelle. My sister's kind of the queen. And she may be . . . might be . . . causing this storm," Anna said, her confidence melting away the farther she got into her story. Instead of trying to explain anything more, she turned the question back around on her guide. "And I suppose you're some super-special master ice harvester?"

"The name's Kristoff," he replied. "And I do happen to be a pretty great ice harvester, now that you mention it. In fact, I hold the Arendelle record for the most ice delivered in one day!"

Anna raised an eyebrow. "Is that supposed to be impressive?" Anna thought about her life in the castle. Ice had always just been there when she needed it. She'd never really thought about how it got there. Or what it might be used for other than cooling drinks. "I mean, people can't need *that* much ice, can they?" she asked.

Apparently, that was not the right thing to say. Kristoff's already red cheeks grew redder, and he sputtered in disbelief. "People can't need that much ice?" he repeated. "Lady, people need *loads* of ice. Loads and loads. And harvesting it is not exactly easy. Have you ever tried to move a block of ice?" Anna shook her head. "I didn't think so. They are heavy! Really heavy. Right, Sven? Sven?"

Anna turned her head. The reindeer had emerged from the barn, still chewing on a ridiculously large clump of hay. Hearing his name, he looked up. Wisps of hay dangled from his antlers and out of his mouth, making him resemble a reindeer-shaped scarecrow.

"I can tell it's a very serious business," Anna said, trying not to laugh.

"It *is* a serious business," Kristoff snapped, his temper flaring. It only made Anna smile more. "How do you think your precious food at the castle stays cool? Magic?"

Anna cringed, the words hitting too close to home. Kristoff's mention of magic had brought it all rushing back. "I didn't know," she said softly. "I'm sorry."

"No, no," Kristoff said, realizing that he had touched a nerve. "I'm the one that's sorry. I didn't mean it . . . I just, well . . . sometimes I say the wrong thing. I spend a lot of time with just Sven, and, well, he's not always the best conversationalist. . . ."

The reindeer let out a loud harrumph and knocked the ice harvester to the ground.

Despite the somber turn the conversation had taken, Anna had to laugh. The reindeer was adorable, and Kristoff struggling to apologize was pretty cute, too. "Well, do you want to make it up to me?" she finally asked.

Kristoff smiled as he threw their supplies into the back of his sled. "Let's get going."

CHAPTER 16

AFTER THE SLIGHTLY rocky start, Hans was now getting quite comfortable as temporary leader of Arendelle. With the help of Gerda and the other household staff, he had turned the Great Hall into a relief station, complete with warm clothes and food to comfort both the townsfolk who couldn't reach their homes and the many foreign guests who were now trapped in the frozen kingdom. He just had a few more things to take care of inside before he could go back out and announce that the relief station was open.

It had only been a few hours since Queen Elsa had turned the world white, and already things inside the kingdom's walls were beginning to descend into chaos. In the courtyard Hans had seen men and women fighting over scraps of wood while their children stood by, shivering. He had seen one sneaky-looking young man blatantly take a pile of wood when the people fighting were too busy to notice. And really, it wouldn't matter if they were fighting or not. Wood was scarce. He had considered sending men out to gather firewood, but it was the dead of night, and he didn't want to risk losing anyone in the darkness. When their supply of wood ran out, that would be it till morning.

That was why Hans was pleased to offer people a warmer place to go for the night. True, the Great Hall was drafty in the relentless wind, and even the thickest of windows and curtains couldn't keep out the strong chill, but it was better than nothing. *Yes,* Hans thought as he checked the glogg one more time to make sure it was hot, *this will be just what the people need. And just what* I *need,* he mused, *to ensure that my position becomes less temporary and more permanent.*

I wonder how Anna is doing, he thought suddenly. Pondering his future position here in Arendelle made it impossible not to think of his fiancée. She clearly hadn't found her sister yet, as the snow was still falling. Or if she had, things weren't going well. Elsa's powers were impressive. And Anna had none. If the pair were to face off . . . Well, it most likely wouldn't end well for his betrothed. The thought of something happening to Anna sent a shiver down his spine. If she didn't come back, how would he secure control of Arendelle?

Hearing a noise behind him, he turned and saw Gerda entering the Great Hall. She was holding out a pile of cloaks. He nodded. It was time to get outside and help "his" people.

Hans made his way out of the castle and down into the crowd. "Cloak," he called out. "Does anyone need a cloak?" The people flocked to him, their arms outstretched. Soon people were thanking him and trying to hug him. They were no longer questioning who he was. Now Hans heard people calling him "savior" and "hero."

"Arendelle is indebted to you, Your Highness," Gerda said. She had been beside him the entire time, and now she looked up at him, a smile on her face.

Hans smiled back at Gerda, pleased by how natural "Your Highness" sounded as she addressed him. He looked back at the crowd. "The castle is open," he said, his voice loud and steady. "There's soup and hot glogg in the Great Hall. Please, go in and get warm."

Instantly, a wave of people rushed past Hans, jostling to be the first ones inside. However, not everyone was eager to get to the soup. Hans spotted the Duke of Weselton and his two men lurking nearby. A few of the other visiting dignitaries stood across the courtyard from him. While most of them looked genuinely concerned about the state of Arendelle and its people, the Duke had his hands on his hips and was watching the scene unfold with disdain. It seemed now was a good time to take a few moments to visit Arendelle's esteemed guests. The last thing Hans wanted was the Duke talking to them first. Turning to a guard who stood nearby, Hans handed the man a stack of cloaks. "Here. Pass these out to anyone who still needs them," he ordered.

As Hans approached the dignitaries, he mentally reviewed quick backgrounds on each. Once again, it seemed all his preparation for this visit was paying off. He saw the representative from Zaria, a thin, reedy man with a huge beard that reached past his belt. That,

Hans knew, was a sign of wealth in the man's kingdom. He would be good to have as an ally. He was one of the most respected men here, although not exactly the most outgoing of sorts. Next to him was Prince Wils, who certainly *was* the outgoing sort. Despite the rather dreary situation, he made a comment to Prince Freluke that Hans couldn't make out and then burst into laughter. Hans tried not to smile. The man's laugh sounded like a little girl's. Gaining his support was not of great importance to Hans. Vakretta was a small kingdom with little to offer in the way of power or trade. Moving on, he spotted the lord of Kongsberg as well as the representatives from Blavenia and Eldora. Of the three, these were the two dignitaries who Hans wanted to win over. The lord of Kongsberg was too powerful. He wouldn't need to listen to Hans, whereas the dignitaries would be more eager to gain power. The Blavenian was practically his already—their country was significantly in debt to the Southern Isles. And Hans was skilled at collecting what was owed him.

Hans smiled to himself. Knowing a little bit about each of the men put him at a distinct advantage. They, he was sure, knew nothing of him. Why would they? Up until today he had been nothing more than a thirteenth son.

But he was about to prove how little that mattered now.

Stopping in front of the group of men, Hans bowed. The men followed suit. "Good sirs," Hans began. "I'm sorry that this is not quite the celebration we had in mind. I do hope we have been able to make you as comfortable as possible given the situation."

"Quite so, quite so," bubbled Prince Wils. "Who doesn't like a little snow in summer?"

"I, for one," the lord of Kongsberg replied. "Prince Hans, have you any word from the princess? How much longer do you suppose we will have to wait for her return? I have people at home who will not be pleased by a long absence, and I find the whole thing rather suspicious. What is your role in all of this?"

"I am doing all in my power to—"

"What power?" the lord snapped back. "You have no real power besides what was handed to you by a silly little princess in over her head. I will not be made a fool. If this is all some grand scheme to keep us trapped here in Arendelle, I will make you suffer."

"Now, now," Prince Wils said, his face distraught at the lord's words. "There is no need for such threats, is there? What point would there be in keeping us here? I'm sure Prince Hans is doing everything he can."

"Prince Hans?" the lord shot back. "I have never heard that name before today and yet look at him. Running around as though he were king. It makes one suspicious. . . ."

Hans knew he had to regain control of the conversation—and fast. If the lord convinced the others of his doubts, it could mean ruin. A sudden surge of anger welled up in Hans and he forced it back down. This was not the time to let emotion rule. So the lord of Kongsberg was a bully. Hans had grown up with twelve bullies! He knew just how to deal with them—and the number one rule was never let them see you sweat. Turn the bullying back on the bully. Like his father had taught him, the best thing to do in a situation like this was act like a mirror.

"Enough!" Hans said, silencing the lord instantly. "Do not

think for a moment that just because you hold power in some faraway kingdom you can come here and treat me like a child. I am a prince! I am a prince betrothed to the princess of this kingdom. Do not dare question me or my motives. My motives are simple—protect Arendelle. We should be working together to help Arendelle, not fighting amongst each other like whales over a seal." He stopped and took a breath. "Now, instead of throwing barbs, don't you think our time would be best spent offering up suggestions on how to fix our current problem?"

For a moment, the lord said nothing. He just looked at Hans as though for the first time. Then he bowed his head ever so slightly. "I'm sorry, Prince Hans. You do indeed seem to have the situation well under control. I suppose all we can do is wait for Princess Anna's safe return."

"Yes, that was my thought exactly," Hans said, trying not to smile. Bullying the bully. He would have to remember to thank his brothers the next time he saw them. This was probably the first time in his whole life they had actually helped. Now the whole group was looking to him for guidance. He would just have to spend a little more one-on-one time with a few of them, and then he would have not only control of Arendelle, but allies to boot.

Unfortunately, there was still one large, or rather one quite small, person who could get in his way. Hearing footsteps behind him, Hans turned to see the Duke of Weselton approaching. "Well, this should be interesting," he said over his shoulder to the other men.

"I've never trusted that man," Prince Wils said softly. "Never trusted him one bit."

"Neither do I, Prince Wils," Hans said. "But I suppose we should hear him out."

"His mustache worries me," the Eldoran dignitary added. "It's just so . . . bushy. It looks like an animal."

Laughing in agreement, Hans squared his shoulders and, with newfound confidence, turned back just as the Duke came to a stop in front of him.

"Prince Hans," the Duke began immediately. "Are we expected to sit here and freeze while you give away all of Arendelle's tradable goods?"

And now to shut down bully number two, Hans thought. "Princess Anna has given her orders and—"

The Duke cut him off. "That's another thing," he said, sneering. "Has it dawned on you that your princess may be conspiring with a wicked sorceress to destroy us all?"

Instantly, Hans's expression went from obliging to icy. "Do not question the princess," he said, his tone as dark as when he had cut down the lord of Kongsberg. "She left me in charge, and I will not hesitate to protect Arendelle from treason."

"Treason?" the Duke repeated, looking confused and suddenly slightly scared.

Hans nodded and was about to explain just what he meant when he heard the sound of hooves clattering over ice. A moment later, Anna's horse galloped into sight. He was covered in sweat and breathing heavily. The saddle was tilted to the side, and one stirrup was missing.

Grabbing the reins, Hans began to soothe the horse. But he needed soothing as well. Something had happened to Anna. Turning, he saw that the men were now looking at him, their frightened faces mirroring his own. Without Anna, he had nothing. What was he going to do now?

CHAPTER 17

"HANG ON! We like to go fast!"

As Kristoff shouted his warning to Anna, he slapped the reins against Sven's neck, urging the reindeer on. Up ahead, the North Mountain rose into the night sky, blocking out the stars and casting long shadows on the woods below.

If Anna had stopped to think about what she was doing, she might have been scared—or at least a bit nervous. After all, she was racing toward Elsa on a sleigh of questionable quality with an ice harvester she had just met. But she didn't have time to think.

"I like fast!" Anna shouted back, the wind whipping her long braid behind her and flakes of snow pelting her cheeks. Leaning back on the bench seat, she put her feet up on the dashboard and her hands behind her head. She looked up at Kristoff and smirked, daring him to drive faster. *Take that, Mr. Ice Man. You're not the only one who is adventurous. I'm* all *about adventure.*

"Whoa, whoa!" he shouted, pushing her feet back to the floor. "Get your feet down." For a moment, Anna was surprised that he actually seemed concerned for her safety. But then he added, "This is fresh lacquer. Seriously, were you raised in a barn?" Then he spit on the dash and shined it with his shirtsleeve.

Anna raised an eyebrow. The irony of Kristoff asking if *she* was raised in a barn was not lost on her. Nor was the spit that flew in her face as Kristoff continued to clean his precious sleigh. *And he thinks* I *have no manners?* "Um, ew!" she said, wiping her face and giving him a look of disgust. "And no, *I* was raised in a castle."

"So tell me," Kristoff said. "What made the queen go all ice-crazy?"

Anna sighed. She had known sooner or later she would have to tell Kristoff the whole story. She had just hoped it would be later. "It was all my fault," she explained. "I got engaged, but then she freaked out because I'd only just met him, you know, that day. And she said she wouldn't bless the marriage—"

"Wait," Kristoff said, cutting her off. "You got engaged to someone you just met?"

"Yeah," Anna replied with a shrug. "Anyway, I got mad and so she got mad and then she tried to walk away, and I grabbed her glove—"

Once again, Kristoff interrupted her. "Hang on. You mean to tell me you got engaged to someone you *just* met?"

Anna wondered if Kristoff had a hearing problem. She had just told him yes less than a minute before. And why was he looking at her like she had two heads? If he was going to insist on asking her the same question over and over again, they really weren't going to get far. "Yes," she finally said. "Pay attention."

As she continued to describe what had happened, she felt Kristoff's gaze on her. It made her uncomfortable and she wiggled away a bit, talking faster. Still, he continued to stare at her. *Do I have something on my face?* Anna wondered. *Or in my teeth? And why won't he watch where he's going?* She shook her head as she finished telling him what had led to Arendelle's winter in July.

But Kristoff didn't seem interested in Elsa and her magic at all. "Didn't your parents ever warn you about strangers?" he asked.

"Yes, they did," Anna said, pointedly looking at Kristoff, the strange ice harvester she had just met that day. "But Hans is *not* a stranger."

Kristoff raised an eyebrow. "Oh yeah? What's his last name?"

Ha! His last name. What a stupid thing to ask! Of course I know his last name. It's . . . it's, uh . . . I have it. I know it! Anna frowned. She didn't have it. "Of-the-Southern-Isles?" she replied, hoping her answer sounded the least bit convincing.

"What's his favorite food?" Kristoff asked, clearly not buying the last name.

"Sandwiches," Anna retorted. What was this? Twenty Questions? What did it matter, anyway? So she didn't know a *few* things about him. She had plenty of time to learn that stuff. But as Kristoff continued to grill her, it became clear that it was more than a few things she didn't know.

"Best friend's name?"

"Probably John."

"Eye color?"

"Dreamy."

"Foot size?"

Anna shot him a look. "Foot size doesn't matter."

Kristoff shrugged. He paused, and for one brief moment Anna thought maybe he was going to stop with the inane questioning. But then he kept going. "Have you had a meal with him yet? What if you hate the way he eats? What if you hate the way he picks his nose?"

"Picks his nose?" Anna repeated, repulsed at the thought.

Kristoff nodded. "And *eats* it?"

"Excuse me, sir. He's a *prince*."

"All men do it," Kristoff said, shrugging.

What he clearly means is that he does it, Anna thought. *Which doesn't have any bearing on what my Hans does. And if on the slim, slim,* slimmest *chance Hans ever has done such a thing, I'm sure it was done gracefully and that he didn't then eat it.*

"Look, it doesn't matter," Anna said, trying to put an end to the conversation. "It's true love."

"Doesn't *sound* like true love."

Anna nearly laughed out loud. "Are you some sort of love expert?" she asked, looking the burly man up and down. She was willing to bet that the only thing he had ever loved—besides himself, obviously—was his reindeer.

"No," Kristoff acknowledged. "But I have friends who are."

"You have friends who are love experts?" she said. "I'm not buying it. . . ."

Suddenly, the sleigh began to slow down. Sven's pace grew more hesitant as he raised his head, ears perked and nostrils flared.

"Stop talking," Kristoff whispered. When she opened her mouth, he clamped his hand over it. "I mean it! *Shhh!*"

Well, I never! Anna fumed. *Just because I was winning that argument doesn't mean . . .*

But then Kristoff stood up and raised his lantern. Anna gulped. The light had illuminated the woods that surrounded them—and revealed several pairs of yellow eyes. Several pairs of yellow eyes that were moving closer. *This,* Anna thought, *is probably not good.*

"Sven, go!" Kristoff shouted, giving voice to Anna's fears.

"What are they?" Anna asked as she was thrown back onto the sleigh's seat.

Beside the moving sleigh, she could see flashes of white as the creatures, whatever they were, moved in and out of the trees, keeping pace with Sven.

"Wolves," Kristoff said, throwing the reins over the dashboard and jumping into the back of the sleigh.

Wolves. Okay, I can handle wolves, Anna thought. *They're just like dogs—only bigger and meaner and I think they have sharper teeth.* She shuddered. Then, taking a deep breath so Kristoff wouldn't see she was scared, she called out to him, "What do we do?"

The sleigh lurched to the right as Sven swerved, barely avoiding a huge tree stump in the middle of the path. Kristoff was thrown off-balance. His arms waved wildly in the air, and for a moment it looked as if he was going to go flying. Then he steadied himself and shot Anna a stern look. "I've got this. You just . . . don't fall off and don't get eaten."

"But I want to help," Anna protested.

"No!" Kristoff shouted over his shoulder as he rummaged through the sleigh's supplies, looking for makeshift weapons.

"Why not?"

"Because," Kristoff said. "I don't trust your judgment. Who marries a man she just met?"

The words hit Anna like a slap in the face. Kristoff sounded like Elsa. Who did he think he was? Her sister had already made her feel foolish, and now this man-child was acting all high and mighty. And on top of that, he didn't think she could handle herself against the wolves! For a moment she was too stunned to speak. Then she sat up straight, eager to prove him wrong.

Scanning the sleigh, she saw a long lute. It wasn't perfect, but it was made of strong wood and, in this situation, could pass for a weapon. Anna looked back up just in time to see a wolf leaping toward Kristoff. With a cry, she drew back the lute and swung. . . .

"Whoa!" Kristoff shouted as the lute whizzed by his head and slammed into the leaping wolf, knocking the creature back down to the ground. He looked over at Anna, surprise on his face.

Ha! she wanted to say. *Bad judgment? Look whose judgment just saved you!* But there was no time to gloat. The wolves were coming at them faster and faster. With a howl, one leaped up and grabbed Kristoff by the sleeve. Anna watched in horror as Kristoff was pulled clear off the sled. Grabbing a torch that had gone flying out of his hand, she raced to edge of the sleigh and looked over. Somehow, the man had managed to pull free from the wolf and grab hold of a loose rope.

Behind him, the wolf that had grabbed him kept coming, determined to get his prize. As Kristoff let out a bloodcurdling scream, Anna frantically looked around the bottom of the sleigh. There was some hay, a few loose carrots, what looked like an old sandwich . . . *Kristoff really ought to clean this thing out more often,* Anna observed. *What I really need is a— Aha! Yes! A blanket.* Reaching down, she grabbed an old blanket from the floor of the sleigh and touched the tip of the torch to the material. Instantly, the blanket burst into flames.

"Duck!" Anna shouted, throwing the blanket in Kristoff's direction. It flew right over his head and hit the wolf, knocking it off Kristoff and into the others that were following.

"You almost set me on fire!" Kristoff shouted as Anna reached out her hand and pulled him back into the sleigh.

"But I didn't," she replied.

Hearing a loud snort from Sven, both Anna and Kristoff turned back to face front. As soon as they did, Anna wished they hadn't. Up ahead, and getting closer by the second, was a massive gorge. It had to be at least thirty feet across, and Anna didn't even want to imagine how far down it went. Anna looked over at Kristoff, hoping he might have some brilliant plan. But he just stared at her blankly.

Okay, so we have a gorge. And we have a reindeer. Her mind flashed to the first time she and her horse had jumped over a creek. It had looked so wide and terrifying, and yet after they had leaped over it, Anna had been ready to go again. This would just be like a really, really . . . *really* big creek. "Get ready to jump, Sven!" Anna shouted.

"You don't tell him what to do!" Kristoff shouted. For a brief moment, Anna thought he was going to offer up an alternate suggestion. But then he shoved a bag in her arms and scooped her up. "I do!" he said, throwing her forward so that she landed on Sven's back. He quickly unhooked the sleigh from Sven's harness.

"Jump, Sven!" he shouted just as they got to the lip of the gorge.

Anna grabbed hold of the reindeer's mane and braced herself for the impact of Kristoff landing behind her. But the impact never came. As the reindeer pushed off into the air above the gorge, Anna looked back. Kristoff was still on the sled! He hadn't gotten free in time! Luckily, the momentum of the high-speed chase had sent the sleigh flying out over the middle of the gorge. It looked like he was going to make it to the other side after all.

As soon as Sven's hooves touched down on the other side, Anna slipped off the reindeer's back and turned to look at Kristoff. *Just a few more feet. Just a few more feet,* she thought, watching the sleigh arc through the air. And then it began to lose momentum. Anna watched helplessly as Kristoff raced to the front of the sleigh and jumped.

Arms and legs flailing, he flew through the air. And then, with a loud thud, he slammed into the snowy edge of the cliff. Anna let out her breath. Behind him, the front of the sleigh nosed down and plummeted to the ground far below. A moment later there was a loud bang as what was left of the sleigh went up in flames.

Kristoff looked down and let out a loud groan. "But I just paid it off!" he said.

Anna didn't care. A sleigh was replaceable. Annoying as he was, she was beginning to suspect that Kristoff was not.

Looking at Kristoff, Anna realized that his fingers were beginning to slip. *If I don't do something fast, he'll be following his sleigh,* Anna thought. Quickly, she opened the bag that was still clutched in her hands. Rummaging around, her fingers closed on something metal. Something metal with sharp points at the end. Pulling the item out, she let out a happy cry. It was exactly what she needed—an ax. Anna's smile broadened as the bag of goodies revealed another prize—a long piece of thick rope. Kjekk had been a master escape artist when he was younger, and after his twentieth escape, she had asked Old Narn, the stable hand, how to make the tightest knot possible.

"Thank you, Narn," she whispered under her breath now as she began to attach the rope to the ax.

Anna's fingers were trembling by the time she completed the knot and checked that it was tight. Satisfied, she ran over to Sven. "Okay, buddy," she said, trying to sound confident. "I'm going to need your help here. I'm going to tie one end of this rope to you." As she spoke, she began to do just that. "And the other end I'm going to throw to Kristoff. Sound good?" The reindeer appeared to nod. "Okay then, let's do this."

Slipping and sliding her way as close to the edge as she could, Anna took a deep breath. "Kristoff!" she shouted. A muffled groan sounded from below the cliff's edge. That was all she needed to hear. Pulling back her arm, she began to swing the rope in a circle. The ax whizzed by her ear, narrowly missing her. With each rotation of her arm it went faster and faster. Finally, with a shout, she let it go.

The ax flew through the air and began to fall, the rope ripping through her gloved hands. Anna held her breath as it flew right at Kristoff. There was a ping as the ax made contact with the snow-covered rock, and then the rope went taught.

"Now, Sven!" Anna shouted. Behind her, the reindeer began to pull. And pull. And pull harder. With each step he took, the pit of worry that had formed in the bottom of her stomach grew larger. What if the rope wasn't strong enough to pull Kristoff back to safety? What if her knot wasn't tight enough after all?

But Anna and Sven made a good team. With the help of a few pulls on the rope, Kristoff clawed his way back over the cliff and onto level ground.

With Kristoff safe, Anna peeked over the edge of the cliff to check on the sled. It was completely smashed to pieces. And on fire.

Everything Kristoff owned was going up in smoke.

Anna waited for a moment, not sure what to say. The ice harvester seemed heartbroken, as if he had lost a friend, not an inanimate object. "I'll replace your sled. And everything in it," she finally said apologetically. "I understand if you don't want to help me anymore. . . ."

Anna waited for Kristoff to respond. When he didn't, she nodded. It looked like she was on her own. Turning, she began to walk away from Kristoff and Sven.

So I don't know where I'm going, she thought as she walked. *I didn't know where I was going before, and I managed to find Oaken's. And so I probably won't see Kristoff again. No big deal. I was getting tired of all his questions. I'm sure I'll be just fine without him. I'm sure I won't get lost or run into those wolves again or—*

"Hold up!"

Anna spun around at the sound of Kristoff's voice. He and Sven were making their way to her. "We're coming!"

"You are?" Anna shouted, relief washing over her. She took an excited step toward the pair, and then stopped herself. She had gotten Kristoff to agree to take her up the North Mountain by seeming strong and in charge. She needed to keep up that bravado now. No reason to let him know how much she actually needed him. Anna tamped down her smile and waited for them to reach her. "I mean, sure," she said, trying not to show her relief. "I'll let you tag along."

But as soon as her back was to Kristoff, she smiled wide. For as much as he pretended to be a tough guy, she was beginning to think Kristoff was just a big softy. Which was fine by her, especially if it meant getting back on track and finding her sister.

CHAPTER 18

ANNA WAS MISSING. Her horse had returned but she, the princess of Arendelle, had not.

Hans plastered a look of concern on his face as he stood holding the reins of Anna's horse. He keenly felt the eyes of Arendelle's people upon him and knew his every movement and every expression was being watched—closely.

Of course, it wasn't hard to look concerned. When the horse had first returned, Hans had been genuinely frightened. His heart had lurched and his palms had grown sweaty. Letting Anna race up into the mountains unaccompanied had not felt right to him in the first place. With her out of his sight, he had no control over the one person he needed the most control of. If Anna was missing—or worse, hurt—everything was in jeopardy. He couldn't become king without a princess to become queen.

Taking a deep breath, Hans took in the reactions of those around him. The villagers who still remained in the square looked concerned. That he had expected. But he was pleased to note they were looking to him for help. The dignitaries, too, were watching him process this sudden turn of events. Some, like his new allies, wore expressions of concern, while others, such as the Duke, looked far too pleased for Hans's liking. The Duke was busily whispering to one of his men, who in turn looked Hans up and down before nodding. Saying something back to the Duke, the two men smirked.

"Princess Anna's horse," he heard someone shout.

"What happened to her?" another villager cried out. "Where is she?"

Then another, older voice called out shakily. "Why hasn't she stopped the winter?"

The words chilled Hans to the core. The thought had not crossed his mind until that very moment. So focused on what Anna's disappearance might mean for his chance at the crown, he had failed to think of the bigger picture. If Anna was gone, there was a very good chance that their ability to end the winter was gone as well. Elsa felt no warmth for Hans, that was clear. Even if he *was* to go after her himself, what incentive would she have to listen to *him* when he begged her to end the winter? The only reason he had felt comfortable letting Anna go in the first place was because he believed she was the only one capable of putting an end to this winter. And now that chance might have slipped through his fingers. His stomach dropped.

Raising his eyes, he saw that while he had been lost in thought, the crowd had been silent, waiting to see what he would say. Looking out over the sea of faces, the knot in his stomach began to ease. They were all looking to him—Prince Hans—to fix this. From the oldest man to the youngest girl, they all had hope and trust written across their faces. If they thought him responsible and brave, he would have to act responsible and brave. He would deal with the issue of winter as it came. First he needed to find Anna.

"Princess Anna is in trouble!" he announced to the people. "I need volunteers to go with me to find her!"

Instantly, a flood of people rushed forward, offering their services. Some were farmers, others castle staff. Some were old while others looked like they had only just left their mothers' sides.

Hans couldn't help wondering: if the situation were different and it were Hans who had disappeared somewhere in the Southern Isles, would there would be such an outpouring of love? *Probably not. Yet here these people are, offering to risk their lives for a princess they have hardly seen for years.*

Focusing on the crowd, Hans quickly sized up who he thought would be the most help. "You," he said, pointing to a young man who looked roughly his age. "I'll take you. And you, sir," he added, pointing to a slightly older farmer with strong arms. "You can come as well." As he continued to handpick a group, he was met with some resistance.

"Why won't you take me, Prince Hans?" a boy who looked no more than ten asked, looking up at him with big weepy eyes. "I want to help."

"I do, too," a little girl said, stepping up. She clutched a tattered blanket in her hand and had to take her thumb out of her mouth to speak. "I love Princess Anna. She's so brave."

Hans knew he was being watched, his every move scrutinized. This was his moment to impress the people of Arendelle. To win them over. He crouched down so he was at eye level with the little girl. "I wish I could take you with me," he said, trying to be as kind as he knew Anna would be in this situation. "But I need you to stay here and be my eyes and ears in case she returns. I'll need you to tell her I love her very much and that I'll be back soon. Can you do that?"

The little girl nodded shyly.

"Thank you," Hans said, pinching her cheek gently.

Then, standing up, he addressed the rest of the crowd. "Princess Anna would be touched by your concern, and as her representative, I thank you for your willingness to join me. But I cannot take everyone. The mountains are treacherous and a large group would only slow us down. I ask that those of you who stay behind continue to keep the fires going as best you can and wait for my return. I promise, I'll bring the princess back."

Hans turned to the visiting dignitaries and raised an eyebrow. They had been surprisingly quiet when the townsfolk stepped up to the task. *Where has their support gone?* Hans wondered. Only a short time ago, some of them had been pledging their loyalty and making vows to support Arendelle under its new leadership. Now they were acting like schoolchildren hiding in the back of the class, hoping not to be called upon.

"Lords? Sirs?" Hans implored. "Will none of you offer help?"

Hans could hear the creaking of the ice underfoot in the silence that followed. Finally, the lord of Kongsberg spoke up. "I have with me only a few men, Prince Hans. If I were to send them with you . . ." His voice trailed off, the excuse weak even to his ears.

"I, too," said Prince Wils, "would love to help, but do we really believe the princess can be saved? Look at the mountain." All eyes turned to view the monster looming in the distance. "A soldier would have a hard enough time traversing the terrain. I doubt the princess could." He lowered his eyes. "I'm sorry, Prince Hans, but I don't believe in wasting time or lives on a fool's errand."

Hans narrowed his eyes. "I appreciate your candor. But I'm not quite as willing as you to just give up."

"Prince Hans," the Eldoran dignitary said hesitantly. "I think what Prince Wils is trying to say is that *you* should not be leaving at a time like this. Arendelle is holding on by a thread, and as you were quick to tell us earlier, *you* were chosen to lead in the princess's absence. If you were to go now . . ."

Instantly, the men around him began to mumble. Some agreed, while others thought the right thing to do was for Hans to go after the princess. As their voices began to increase in volume, the townsfolk took notice and began to nervously shift on their feet.

Soon Hans could hear them murmuring words of doubt over his leaving.

Hans loved every minute of it.

"That's enough!" Hans shouted, silencing the men. "I realize that leaving now is not the best of options. But I have no choice. I must go after my fiancée and return her to her people. And I expect all of you, in my absence, to stay strong. Do not mistake this decision as a sign of weakness on my part. See it for what it is, the act of a man in love with both the princess and this kingdom. I must get to the stables and be on my way—immediately."

Hans was turning to go when he heard the Duke's little voice. Up until then, the Duke had been silent, watching Hans and the other dignitaries closely but not adding to the debate. Now he stepped forward. "I volunteer two men, my lord!" he said.

As the Duke ushered his two men forward, Hans sized them up. They looked like thugs, with deep-set eyes and frowns on their lined faces. Hans carefully noted that each of them rested a hand on a long, sharp sword.

Keeping an eye on the Duke's obvious spies was hardly a distraction Hans needed at the moment. But he couldn't say no to the Duke's offer without raising suspicion. With a nod, Hans welcomed the men to his group.

Telling the others he would meet them at the stables, Hans made his way over to the Blavenian dignitary. He was the only one Hans completely trusted, and Hans was going to need his help. Pulling him aside, Hans made sure no one was listening. Then, lowering his voice, he whispered into the man's ear. "Keep an eye on the Duke," he said. "I don't trust him. I think he is trying to undermine me. If he does anything, you will let me know as soon as I return, yes?"

"Of course, Prince Hans," the man replied.

"Good," Hans said back. "Because I have enough problems to deal with without adding a weasel to the mix."

CHAPTER 19

WHILE SHE WASN'T quite willing to admit it out loud, Anna was happy to have Kristoff and Sven for company. For one thing, the woods were kind of scary, and for another, she honestly didn't know where she was going. Having Kristoff as a guide was turning out to be rather helpful. And Sven was doing a good job taking the scary out of the forest. *He reminds me of a puppy,* she thought as she watched the reindeer prance through a particularly high snowdrift.

Since leaving the gorge, Anna and Kristoff had kept up a steady pace despite the deep snow, dark skies, and icy temperatures. But now the sky was turning from dark blue to soft yellow as the sun began to rise over the horizon.

"How long have you had Sven?" Anna asked, catching Kristoff

watching his reindeer play. She hadn't failed to notice the intense bond between the two or the way Kristoff's expression softened every time he looked at the reindeer.

"We've been together since he was a calf," Kristoff said. "Well, since we were both calves, really. I was just a kid when we found each other."

Anna smiled. "It must have been nice to have someone to count on, even if he's just a reindeer," she said. Sven looked up and grunted at her. "I'm sorry, Sven. You're a wonderful reindeer."

Looking pleased, Sven went back to chasing shadows thrown by the trees around them.

"Yeah, I don't know what I would have done without him. Most times, it was just the two of us." Kristoff paused and looked over at Anna. "I'm sure you don't know what that's like, what with living in the castle and all."

Anna didn't respond right away. Images of sitting in front of Elsa's door, hoping it would open and Elsa would be her friend again, flashed through her mind. "I would have loved to have a friend like Sven," she finally said. "I wasn't exactly surrounded by people growing up."

"What about your sister?" Kristoff asked.

Anna shook her head. "She isn't quite the warm and fuzzy type, if you couldn't tell," she said, gesturing at the winter wonderland around them. "But you know, having a lot of me time wasn't such a bad thing." When she saw Kristoff's skeptical look she added, "No, seriously. Like, I'm really good at playing solitaire. Really, really good. And I'm a mean knitter. I can make a scarf in less than a day. Well, usually. Sometimes the yarn gives me trouble. It gets all tangled together and then when I give it a yank . . ." She stopped speaking when she realized Kristoff was laughing. "What?" she asked.

"Nothing," he said, still chuckling. "It's just . . . well, has anyone ever told you that you have a tendency to ramble?"

Anna shrugged. "Not until now," she said. "I told you, not a whole lot of people for me to talk to growing up. Guess I'm making up for lost time."

"Well, don't let me stop you," Kristoff said, gesturing for her to continue. "Tell me more about what a young princess does growing up in a castle without too many friends."

"Only if you really want to hear it," she replied.

"I'm on pins and needles," he said.

Anna let out a laugh. She hadn't realized how funny Kristoff could be. She also hadn't realized he had a dimple in his right cheek when he smiled. Looking away from the ice harvester, Anna went on.

"I read—a lot. Which can be super fun if you have the right book. It wasn't entirely terrible. So I didn't get to play games with Elsa or share secrets or any of that sister stuff. Who needs that, anyway . . . ?" As her voice trailed off, Anna realized this whole time she had been trying to convince herself more than Kristoff. The smile faded from her face and she felt tears well up in her eyes. She turned away, hoping Kristoff wouldn't notice.

But he had. "Yeah, that sister stuff isn't all it's cracked up to be," he said gently. "I don't have a sister, either, and I think you and I are both doing just fine."

Anna smiled. It was sweet of Kristoff to try to make her feel better.

For a moment, they were both silent. Kristoff kicked at a ball-shaped piece of ice while Anna fiddled with the streak of white in her hair. She didn't know what to say. She wasn't used to opening herself up to someone this much. It felt nice, and she realized with a jolt that it felt nice because she was sharing it with Kristoff. The ice harvester might have teased her earlier, but he seemed to understand what it was like not to have the most normal of upbringings.

"You don't have *any* sisters?" Anna finally asked.

Kristoff shook his head. "Not really," he said vaguely.

"What about brothers? Do you have any brothers?" Anna asked. "Hans has twelve!"

"He must be a lucky guy," Kristoff said, his tone hard to read. "Twelve brothers and now you. Impressive."

Anna blushed. For some reason, hearing Kristoff talk about her as though she belonged to Hans made her feel funny. She didn't know why she had mentioned him in the first place. She supposed she just liked the idea of having someone to talk about. Just saying Hans's name made her feel all warm inside.

"Anyway," she said, trying to change the subject back to something a little less awkward. "I guess I just wish that I had had the chance to get to know Elsa before this all happened. I could have been there for her, stopped all of this from ever happening." Anna paused. "But now we're going to find her. She'll come back to Arendelle and we'll fix everything. Together."

Anna glanced over at Kristoff. "Well, if she can ever forgive me, that is."

"I think you would be surprised at how forgiving family can be," Kristoff said. "No matter what kind of relationship you might have."

Anna was just about to ask him what he meant and why he was being so evasive about his own family when the forest thinned and they stepped into a clearing. The sun was up now and the glare off the snow momentarily blinded Anna. When her vision cleared, she let out a gasp. From their vantage point, they could just make out Arendelle in the distance.

"It's completely frozen," Kristoff said, coming to stand beside her.

He was right. The gray stone of Arendelle's walls and castle had disappeared under a layer of snow, and the ice had begun to spread beyond the fjord.

"It'll be fine," Anna said. "Elsa will thaw it."

"Will she?" Kristoff questioned.

"Yeah," Anna said with a little less confidence. "She has to." Then she took a deep breath and squared her shoulders. They weren't doing Arendelle any good just standing there with their mouths open. "Come on. This way to the North Mountain?" She turned from her kingdom and pointed straight ahead at a gentle slope leading up.

"More like this way," Kristoff corrected, reaching over and moving her finger—in the direction of a very tall, very steep, very dangerous-looking mountain.

Anna gulped. What had she gotten herself into?

So, Elsa . . . you have powers, huh? That must be pretty neat.

Neat? Neat? *My sister reveals that she has magical ice powers, and the best I can come up with is* neat? Anna thought as she walked beside Kristoff and Sven. To distract herself from the giant mountain she was apparently going to have to climb, Anna had been silently practicing what she would say to her sister when they finally found her. So far, "neat" was as far as she had gotten.

Hearing a soft tinkling sound, like chimes moving in the wind, Anna looked up and smiled in delight. They were in the middle of a grove of willow trees, which, like everything else, was frozen. But unlike the rather monotonous fir forest they had been making their way through, *this* place was breathtakingly beautiful. The willows' branches hung down, their long leaves glistening like tiny lights that created curtains, separating the grove from the rest of the forest. Inside the grove felt like its own little world. Hearing the tinkling sound again, Anna saw that Sven was playfully knocking into the branches with his antlers. Each time he did, the branches hit against one another, causing the ice to make its cheery sound.

Elsa did all this, Anna thought in wonder as she gently waved her hand through the branches. *I've been so focused on the damage she created, I never stopped to think about the wonderful things she could do with her powers.*

"I never knew winter could be so beautiful," Anna said softly.

"Yeah, it really is beautiful, isn't it?" a voice, which was not Kristoff's, said, startling Anna. "But it's so white," the voice went on. "How about a little color? I'm thinking like maybe some crimson, chartreuse . . ."

Anna looked over and exchanged a confused look with Kristoff. Where was the voice coming from? The only other being in the grove with them was . . . No. It couldn't be. Could it? Together they looked over at Sven. The reindeer was staring at them blankly, his large antlers completely tangled in willow branches. They were still staring at him when the voice piped up again.

"How 'bout yellow—no, not yellow," the voice said as though disgusted by the thought. "Yellow and snow? Brrr . . . no go."

The voice was now coming from right between Anna and Kristoff. Anna looked down. Then she looked back up at Kristoff. Then, together, they both looked back down, their eyes wide as saucers.

Standing between them, as though it were the most natural, non-weird thing in the world, was a small snowman. A small, *talking* snowman made up of three snowballs and two short little stick arms.

"Am I right?" he asked when he saw Anna and Kristoff looking at him. Then he smiled.

Anna couldn't help it: she screamed. Kicking out, she sent the little snowman's head flying right into Kristoff's arms.

"Hi!" the snowman said cheerfully.

Kristoff was not charmed. "You're creepy," he said, tossing the snowman's head back to Anna.

"I don't want it," Anna shouted.

The two began to throw the snowman's head back and forth, neither one at all eager to be left with their version of a hot—or in this case, cold—potato. The remaining two balls of snow that made up the little creature danced back and forth between Anna and Kristoff, stick arms waving wildly in the air.

"Ew, ew, the body!" Anna shrieked, catching the snowman's head one last time before slamming it—upside down—back onto his body. *What is going on?* Anna thought as she tried to catch her breath. *A talking snowman? How is that even possible?*

But it was, it seemed, entirely possible. "Wait," the snowman said, confused. "What am I looking at right now? Why are you hanging off the earth like a bat?"

Anna couldn't help it. She laughed. That was followed by a wave of sympathy as she looked at the little guy trying to make sense of the world. Because his head was on upside down, he was looking at everything *upside down*. "Okay, wait one second," she said, kneeling down in front of the snowman. Gently, she picked up his head and flipped it right-side up before placing it back on his body.

"Oooh! Thank you!" the snowman said.

Perhaps I was a little quick to judge, she thought as he smiled up at her like a loyal puppy dog. *He's just a sweet, lovable, innocent little guy. Who happens to be made of snow.* "You're welcome," she said warmly.

"Now I'm perfect," the snowman said proudly, wobbling beneath the willows.

Watching him, Anna had to agree that the snowman was pretty perfect as far as snowmen went. He had the requisite three balls of snow. Two arms made of sticks and eyes that appeared to be made of coal. But he was missing one very important part. Reaching into Kristoff's satchel, Anna pulled out one of Sven's carrots. Then she turned, ready to add it to the snowman's face. Unfortunately, the snowman chose that precise moment to turn around as well. He collided headfirst with the carrot. With a small crunch, the carrot went all the way through the snowman's head so that only the tip was visible on his face. The rest of the carrot protruded out of the back of his head.

"Oh!" Anna cried. "Too hard! I'm sorry! I was just . . ." Her voice trailed off. She didn't think explaining her motives would do much good. "Are you okay?" she asked instead.

Looking down, the snowman saw the tip of the carrot and his eyes lit up. "Are you kidding me?" he cried happily. "I am wonderful! I've always wanted a nose!" He went cross-eyed as he tried to take a better look. "So cute! It's like a little baby unicorn!"

While he was clearly unperturbed by the chunk of carrot sticking out of the back of his head, Anna couldn't let just let him wander around the woods that way! For some reason, that seemed like bad snowman etiquette. Reaching behind him, she pushed the carrot forward. Instantly, the tiny nose became a large orange nose.

"Hey! Whoa!" the snowman cried. Anna cringed. Maybe she had gone too far. But then, the snowman clapped his stick hands together in glee. "I love it even more!" He smiled up at Anna and Kristoff. "All right, let's start this thing over. Hi, everyone. I'm Olaf. And I like warm hugs." Opening his arms wide, he stood, waiting for a hug.

"Olaf?" Anna repeated. That name sounded so familiar . . . *Did I read it in a book?* she wondered. *Or maybe it was a name of someone in one of the gallery portraits? I swear I've heard it before . . .*

And then she remembered. "That's right!' she said. "Olaf!" She and Elsa had made a snowman once—long ago—named Olaf. He had been just like this Olaf. *I even remember Elsa holding out the fake snowman's arms and saying, "I like warm hugs."*

"And you are?" Olaf asked, breaking into Anna's thoughts.

"Oh, um . . . I'm Anna," she said.

"And who's the funky-looking donkey over there?" Olaf asked, pointing toward Kristoff and Sven.

"That's Sven," Anna said.

Olaf nodded. "Uh-huh. And who's the reindeer?"

". . . Sven," Anna said again. Then, realizing that Olaf had called Kristoff a funky-looking donkey, Anna laughed to herself. She waited as Olaf said his hellos and then asked the question that was burning a hole in her throat. She needed to know—"Olaf," she said, "did Elsa build you?"

"Yeah," he replied breezily. "Why?"

So she had been right. Olaf was here now, alive and talking—because of Elsa! Because of her magic! *I wish the people in Arendelle could see Olaf,* she thought. *Then they could see how amazing Elsa's powers can be.*

"Do you know where she is?" Anna asked, shooting Kristoff a look. He had taken one of Olaf's arms off and was holding it up, fascinated by how it continued to move even when disconnected from the body. *Olaf wasn't entirely off point,* she thought. *Kristoff* can *be a donkey sometimes.*

Unaware of, or at least not bothered by, his detached arm, Olaf nodded. And once again, he said, "Yeah. Why?"

"Do you think you could show us the way?" Anna asked eagerly. This was the closest they had come to figuring out exactly where Elsa was hiding. If Olaf could bring them to the queen, they would be one step closer to putting a stop to this winter. And maybe to mending Anna's relationship with her sister.

She looked up at Kristoff, hoping he would be as excited as she was. But he was still too busy playing with Olaf's arm. To their surprise, the arm suddenly reached out and slapped Kristoff across the face. "Stop it, Sven," Olaf said to Kristoff. "Trying to focus here." Then he looked back at Anna and once again asked why.

"I'll tell you why," Kristoff answered instead. "We need Elsa to bring back summer."

At the word "summer," a huge smile spread across Olaf's face. Summer, it turned out, was something Olaf really, *really* liked. While Anna found the idea of a creature made of snow liking a season known for being warm adorable and endearing, Kristoff did not.

"I'm guessing you don't have much experience with heat," he said.

"Nope," the happy-go-lucky snowman said. "But sometimes I

like to close my eyes and imagine what it'd be like." As Anna and Kristoff watched, the snowman did just that. He closed his eyes and drifted away, lost in images of lying on the beach or frolicking through a field full of dandelions.

"I'm going to tell him," Kristoff whispered to Anna as the snowman continued to narrate his daydream.

"Don't you dare," Anna hissed back. There was no reason to dash the little guy's hopes. So what if he believed he could walk around in the sun and not melt? If the weather stayed like this, he would never have to learn any different.

Opening his eyes, Olaf looked over at them and smiled. "Come on!" he said. "Elsa's this way. Let's go bring back summer!"

Turning, he began to wobble away from the willow trees. A moment later, Anna followed. Behind her she could hear Kristoff grumbling about snowmen and summer and melting, but she ignored him. He could mumble and grumble all he wanted. They were about to find her sister!

Anna's excitement was short-lived. As they left the willow grove and neared the base of the North Mountain, the terrain began to change. The beauty that had awed Anna just a short while ago was gone. In its place was something far more menacing. Icicles stuck out horizontally from the mountain, like spears on the front lines of battle. The wind was stronger now, too, whipping at Anna's face and stinging her cheeks. It was like seeing the other side of her sister's personality. The willows and Olaf were the kind, sweet part of Elsa. This was the scared and lonely part.

"So how exactly are you planning to stop this weather?" Kristoff asked, gesturing to their surroundings.

"Oh, I'm going to talk to my sister," Anna said, feigning more confidence than she actually felt.

Kristoff stopped midstride and stared at her. "That's your plan?" he asked in disbelief. "My ice business is riding on you *talking* to your sister?"

"Yup," Anna replied, stopping to return his stare.

Kristoff groaned and resumed trudging through the snow. Anna was surprised he had let the conversation just drop like that and was about to say so when she heard him shout. Whipping around, she saw that he was standing perilously close to an icicle. One more step and it would have stabbed him right in the nose.

"So you're not at all afraid of her?" he asked, reaching up to make sure his nose was okay.

"Why would I be?" Anna retorted. "She might have crazy ice powers, but this is still Elsa we're talking about."

Anna confidently strode forward . . . all the way into a dead end. On the plus side, they had arrived at the base of the North Mountain. On the downside, the spot they had come to was a spot that rose straight up into the sky.

"What now?" Anna asked, turning to Kristoff, Olaf, and Sven.

Kristoff craned his head back as he examined the mountain. Then he looked at Anna's hopeful face. He sighed. "It's too steep," he said. As he spoke, he opened his bag and began digging around in it. "I've only got one rope, and you don't know how to climb mountains."

"Says who?" Anna replied, pleased to see the surprised expression on Kristoff's face when he looked up and found her clinging to the mountain. She hated when people doubted her, and really, how hard could climbing be? You find footholds for your feet and handholds for your hands. Then you climb. *Although,* she thought as she scanned the rock face in front of her, *I don't really see that many places to hold on. . . .*

"What are you doing?" Kristoff asked.

Anna didn't risk turning around, but she could hear the mocking tone in Kristoff's voice and it only served to spur her on. "I'm going to see my sister."

"You're going to kill yourself," Kristoff replied.

Ignoring him, she reached her leg out, straining for a small ledge.

"I wouldn't put my foot there."

Anna ignored his warning and placed her foot on the ledge. Her legs shook as she tried to steady herself, but she was thrilled when she was able to move a little farther up the mountain. *Ha! So there, Mr. Know-It-All. A few more slick moves like that and I'll be on my way!*

"Or there," Kristoff said as she once again moved her foot. Then he added, "How do you know Elsa even wants to see you?"

"I'm just blocking you out 'cause I have to concentrate here," Anna said over her shoulder. *And because I don't need to be reminded that my sister basically ran away from me,* she added silently.

Failing to pick up on the fact that Anna was clearly not in the mood for self-reflection, Kristoff kept pushing. "You know," he said, "most people who disappear into the mountains want to be alone."

"Nobody *wants* to be alone. Except maybe you," Anna shot back. Her fingers were beginning to go numb and she was pretty sure that if muscles could scream, hers would be shouting horrible things at her right now. The last thing she wanted to be doing was talking to Kristoff about relationships—again. Just because he had so-called "friends" who were "love experts" didn't make him a genius on the subject. And *seriously*, why did this mountain have so few handholds?

There were no more places to put her hands or her feet. Anna was stuck.

"Please tell me I'm almost there," she asked. Sadly, risking a look down, she saw that her "big climb" had taken her up—about six feet. *Okay, that's a little bit embarrassing,* Anna admitted silently.

"Hey, Sven?" Olaf shouted, addressing Kristoff. He and Anna turned and looked over at the little snowman. "Not sure if this is going to solve the problem, but I found a staircase that leads exactly where you want to go."

"Thank goodness!" Anna said. "Catch!" Then, without even looking down, she let go of the mountain and threw herself backward—right into Kristoff's arms. Looking up at him, she smiled. "Thanks. That was like a crazy trust exercise!" Then, jumping free, she ran after Olaf.

Behind her, she could feel Kristoff's gaze following her, and it made her flash hot for a moment. She hadn't failed to notice when she landed in Kristoff's arms that it felt kind of nice to be held by someone so big and warm. But just like that, Anna pushed the feeling aside. Catching up to Olaf, she grabbed his little stick hand, and together they began the long climb up the stairs that would hopefully lead to Elsa!

CHAPTER 20

HANS WAS PLEASED. The group of men he had put together were more than capable and had so far offered up no resistance to his leadership. Except for the Duke of Weselton's men. *Those two,* he thought now, glancing back at the men, *are going to be trouble unless I figure out a way to change their loyalty.* For the moment, though, Hans was content to just wait and see how things played out. It would do him no good to focus his attention on anything other than finding Anna.

They had been following Anna's tracks for a few hours. At first, it hadn't been too difficult. Her horse had left a clear path of broken branches on his gallop back toward Arendelle. But they had come to the point where Anna and her horse had clearly parted ways. A distinct human-sized impression could be seen in the white powder beneath a tree, and the tree itself was one of the few without snow covering its branches. *She must have fallen off here,* Hans thought, jumping off his own horse to examine the area. *Yes, she most definitely landed beneath this tree.* He reached up, his fingers brushing the soft needles of the fir tree.

"She was probably stunned," Hans said to the men who sat astride their horses, waiting. "But then she would have tried to stand up." He lay down on the ground, reenacting the scene as he saw it play out in his head. "She would have used these branches for support. They would have been covered in snow and hanging low to the ground, you see. When Anna grabbed on, the snow would have been knocked loose, which is why the tree looks bare now. And then, then what would my Anna have done . . . ?" His voice trailed off as he looked around.

Hans loved that the men were all looking at him, seemingly awed by his impressive tracking skills. The only problem was, he actually wasn't very good at tracking at all. He had just been following the horse's path up to this point. The heavy beast had left plenty of clues to follow, but now he would have to follow Anna. And she was far more delicate than the horse.

"Sir!" one of the men called out. "Could she have gone this way?"

Looking over, Hans let out a soft breath. The man was pointing at tracks in the snow. They were barely visible, but they were clearly those of a human. Following them, Hans saw that they led away from the tree and toward a small stream. And in the distance, rising up over a small hill, was smoke.

"Princess Anna must be over there!" Hans shouted, jumping back on his horse. Kicking the horse into a trot, he headed toward the smoke. Behind him, the jingle of bits and stirrups let him know his men were following.

A few minutes later, Hans found himself standing in front of a wood cabin. A small set of stairs led up to a porch and the front door. A sign reading WANDERING OAKEN'S TRADING POST hung down, with a smaller sign attached that read AND SAUNA. Hans smiled. *Hopefully Anna is inside. Then we can head back to Arendelle and get out of this wretched snow. And if she's moved on, well . . . perhaps someone inside knows where she's gone.*

"Men, you wait here. Keep an eye out while I go in and see if the princess is here," Hans commanded. Dismounting, Hans tied up his horse and moved toward the stairs. Then, thinking better of it, he paused and turned back. "You two," he said, pointing at the Duke's men. "You come with me." He didn't want them out of his sight.

Hans walked up the stairs and pushed open the door. "Hello?" he called out.

It took a moment for his eyes to adjust. The sun on the snow had been blinding. In comparison, the interior of the trading post was dark. Slowly, shapes began to emerge. He could make out shelves, dry goods, a door that, due to its steamy nature, had to lead to the sauna, and . . . a mountain? Hans shook his head and blinked his eyes rapidly. When his vision cleared, he realized he wasn't looking at a real mountain. He was, instead, looking at a mountain of a man.

"Hoo-hoo! Big summer blowout!" the human mountain said.

He was standing behind the counter, his fingers drumming on the wood. "Perhaps you would like some sun balm of my own invention?" He held up a brown bottle and smiled hopefully.

Hans smiled back, mimicking the man's expression. He was hopeful as well. But while this man was eager for a sale, Hans was eager for information. Glancing around the room, Hans quickly tried to get a sense of this huge man. *The more I know,* he mused, *the easier it is to manipulate.* He quickly deduced several things. One—the man had terrible taste in sweaters, and two—he clearly fancied himself a businessman. While the first thing was only useful in that Hans now knew what sweater to never wear if you were a seven-foot man who was at least three feet wide, the second item was valuable. Businessmen were driven. They knew the worth of money, and they usually knew a good deal when they saw it. They also, Hans knew from experience, tended to do what was best for their business. And themselves. While that character trait might not always win them friends, in this situation, it was certainly going to help Hans get what he wanted from the man.

"Hello, there," Hans said, approaching the counter and holding out his hand. "I am Prince Hans, of the Southern Isles. I am looking for someone and hoping you might be able to help me."

The big man's smile did not grow bigger or smaller. It stayed exactly the same. He was clearly not impressed with Hans's title. "I am Oaken," he said. "Would you like some pants without legs? My own invention! Half price? Maybe some for you two big fellas?" He waved at the Duke's men, who were standing back, stone-faced.

Hans shook his head. "We're actually all set for pants," he

said. "We just stopped in because I have reason to believe that my beloved, Princess Anna, may have stopped in here not so long ago."

"Ah, love," Oaken said. "That is nice. Maybe you will be wanting some books on love? I have many!"

Hans grimaced. "I am sure your selection is wonderful, but I don't really need any books. What I *do* need is my beautiful Princess Anna. . . ." Hans's voice trailed off as Oaken remained impassive. This was getting him nowhere. "Fine, fine. I would love a book."

Instantly, Oaken's blank expression disappeared and was replaced by a huge grin. "Hoo-hoo! That is good! Of which story would you like?"

Hans could feel the Duke's men watching him, judging his inability to get an answer, and it infuriated him. He didn't want anyone to see him as ineffectual—especially the Duke's men, who would be all too happy to report their observations back to the man who'd sent them. But he hadn't trusted them alone outside. So now he was stuck with them as witnesses to what was turning into a colossal headache. Hans clenched his fists. *Businessman,* he reminded himself. *Oaken is a businessman. So why don't I do a little business and see where that gets me?* Clearly, the big man was obliging when people were buying things. So Hans would just have to buy things—lots of things!

"Oaken, on second thought," Hans said, mirroring the big man's grin, "I do think we will take some pants without legs." Hans scanned the store, looking for more things to purchase. "Oh! And some carrots. The horses would appreciate carrots I'm sure."

"Hoo!" Oaken cried, pleased with his sudden windfall. He

began to bag up the items. As he held up the carrots, he added, "That is true! Horses do enjoy tasty treats. So do reindeers. In fact, I just sold some carrots to a pretty girl with a white streak in her hair a few hours ago. . . ."

"A girl with white in her hair," Hans repeated. "She was here? Why didn't you say so in the first place? *That* is the princess. *My* princess."

Oaken shrugged. "Apologies." Then he held up a bag. "Perhaps you would like a bag, ya?"

Hans sucked in his breath as he tried to remain calm. "I don't care, I don't care!" He threw a large pouch of coins on the counter. "Please, just tell me where the girl went."

Picking up the pouch, Oaken emptied it on the counter and began to count the coins very carefully. "She bought some supplies for that sneaky ice harvester," he said. "And then they left for the North Mountain." He finished counting and handed Hans his change. "Have a good day!"

Mumbling a thank-you, Hans turned and headed back outside in a bit of a fog. It didn't make sense. Anna had left the store with another man. Who was he? Was someone else trying to win Anna's hand and the throne? Well, that man had no idea what he was up against. Hans hadn't made it this far to walk away without a fight.

"Sir?"

The sound of one of his men's voices broke into Hans's internal monologue. Looking around, he saw that everyone was waiting on his orders.

"I just learned, after a quick and easy interrogation, that

Princess Anna has gone to the North Mountain." He ignored the Duke's men, who both raised their eyebrows, and instead pointed at a group of the townsfolk who had volunteered. "Let's split up. You five go west and look for a way to the mountain. The rest of us will go east. With luck, we shall meet atop the North Mountain and rescue Princess Anna."

Hans held back to make sure that both groups seemed sure of where they were going. When he was certain, Hans kicked his horse forward. Coming up behind the Duke's men, he was surprised to hear his name. He pulled back on the reins.

"Did you see him trying to get answers from that big oaf?" the taller one said. "It was pathetic. If the Duke were here he would have had the guy talking in no time."

The shorter man twirled his long mustache in his fingers and laughed. "He would have had him screaming in no time, you mean!" he said gleefully.

The rest of the men's words were lost to Hans as the wind picked up and the pair trotted ahead. But he had heard enough. *So the Duke would have resorted to violence? How ironic that his men are calling me the idiot, when clearly he doesn't have the forethought to think about what reacting calmly and rationally can achieve.* True, violence could work, but only brutes used violence. Brutes like his brothers, who wouldn't have known how to talk out a problem if they put all their brains together. Hans couldn't count the number of times he had tried to find the peaceful way out of a situation only to find himself being pummeled, or stuck in the pigsty, or thrown off a moving cart. And his father had been no better. His "solution" when one of his farmers had a problem he didn't like had been to burn the man's barn down. Or take all his livestock. It never failed to surprise Hans that a man who ruled such a vast kingdom could be so stupid. Violence begat violence. It was inevitable. Yet that was all his family knew.

Hans shuddered. No, he had had enough violence to last him a lifetime. He would not sink to his brothers' level. He would not let himself be like them—not if he could help it. So maybe a well-thought-out plan didn't yield the swiftest result. It still yielded one eventually. Hans nodded, reassuring himself. *Yes. I got what I wanted. I know where Anna is heading, and I know I can get more information from Oaken if I ever need it in the future.* The same could not be said if the Duke had "dealt" with it himself.

Looking ahead, Hans watched the two men who had so easily mocked him. So they didn't respect him. That was fine. It just meant that their guard was down and that they wouldn't interfere with his plans. But if they did? Well, while he didn't favor violence, it could certainly have its benefits when used wisely. . . .

CHAPTER 21

WHEN OLAF HAD told them about a "staircase" leading up the mountain, Anna had pictured a steeply sloping path of jagged rocks. So when the little snowman led them to a beautiful, intricate staircase made completely of ice, Anna was at a loss for words. Even more breathtaking was the frozen palace at the top of the steps. Glistening spires reached toward the clear blue sky above them. Each frosty turret had the detailed look of being hand-sculpted. Which, Anna realized, they probably were, in an icy magic kind of way.

"Whoa," Anna breathed out in awe.

Beside her, she heard Kristoff gasp. When she looked over, he had his hand on his heart. "Now that's ice," he said, reverently. "I might cry."

"Go ahead," Anna replied. "I won't judge." And she was being honest.

Stepping forward, Anna gingerly put one foot on the bottom step of the icy staircase and pushed. *Better safe than sorry,* she thought, waiting to see if the ice would crack under the pressure. It didn't, and she began to climb, one hand holding tight to the railing. As she got closer, Anna could make out more details. Elaborate carvings of snowflakes were etched in the sides of the palace, which glowed and shimmered in the light. To the left, she saw a balcony and wondered if her sister was up there somewhere.

Reaching the top of the stairs, Anna paused in front of the palace's large doors. Like everything else, they were beautiful and intricate, the result of something deep and wonderful inside Elsa. *I wish everyone back in Arendelle could see this place,* Anna thought. *They have only seen the devastation Elsa can cause. But that was because they saw only what Elsa can do if she is lashing out in fear. This place is what comes from letting go and following her heart. This is the Elsa I know will want to make things right in Arendelle.*

Hearing heavy breathing beside her, Anna turned and saw that Kristoff and Olaf had followed her.

"Flawless," Kristoff said, staring at the doors.

Anna nodded in agreement. Her fingers reached out, tracing the delicate etchings carved into the ice. She could see pieces of her sister in every detail. One long line of ice curved around and around itself, reminding Anna of Elsa as a young girl, when she would twirl in circles, laughing as the skirt of her dress billowed out around her. Small carved snowflakes brought back a memory of Elsa sticking out her tongue and giggling. "Look, Anna!" she had cried. "It's snowflake candy!" Anna had laughed and laughed, sticking out her own tongue. It was a vague memory, but it still filled Anna with warmth—and sadness.

She raised her hand, preparing herself to knock. But she hesitated. How many times had she stood in front of a closed door, hoping Elsa would let her in? And here she was, same situation, very different type of door. The thought of being shut out again was almost unbearable. Then she shook her head. How could she ask the people of Arendelle to give her sister another chance if she couldn't even do it herself? She had come all this way because she *wanted* to give Elsa a chance. . . .

"Knock," she heard Olaf say encouragingly. Her hand came closer. But still, she didn't touch the door. "Why isn't she knocking?" Olaf asked Kristoff. "Do you think she knows how to knock?"

This is getting ridiculous, Anna scolded herself. *What's the worst that can happen? She doesn't answer? It's not like you don't know how that feels. So just go ahead and . . .*

KNOCK! KNOCK!

On the other side of the door, Anna could hear the sound echo through the palace. She held her breath, waiting for the usual to happen. But this time, instead of staying shut, the doors to Elsa's world swung open.

"Ha!" Anna shouted, clapping her hands together happily. "It opened! That's a first." As she moved to step inside, Anna's foot paused on the threshold, and she turned to look at Kristoff. "You should probably wait out here," she said gently.

"What?" Kristoff asked, confused.

"Last time I introduced her to a guy, she froze everything," Anna replied.

"But it's a palace made of *ice*," Kristoff said, as though Anna were insane. "Ice is my life!"

Anna felt bad, but she knew she couldn't risk his life just so he could see what was, in essence, the world's most elaborate ice sculpture. Besides, this conversation with Elsa was one she needed to have alone.

"You too, Olaf," she said, stopping the snowman as he began to walk through the door. He looked up at her with big, hopeful snowman eyes. She shook her head. "Just give us a minute."

A minute is all I'm going to need to find out just how upset Elsa is, Anna added silently. Taking a deep breath, she stepped into the grand hallway. It was showtime.

"Elsa? Elsa! It's me . . . Anna!"

Inside the palace, Anna's words bounced off the frozen walls, loud in the otherwise eerie silence. It was as beautiful inside as it was outside, but there was something lonely about it. The doors had opened into a huge entryway with a soaring ceiling. An elaborate ice chandelier hung down and, across the room, a carved staircase led up to another floor. But there were no pictures, no personal touches. It was, for lack of a better word, cold.

Taking one more glance around the room to make sure Elsa wasn't hiding in the shadows, Anna made her way across the icy floor toward the staircase. The stairs were slick and the railing thin and hard to hold. As she climbed, Anna held her breath, sure that each step she took would have her slipping and sliding back down.

As if on cue, Anna's foot slipped and she lost her balance. Clutching the railing, she struggled to steady herself. When she was finally sure that the worst was over, she looked up. To her surprise, Elsa stood at the top of the staircase.

"Anna?" Elsa said, as though she couldn't quite believe what she was seeing.

As for Anna, she *definitely* couldn't believe what she was seeing. "Elsa, you look different. . . . It's a good different but . . ." Her voice trailed off. Her sister wasn't just different, she was *transformed.* The woman standing there was the most beautiful person Anna had ever seen. Elsa's white-blond hair was no longer pulled back in a tight bun. Now it hung in a loose braid over her shoulder, the silvery strands catching the light and shimmering as if lit from within. The last time Anna had seen her sister, Elsa had been wearing her coronation dress, with long sleeves and a high neckline. It had been a lovely dress, Anna admitted to herself, staring up at her sister in awe, but now Elsa looked, well, stunning. *No, it's more than the dress and the hair,* Anna realized. *She looks . . . free.* Anna smiled and took a few steps closer to her sister. "This place is amazing," she said as she walked.

"Thank you," Elsa said, tucking a strand of hair behind her ear nervously. "I never knew what I was capable of."

You and me both, Anna wanted to say. But instead, she apologized.

"I'm so sorry about what happened. If I had known—" She reached out her hand hopefully.

Elsa recoiled as though Anna were a viper. "No, it's okay. You don't have to apologize. But you should probably go," she said, backing away. "Please."

"But I just got here," Anna said, climbing another step.

"You belong down in Arendelle," her sister said, backing up still more. "I belong here. Alone. Where I can be who I am without hurting anybody."

"Actually, about that," Anna began, ready to clarify that Elsa probably *had* hurt somebody already. *And I'm not even counting myself and the loneliness I felt from all those years of silence,* she thought—but she stopped herself. She wanted her sister to come home, not to scare her so badly that she stayed hidden up here for the rest of her life. She closed her mouth as she tried to figure out the best way to respond to her sister's stubborn need for isolation. But before she could come up with anything, she was interrupted by the sound of Olaf counting.

"Fifty-eight . . . fifty-nine . . . sixty!"

Despite herself, Anna smiled. The cute little guy had taken her quite literally when she said she needed a minute.

Bursting into the great hall, Olaf saw Anna and Elsa and waved. "Hi! I'm Olaf, and I like warm hugs."

As he wobbled up the stairs, Anna watched her sister. Confusion flashed across Elsa's face, followed by fear, and then shock. But the good thing was, the last emotion on Elsa's face before Olaf reached Anna was wonder.

"Olaf?" she said. "You're alive?"

The little snowman hesitated, then shrugged. "I think so?" he answered uncertainly.

Anna knew what her sister must be thinking. She had been thinking it herself, not so long ago. "He's just like the one we built as kids," Anna said, kneeling down next to Olaf. "We were so close. We can be like that again."

To Anna's surprise, Elsa smiled. But as quickly as it came, the smile faded, replaced by a look of pain. Whatever Elsa was thinking about, it wasn't the warm and happy memory Anna had envisioned when she first met Olaf.

"No, we can't," Elsa said. Turning, she headed toward another flight of stairs.

"Elsa! Wait!"

"I'm just trying to protect you," Elsa called over her shoulder.

"You don't have to protect me," Anna said, following her sister. "I'm not afraid. Please don't shut me out again."

Why can't she just understand? Anna thought as she pursued her sister up the stairs. *I get it. She had to grow up with powers she didn't understand. It must have been terrifying. But if she had let me in then, maybe we wouldn't be here now. Doesn't she see that I'm as alone as she is? And it doesn't have to be that way. Neither of us has to alone or afraid. We could have each other—if Elsa would just let me in.*

Maybe Kristoff was right. Maybe Anna was being naive to think she could just walk in there and make everything all right. *Even if she doesn't want to forgive me, I thought that at least she would be concerned about the people back in Arendelle. Unless . . . Maybe she doesn't know.*

Anna caught up to her sister just as Elsa walked out onto the huge balcony Anna had spotted from outside. In the distance, the sun was sinking in the sky, causing the ice underneath their feet to shimmer in shades of gold, purple, and red.

Anna's movement caught Elsa's attention, and Elsa spun around.

Anna gulped. It was now or never. Sighing, she pointed down at the frozen ground. "You kind of set off an eternal winter . . . everywhere." Her sister's face filled with fear, breaking Anna's heart. "It's okay. You can just unfreeze it," she said.

"No, I can't."

"Sure you can," Anna said, not willing to give up on her sister. "I know you can." And she *did* know it. Elsa could come home and fix it. It would all be okay.

But it wasn't okay. It wasn't okay at all.

As Anna watched, Elsa began to twirl nervously around the room. "I'm such a fool!" she shouted as a strong wind began to whip around her legs. Snow began to fall from the ceiling, and the room's temperature dropped instantly. Beneath Elsa's feet, another layer of ice began to form.

"Don't panic!" Anna cried, trying to calm her sister. The last time her sister had gotten like this, Arendelle had ended up in deep, deep snow.

It was no use. Elsa was beyond listening. Ice was beginning to form on her fingertips, and the gently falling snow had turned into a full-blown blizzard. Raising her arm to protect her eyes from the sting of the snow, Anna tried to find her sister. But all she could hear was the howling wind. "Elsa! Please!" she shouted. "We can change this!"

"I CAN'T!"

As if in slow motion, Anna watched as Elsa's scream caused the blizzard to swirl out of control. There was a tense pause and then—the snow shot out at Anna. She sank to the floor, grasping her chest in pain.

Instantly, it felt like her body was turning to ice from the inside out, and she began to shiver. Reaching a hand down to steady herself, she was only vaguely aware of Elsa's tortured cry and the sound of footsteps as Kristoff burst into the room. All she could hear was her own heart pounding painfully in her chest.

"Anna?" Kristoff's worried voice broke into her thoughts. "Are you okay?"

Raising her eyes to meet Kristoff's, she was surprised to see that he looked scared. "I'm fine," Anna said, pushing herself to her feet. True, she felt like she was going to be sick. But she wasn't going to let anyone see how much pain she was in. She was there for her sister, and Elsa still needed her.

"Elsa," she said softly, "I know we can figure this out together—"

But it was too late to try to reason with her sister. Anna knew it even as the words came out of her mouth. Her sister's shoulders had tensed, and her hands were now clenched at her sides. She was on the defense.

"How?" Elsa shouted desperately. "What power do you have

to stop this winter? To stop me?" As she spoke, sharp spikes of ice began to creep down the walls and pop up on the floor.

"Anna, I think we should go," Kristoff said as he wrapped a protective arm around her shoulder.

She shrugged him off. "No. This isn't who Elsa is. She's just scared."

"*She's* scared?" Kristoff repeated. "You're joking right? I'm pretty sure she has nothing to be scared of."

But Kristoff was wrong. Elsa *was* scared. Anna could see it. Not in the tense way she held her body, but in the desperate look in her eyes. In the way her glance kept going to Anna. It might have been years since the two had confided in each other, but Anna still knew what Elsa looked like when she was terrified.

"Elsa, you didn't mean to do any of this," Anna finally said aloud. "It was an accident. We can fix this. We can fix it all. Together. I'm not leaving without you, Elsa."

"Yes," Elsa said, sounding heartbroken, "you are."

Waving her arms in the air, Elsa began to pull the snow off the floor, moving and shaping the powder until finally—standing between her and her sister—was the largest, strongest, scariest-looking snowman Anna had ever seen.

As the creature took one menacing step toward them, Anna and Kristoff exchanged looks. They clearly had only one option—RUN!

CHAPTER 22

HANS KNEW the search party was beginning to lose hope. He knew they were tired and hungry. He knew that they wanted to stop. But he didn't care. He needed to find Anna.

Since leaving Wandering Oaken's Trading Post, Hans had been pushing the group relentlessly. Despite the deepening snow and the increasing wind, he kept the pace fast and the distractions to a minimum. With every step they took, he felt the Duke's men watching him, their gazes cold and judging. He knew that they would report everything that had happened to the Duke. It could be Hans's undoing. So he kept his guard up and his back straight and did his best to focus on the task at hand. Which meant keeping everyone moving—fast.

"Your Highness?"

Hans whipped around in his saddle but did not pull back on his horse's reins. One of the younger volunteers was trotting a few steps back. His horse's head hung low, and the boy was shaking. "Your Highness, I know you told us we must keep going, but, well . . ."

"What is it, Thomas?"

"Well, not me, Your Highness, but some of the older men . . . they are growing tired. We were thinking maybe we might stop? Just for a few minutes? Give the horses a chance to rest and then we can move on? There is a grove up ahead. I took the liberty of riding ahead and, well, it is a good place to stop. It's actually quite beautiful. . . ."

Hans raised an eyebrow. Did the boy honestly think he cared about seeing something beautiful? All he cared about was finding Anna and forcing Elsa to stop this winter. Then he would return to Arendelle the conquering hero. He would be applauded and hailed as the kingdom's savior. Elsa would be forced to abdicate her throne, and he would marry Anna, become king, and finally accept control of the throne and the kingdom from his bride.

Stopping to see beautiful groves did *not* fit in that scenario.

But as he looked at the young boy shaking in his saddle, Hans realized he had little choice. He had to stop. At least for a moment. To insist they press on would make him look inhumane. His best option, his only real option, was to reassure the men that he was one of them. That he, too, felt the cold and that he, too, was tired. If he showed them all that he could power through it, they would have to do the same. Plus, if he were to return to Arendelle with Anna but without some of the kingdom's beloved townspeople, it might put a dent in his glowing reputation.

"Very well," he said. "We will go to this grove and rest. But only for a short while. And warn the others, this stop means we will only ride faster and harder after."

"Thank you, Your Highness!" Thomas said. "Thank you! I'll tell the others." Turning, he trotted back to the men.

Hans watched as Thomas delivered his message and smiled when the men, delighted by the news, began to applaud. It never ceased to surprise him how easily people could be manipulated. He had given up a few moments of time and, in turn, garnered more respect.

And then they reached the grove.

Instantly, Hans's confidence all but vanished. In that moment, he knew that while he wanted to blame his fears completely on the Duke's men, the fault did not lie solely on their shoulders. It lay mostly, he now realized, on the shoulders of the person who had created the masterpiece he was looking at—Elsa.

Hans had been clinging to one single reassuring thought: Elsa was a monster. Elsa was a monster who had covered Arendelle in snow and then abandoned her people to suffer. She had frozen the fjord and cut her kingdom off from any potential help. She had made children go hungry and families freeze. It was this, her utter lack of humanity, which guaranteed Hans his chance to be a hero. If the people of Arendelle feared Elsa, they would want her to be captured and restrained. They would *want* her to abdicate her throne, and in turn, they would *want* Hans to take it. For his plan to work, Hans *needed* Elsa to be the monster.

And yet, looking around him now, Hans had to admit that Elsa's power was not only destructive—it was also beautiful. The grove Hans found himself standing in was surrounded by tall, mature willow trees. On a regular summer day, he imagined that their long, thin branches would have swayed gently in the warm breeze and their distinctive feathery leaves would have made a gentle rustling sound. But it was not a regular summer day, and the leaves did not rustle—instead, they tinkled. Elsa's winter had frozen the trees. The branches hung low and the frozen feathers and small buds were encased in ice. The wind blowing through the glen caused the branches to hit one another, filling the air with the sound of a hundred wind chimes.

It looked as beautiful as it sounded. Even though the sun had long since sunk beneath the horizon, the glen still seemed to glow. Moonlight reflected off the frozen branches, bathing the whole area in a bluish-white light and causing the air around them to shimmer.

If anyone in Arendelle saw this, Hans realized, his anxiety mounting, they wouldn't see Elsa as a complete monster. This place, whatever it was, was something special. Something perfect. Elsa had created something beautiful, something pure, and not in the least bit frightening. If this was any indication, Elsa was more powerful than Hans had thought. And if her magic was this strong . . . well, Hans's plan might not be as easy to execute as he had hoped. Unless . . .

Hans smiled. He had been looking at this all wrong. If Elsa was captured, she would be scared. And clearly, when she was scared, her power was dangerous, not beautiful. All he had to do was make sure she never created anything like this again. He would destroy this glen and any trace of beauty. No one else ever needed to know what she was capable of.

There was just one obstacle in his way—the Duke's men. Their allegiance to the little man was off-putting, and their doubt in Hans was grating. Looking over, he saw that they had moved slightly outside the glen, as though allergic to all that beauty. What he needed was to have them on *his* side. *And the easiest way to get a thug to do what you want? Offer him a reward, of course.*

Kicking his horse forward, Hans trotted over to the men. Both were holding their hands in front of their faces, blowing on their fingers in the vain hope of making them warm.

"Gentlemen," Hans said, nodding in greeting. "I think perhaps we got off on the wrong foot."

The taller of the men lowered his hands. "And how do you figure that?" he asked, his deep voice rumbling loudly.

Hans moved slightly closer and leaned in. "I realize now," he whispered, "I wasn't quite clear on how I can make this little adventure of ours come out to your advantage." He waited to see if the men would turn and ignore him or keep listening. They kept listening. "You are here at the behest of your duke. But if I may ask, is he making it worth your while to risk your life up here on this mountain?"

"The Duke ain't said nothing about making things worth our

while," the shorter of the two men protested. "He just said Erik and I should go with you."

"Shut it, Francis," Erik, the taller thug, said. "We don't need to be telling this guy the Duke's business." Then he looked back at Hans. "And we don't answer to nobody but the Duke. So you can stop your prying."

"You're right," Hans replied. "I'm sorry. You don't have to tell me anything. The Duke is lucky to have two such loyal men. I suppose I can ask some of the other men to help me. I should have asked them in the first place. I just hate the idea of giving them land and title when they clearly are to be my subjects. I thought because you two weren't, you might like a little land and extra money in your pocket. You could make yourself a nice vacation home on the Southern Isles. Get out of Weselton during the winter and enjoy the warmth of my father's kingdoms. But since you aren't interested . . ." Hans paused and shifted the reins as though to go. Who cared if he was offering something he couldn't *actually* deliver on? They didn't need to know that. They just needed to take the bait.

For one tense moment, Hans was sure the Duke's men were actually going to let him walk away. But then Erik, who Hans was quickly realizing was the "brains" of the pair, spoke up. "What do you have in mind?"

Hans smiled. Then, turning around, he wiped the smile from his face so he would appear all business. "I need you to help me capture Elsa—alive."

"But the Duke sent us up here to kill her," Francis said, confused.

"Why would we want to keep her alive?" Erik asked. "Why did we even come up here if we're just going to let her go?"

Hans held back a groan. He hadn't expected so many questions from the pair. He had just hoped he could dangle a reward of some kind in front of them and they would do whatever he told them to do, no questions asked. Yet these two wanted answers. Which he didn't have. Quickly, he tried to think of a believable reason why he would wish to capture, not kill, the queen. A moment later, he had it.

"No, no, no," Hans finally replied. "That is what the Duke wants. But it is not what I want. Killing her would be the worst thing we could do. Look around you. Elsa is more powerful than we imagined. What if she is killed and the magic doesn't die with her? What if Arendelle is trapped in winter forever? I don't want that to happen. And I don't think the Duke would want that to happen to such a lucrative trading partner. We need to capture her—alive—and get her back to the castle in one piece. If you help me do that, I will guarantee you both titles, as well as land on one of my father's isles. Are we agreed?"

"Hold on," Erik said. Then he leaned over and began whispering in Francis's ear.

Hans watched, holding his breath.

At that moment, Erik held out his hand. "We have a deal," he said.

Hans smiled. "Deal," he said, shaking the man's hand.

That, he thought as he turned and went to gather the rest of his men, *was far easier than I expected.* Hans had no idea if killing Elsa would really be disastrous. In fact, he rather suspected the opposite. But disposing of the queen now created far too many variables. Hans was confident that, for now, he could talk his way to a happy ending.

CHAPTER 23

"STOP!" ANNA SHOUTED. "Put us down!"

No matter how much she squirmed or wiggled, Anna could not free herself from the grip of the giant snow monster. *The snow monster my own sister created to throw me out of her ice palace,* Anna thought. A wave of anger rushed over her, immediately followed by a wave of sadness. She could wiggle all she wanted, there was no escaping the truth—her sister didn't want her around.

Next to her, Kristoff struggled to free himself, to no avail. His rosy cheeks were growing rosier as he kicked his legs. Olaf, held tightly in the creature's other hand, was, as usual, seemingly unaware of the danger he was in.

"You are a lot stronger than I think you realize," the little snowman said.

In response, the creature pulled back both of his snowy arms and threw the three down the stairs. "Go away!" he shouted.

Anna hit the middle of the staircase and instantly began sliding down the rest of the way. She let out a little squeak as she saw Olaf's head roll by, followed shortly by his behind. Reaching the bottom of the stairs, Anna and Kristoff came to a sliding stop. The little snowman was not so lucky. His head slammed into a snowbank. The rest of him followed until there were three balls of snow protruding from the bank.

Anna had had enough. It was one thing to have her sister kick her out, but it was another thing entirely to have her *throw* them out—literally. And to let her stupid monster creature thing hurt poor little Olaf. Fuming, Anna turned around. "It is *not* nice to throw people!" she shouted at the creature's retreating back. When the snow giant didn't turn around, Anna moved toward the steps, ready to take him on.

"All right, feisty pants," Kristoff said, grabbing her around the waist. "Just let the snowman be."

Anna struggled. She didn't want to just let the snowman be. She wanted to get him. Throw *him* down some stairs and see how he felt about it. But the more she struggled, the tighter Kristoff's grip became. He was never going to let her go if he thought she was still fuming. Relaxing in his arms, she held up her hands as though admitting defeat. "Okay," she said. "I'm calm."

Just as she had expected, Kristoff let her go. The second he did, she bent down and grabbed a handful of snow. Packing it as tight and as fast as she could, she pulled back her arm and launched it—right at the snow creature. With a little thud, it harmlessly hit the giant on his back and fell to the ground, barely leaving a mark on the big snowman.

So there, ya big meanie! Anna cheered silently. *How does it feel to be the one getting bullied? What are ya going to do about it now? Huh? Huh? Hu—ohhhh . . .*

Apparently, the snow creature was more than happy to do something about it. As Anna watched, long spikes of ice began to form around the creature's joints. Turning back toward them, he let out a roar.

"Now you made him mad!" Kristoff shouted.

"I'll distract him!" Olaf cried out heroically as the creature leaped over the gorge that surrounded the palace. "You guys go!"

Before Anna could protest, Kristoff shoved her away from the snow giant. Looking behind her, she watched as Sven galloped off in the opposite direction, followed closely by Olaf's belly and butt. Only Olaf's head remained in the snowbank. But as Anna watched in horror, the creature blew past Olaf, causing the little guy's head to land facedown in the snow. There wasn't much he could do for them now.

Anna was hesitant to leave Olaf behind, but she and Kristoff needed to get away, and Anna was sure Olaf would be okay. The two raced across the snow, trying desperately to outrun the creature. They slid down a steep slope and ran through a maze of conifers, the branches heavy with snow.

Suddenly, Anna slid to a stop. Her gaze fell on the biggest tree with the heaviest branches, and she smiled. When she had fallen off Kjekk, she had tried to pull herself up using a branch. As soon as she had let go of the branch, it had swung up, sending all the snow flying. It had knocked snow off the surrounding trees. And that had just been a little branch. If she were to use a *bigger* branch . . .

Running over to the nearest tree, she jumped up, trying to grab the lowest hanging branch. She missed. She jumped again, her fingers grazing the wood but still not getting it. Finally, letting out a yell, she jumped with all her might. Her fingers closed around the branch and she pulled it back toward her.

She didn't have to wait long. Almost immediately, the ground beneath her feet began to shake. Anna saw the creature's big hand swipe through a section of trees, ripping them out of the ground as though they were toothpicks.

Anna's hands were trembling, her body shaking from the effort of keeping the branch steady. From somewhere behind her, she heard Kristoff call her name, but she ignored him. Her attention was focused completely on the approaching snow monster. *Three,* she began to count as he got closer. *Two* . . . He was almost where she wanted him. *And one!*

With a shout, Anna let the tree branch go. Free of her weight, it snapped into the air. The snow that had sat heavy on the branch went flying—right at the creature! There was a thud as the pounds of thick snow slammed into the snow giant.

Bull's-eye! But Anna didn't have time to gloat. She and Kristoff raced through trees and past huge piles of snow, putting as much distance between them and the creature as possible. They ran down a small hill and then clambered their way up another. And then they ran out of places to run.

Bursting through the trees, Anna and Kristoff barely stopped themselves before hurtling over the edge of a cliff! Windmilling their arms, they managed to stop their forward momentum just in time. Behind them, the creature let out another angry roar.

"It's a hundred-foot drop!" Anna shouted, peering down into the snowy abyss below.

"It's two hundred," Kristoff corrected.

Anna looked over at him and cocked her head. Now didn't seem like the time for technicalities. And seriously, why on earth was he going through his bag? Couldn't he wait to find what he was looking for—

"OW!" she cried out as Kristoff took a rope from the satchel and tied it—tightly—around her waist. Then he dropped down to his knees and began digging what appeared to be a U-shaped hole. "What's that for?" she asked.

"I'm digging a snow anchor," he replied as though that were obvious.

Anna looked over at him skeptically. Did he mean he was going to anchor *them*? And if he did mean that, did he mean they were going to . . . jump? Anna gulped. "What if we fall?" she asked nervously.

"There's twenty feet of fresh powder down there," he explained. "It'll be like landing on a pillow . . . hopefully."

Hopefully? This was the most insane thing she had ever done. But oddly enough, hearing Kristoff's voice calmed her and she realized, with a jolt, that she trusted him. "Okay, you tell me when," she said as, behind her, she heard the heavy footsteps of the creature coming closer.

"One . . ."

"I'm ready to go . . ."

"Two . . ."

Anna bounced up and down, psyching herself up.

And then a giant tree flew through the air, right toward them. "TREE!" she shouted. Before she could even think about it, she jumped over the edge, taking Kristoff with her.

"AHHHH!" Kristoff shouted.

"AHHHH!" Anna shouted.

"UMPH!" they groaned together as the rope hooked on the snow anchor above and went taut.

For a moment, they both just hung there, swaying gently about fifty feet above the snowy ground. "Well, that happened," Kristoff finally said. He looked down at Anna.

She shrugged. So, that might not have been the *best* move on her part. At least they were alive and away from the snow giant. Opening her mouth to point out that fact, Anna stopped as she saw Olaf's head come falling toward her. As he passed them, the little snowman gave them a big smile. "Hang in there, guys!" he called out.

As the little guy's head disappeared into the snowy mist below, Anna felt a jerk on the rope. Then another one. And another.

Looking up, Anna saw that the creature had grabbed their rope from the anchor and was pulling them up. In another few tugs, they would be back where they started.

"Kristoff!" Anna shouted, looking up to him for help. But at that precise moment, the creature gave a particularly rough tug. Kristoff was flung up and over, his head slamming into the cliff. Instantly, he lost consciousness.

Well, that's great, Anna thought, trying not to panic. *Looks like I'm going to have to get us out of this all by myself.* She scanned the area, hoping to spot something useful. And then her eyes landed on a knife hanging from Kristoff's belt. She reached for it just as the creature pulled them the rest of the way up so they were hanging right in front of his face.

"Don't come back!" the snow giant shouted.

Anna pulled back as the snowman spewed snowy phlegm all over them. "We won't!" she shouted. Then, with one swift move, her fingers closed around the knife handle and she sliced through the rope.

They hung suspended in the air just long enough for Kristoff to come to, and then they started to fall—fast! Anna barely had time to register that she might have just killed them both before she landed with a thud in the snow. The surprisingly *soft* snow.

"Hey!" she said, laughing in relief. "You were right. Just like a pillow." She turned, expecting to see Kristoff beside her. To her surprise, she saw Olaf instead. He was clinging to Kristoff's boots, which were sticking out of the snow.

"I can't feel my legs!" the little snowman shouted. "I can't feel my legs!"

Trying not to laugh at Olaf's genuine fear, Anna watched as, behind the snowman, Kristoff sat up. Shaking his head and spitting out snow, he said, "Those are *my* legs."

Instantly, relief flooded Olaf's face. As the snowman began to put himself back together, Sven appeared, none the worse for wear. In fact, the reindeer seemed unbothered by the run-in with the snow giant. Instead, he just seemed hungry. Anna laughed as he tried to make a snack out of Olaf's nose.

I'm glad that everyone is okay, Anna thought, struggling to pull herself out of the snow. After all that running, Anna felt drained. "Whoa!" she said as Kristoff lifted her out of the snow as though she weighed no more than a feather. Anna felt his hand linger on the small of her back as he placed her gently on the ground. His hand was so warm and reassuring. It felt almost as though it belonged there.

"You okay?" Kristoff asked.

"Thank you," Anna replied. She looked back up at him, and their eyes met. "Um . . . how's your head?" she asked, reaching up to touch the spot where he'd had the unfortunate run-in with the cliff.

"Ow!" he shouted, placing his hand on top of hers. Then, as though embarrassed, he waved it off. "It's fine. I'm good. I've got a thick skull. So . . . now what?" he asked, changing the subject.

"Now what . . . ?" Anna repeated. What did Kristoff mean? Now what between *them*?

Suddenly, Anna felt the blood rush from her face as the real meaning of Kristoff's question hit her like a ton of bricks. "Now what! Oh! What am I going to do? She threw me out. I can't go back to Arendelle with the weather like this. And then there's your ice business—"

"Hey, hey, don't worry about my ice business," Kristoff said, cutting her off. Then he cocked his head and peered closer, as if noticing something for the first time. "Worry about your hair!"

"What?" Anna said, shocked. Reaching up, she smoothed her hair down. "I just fell off a cliff. You should see *your* hair."

"No," Kristoff said. "Yours is turning white."

Anna grabbed her braid, pulling it in front of her face. Kristoff was right. The small piece of hair that had always been white had now disappeared in a much larger piece of white. As she watched, even more of her red hair changed color.

"It's because she struck you," Kristoff said softly. "Isn't it?"

Anna wanted to deny it, but she couldn't. Would Elsa ever stop hurting her? She looked up at him, her eyes filled with sadness.

"You need help," he said, his tone gentle. "Now come on."

Taking her hand, he began to lead her away from the cliff. Behind them, Olaf and Sven followed at a slower pace. "Where are we going?" the snowman called out.

"To see my friends," Kristoff answered.

Looking up at him, Anna smiled, despite the fear that was flooding through her. "The love experts?" she teased.

But Kristoff's response was anything but teasing. "Yes," he said seriously. "And don't worry; they'll be able to fix this."

"How do you know?" Anna asked, surprised by how upset Kristoff seemed to be.

"Because," he said, looking down at her, "I've seen them do it before."

I've seen them do it before.

Kristoff's words echoed through Anna's mind. What did he mean "before"? And who was "them"? What would love experts know about fixing weird white hair?

Anna didn't know what to think anymore. In the last twenty-four hours, her life had been turned upside down. Now here she was walking with a guy, a snowman, and a reindeer toward "love experts" while her hair turned whiter and whiter. And the oddest part about it all? Despite the frightful events that had just transpired, she felt completely at ease with this odd trio.

"Look, Sven," Anna heard Olaf's cheery voice say. "The sky's awake."

Turning her head, Anna smiled. The snowman was lying down on Sven's back, his eyes turned up to the stars above. The Northern Lights were bright, their bluish-green color almost blocking out the stars. Olaf was right. The sky really did look awake. *Awake and very much alive,* Anna thought. Suddenly, she felt a chill rush over her, and she shivered.

"Are you cold?" Kristoff asked, concerned.

"A little," Anna said.

Kristoff reached out his arm and, for a moment, Anna thought he might put it around her. The thought made some of the cold ease from her bones. But he didn't. Instead, he took her hand and pulled her off the path. Then he pointed at the ground. Anna's eyes grew wide. All around her were pockets of snow-free ground. It looked like the area was one big white and brown polka-dotted blanket. From one snow-free patch, a gust of steam vented upward, blowing out warm air.

"Oooh . . . that's nice," Anna said, walking over and placing her hands in the steam. Instantly, she felt less cold. Looking up, she smiled at Kristoff in thanks.

Together, Anna and Kristoff began to walk along the steamy path. "So," Anna asked, breaking the silence. "What's the deal with these friends of yours? Are they really going to know what to do? And what exactly makes them 'experts'?"

Kristoff's face turned bright red. "They . . . ummm. Yes, they know what to do." He stammered a bit more and then fell silent again.

"Well, do these 'experts' of yours have names?" she asked, still curious. "Are they doctors? Should I call them Dr. Love Expert? Or just plain old Mr. and Mrs.?"

"Hardy har har." Kristoff's fake laugh faded into a frown as he shot her a look. For a brief moment, she wondered if she had pushed him too far. Clearly, the guy was sensitive about these people they were going to see. *But why?* Anna wondered. *Does he think I'm going to embarrass him or something?*

Just as Anna was about to explain how polite she could be in a not-so-polite way, Kristoff cleared his throat nervously. "Well, I say friends . . . they're more like family."

Family, Anna thought. *I did not see that one coming.*

"When I was a kid, it was just me and Sven." Kristoff began to ramble. "Until they took us in. I don't want to scare you, they can be a little inappropriate. And loud. Very loud. They're also stubborn at times, and a little overbearing. And heavy. Really, really heavy."

Anna stifled a smile. He didn't know it, and he most definitely wasn't trying to be, but Kristoff was being pretty darn adorable. His family, whoever they were—and they did sound rather odd, but whose family wasn't—clearly meant the world to him. *I wonder if that's why he hasn't talked about them until now,* Anna thought. *If I had something that special, I would want to keep it close, too. I bet he had the most wonderful childhood. I guarantee no one shut doors in* his *face.*

But before that, he must have been so alone. He had said it was just him and Sven. That must have been hard . . .

Realizing that Kristoff was still talking, Anna focused. "But they're fine," he was saying. "You'll get it. They mean well."

Anna couldn't help herself. Overwhelmed with emotion, she reached over and gently laid her hand on Kristoff's arm. "They sound wonderful," she said softly. "I can't wait to meet them."

Kristoff smiled, obviously relieved. "Well, then, follow me!" he said happily. Pulling his arm away, he began to stride ahead.

Behind him, Anna watched him walk, her smile slowly fading. She had meant what she said—she *was* excited to meet Kristoff's family. But just thinking about family had made it impossible for her to not think of Elsa. Elsa, who was back on the mountain somewhere, locked away in her ice palace. Elsa, who wanted nothing to do with Anna.

"I like walking, don't you?"

Olaf's voice cut through Anna's deepening thoughts and, despite the sadness that was settling in her heart, she smiled. "I do like walking," she replied. "Very much."

"Have you ever walked on a beach? In the sun?" he asked. "I hope I get to do that someday."

Anna laughed. "I hope you do, too," she said, even though she knew it was impossible. She paused, drifting back into her thoughts.

"What are you thinking about?" Olaf asked.

Anna smiled. "Family. How nice it must be for Kristoff to have a family that cares about him so much."

"I have a *great* family," Olaf said.

"You do?" Anna asked.

"Sure. You and Sven and Sven. You're my family. I like you and you like me and we all helped each other back there. So isn't that family?" He turned and looked up at Anna hopefully with his big, innocent eyes.

Anna thought about it for a moment. "You know what, Olaf? I think that is exactly what family is."

"I thought so," he replied, wobbling on. "I mean, I think I'd probably do anything for you. Just like how you climbed a whole entire mountain to see your sister. And she's family, right?"

"Yes, Olaf," Anna said softly. "I care about her very much. I'm just not sure how much she cares about me. She didn't want me in her palace . . ."

Olaf looked thoughtful. Then he smiled. "Maybe she was just having a bad day. Do you know what I like to do when I have a bad day? I like to think about summer. And the beaches and the sun and . . ."

As the little snowman continued to talk about his summer dreams, Anna kept thinking about what he had just said. She knew the reason Elsa had kicked them out wasn't just because she was having a bad day. She had kicked them out because she didn't want them there. But maybe she did that . . . because she cared? In her own strange way? For a moment, Anna's heart was warmed at the thought. But then she remembered how coldly Elsa had looked at her, and the warm feeling faded. It wasn't going to do her any good to think the impossible. All she could do now was focus on getting to Kristoff's family and hope they would know how to fix what Elsa had broken!

CHAPTER 24

THIS BETTER BE WORTH IT, Hans thought as he came around another bend and found himself looking at still more snow.

For the past hour, Hans and his men had been making slow but steady progress. Yet Hans could tell the exertion was beginning to take its toll, not just on him, but on his men as well. Quiet grumbling had turned into outright complaining with each turn they made and each hill they climbed. If they didn't find Princess Anna or Queen Elsa soon, Hans worried he would have an out-and-out rebellion on his hands.

Still, Hans didn't want to give up. If they turned around now and went back to Arendelle empty-handed, his hopes of becoming king would be dashed—permanently. No. He needed to find the sisters. He *needed* to find Anna.

"Sir!"

A shout from up ahead startled Hans, and he jolted in his saddle.

"Sir! I think we've found her!"

Urging his horse forward, Hans cantered the remaining steps to where his scout stood waiting. He had sent the small man ahead a few hours earlier to see if he could find a clear trail. It seemed he had.

"What's the report, Anders?" Hans asked eagerly. The young man was a volunteer from the village. He had claimed to have experience tracking wild animals, but from the looks of him, he had been exaggerating.

For a moment, Anders didn't respond as he struggled to catch his breath. He looked terrible. His skin was pale, and his hands were shaking so hard he could barely hold the reins. "I . . . I . . . I followed the trail," he stuttered finally. "Like you asked me t-t-to. And it led to a huge castle, sir. Like nothing I've ever s-s-seen before. I think the queen is there. But there's a m-monster! A huge monster! It's all white and, and, and . . ." The scout's voice trailed off as he was overcome with a fit of shaking.

Hans raised an eyebrow. "A monster?" he repeated. "You're saying you saw a *monster* up there?"

The scout nodded weakly.

Turning back to look at the men waiting a few yards behind him and the scout, Hans weighed his next move. *If I tell them there is a monster, which there may or may not be—and I'm leaning toward not, as clearly this young boy is tired and has a very overactive imagination—then I risk them hightailing it back to Arendelle. If I don't tell them, and there is a monster, they may be caught unaware, but at least I'll have backup.* He shrugged. *At least I'll know what I'm getting into.*

"Men!" he said, turning to face his group. "The scout has brought us good news! The queen's hideout has been found!" The men let out a cheer.

Yanking on his reins, he kicked his horse into a gallop. Behind him, he could hear the sound of the other horses as well as the weak protests of the scout. *Let him protest,* Hans thought as he felt the wind sting his cheeks anew. *Soon I'll have rescued Anna and captured the queen, and I will be heading back to Arendelle the hero.*

The scout had been right. Queen Elsa's castle was unlike anything Hans had ever seen before. It rose into the sky, all shimmering ice and sharp points. Seemingly lit up by the sky itself, it reflected all the colors of the sun rising slowly over the horizon. A beautiful but dangerous-looking set of stairs formed from ice and covered in intricate carvings led up to the castle doors. Despite himself, Hans was impressed.

So this is what you're capable of, Queen Elsa, Hans thought. *The willow grove was just a drop in the bucket. Still, everyone has a weakness, even powerful people like you. I'll find yours sooner or later. A wall of ice won't keep me away.*

Gesturing for his men to gather around, Hans pointed toward the castle. "We are here to find Princess Anna," he reminded them. "Be on guard, but no harm is to come to the queen. Do you understand?"

Hans waited to make sure everyone was in agreement. He needed every single one of them to stick to the plan. He looked over at the Duke's men and narrowed his eyes. Especially those two. He was relieved when, meeting his gaze, the two men gave barely perceptible nods.

Good, Hans thought. Everything was in order. Now all they had to do was walk into the castle and overtake Elsa. It would be as easy as . . .

Hans didn't have time to finish his thought. Suddenly, a huge creature made from snow and ice rose up from the ground. Two beady eyes stared out of its huge marshmallow-shaped head. As it rose to its full height, Hans saw that the creature was nearly twenty-five feet tall! Sucking in a huge breath of air, the creature leaned forward and bellowed, "GO AWAY!" Then he slammed his fist into the ground, narrowly missing Hans.

Signaling to the rest of the men, Hans watched as they all raised their swords into the air. With a cry, they lunged at the monster.

But they were no match for it. As if flicking away gnats, the creature swatted the men, sending them flying.

Hans, however, was proving far harder to get rid of. Ducking and weaving, he stayed just out of the creature's reach. He barrel-rolled away when the monster slammed his foot down and jumped to the left to avoid being hit by an icy fist. Over and over again, the creature came at Hans, and over and over again, Hans slipped away.

That all you got, you big snowy beast? Hans thought as he pulled out his sword and began to swing it skillfully. *Compared to my father when he's angry, you seem like a cuddly bunny.*

Hans ducked as the creature once again tried to hit him. Out of the corner of his eye, he spotted the Duke's men charging up the stairs. *Now where are they going?* Hans thought. And then he saw the queen peeking out the door.

They were going after the queen without him! Hans fumed. That was *not* what they had discussed. With an angry cry, he pulled back his sword and then whipped it in front of him. The monster, who had taken one step too close to Hans, let out a roar as the blade sliced through his snowy body. Thrown off-balance, the creature began to tumble forward. Hans pushed back against the stumbling beast.

Hans glanced over his shoulder, his eyes growing wide. The creature was pushing him right toward the cliff that surrounded Elsa's ice castle. A few more steps and he was going to fall over the edge. Turning back, he swung his sword in the air. But it was useless. He was about to go over.

In desperation, he whipped his sword one last time. The iron pinged as it rushed through the cold air. Hans knew it was too late. He had missed. The sword was just going to keep going and he was going to fall.

And then, the sword hit something solid. The sudden impact caused the sword in his hand to shudder violently, and he almost let go. Hans hung on, smiling, as the sword moved faster and faster through the creature's thick snow leg. His brothers had always gloated about how good it felt to cut down the enemy. Up until now, he had thought they were crazy. But this *did* feel good. And it felt even better to watch as the creature stumbled once more and his whole body leaned to the left. Then to the right. And then, it toppled right over the cliff. *Phew!* Hans thought. *That was a close one—*

"Ahhh!" Hans let out a cry as the creature's hand reached into the air in one last desperate attempt to save itself and smacked into Hans. The prince went flying. For one terrifying moment, he felt nothing but air beneath him and then, at the last second, he managed to grab onto the edge of the staircase. A moment later, the strong hands of some of his men closed around his own, and he was pulled up to safety.

Catching his breath, Hans lay still for a moment. He wanted to lie on the wonderful, snow-covered ground forever. Appreciate the fact that he was alive. But then he sat up. Every minute he sat here was another minute the Duke's men were in the castle—alone. Hans knew better than to trust them. Getting to his feet, Hans brushed the snow off his pants and then rushed up the stairs and into the castle.

Suddenly, he heard a cry from above him. "No! Please!"

Hans had been right to worry. As he made his way up the stairs, he continued to hear the queen's desperate pleas. If he didn't hurry, he would be too late. The Duke's men had done exactly what he had feared they would do—they had turned on him. Instead of trying to capture the queen alive, it sounded like they were trying to kill her.

Just then, Hans heard the unmistakable sound of an arrow being released from its bow.

"Stay away!" Hans heard Elsa scream.

"Get her!" one of the thugs shouted. "Get her!"

Reaching the landing at the top of the stairs, Hans paused. It had just gone eerily quiet. He could no longer hear the bow's string being pulled taut, and the Duke's men no longer shouted words of encouragement to one another. Which likely meant one of two things—they had either killed Elsa *or* they had been killed by Elsa.

Hans took a deep breath. Pushing open the door, he burst into the room.

Hans had been partly right. Things weren't going well for the Duke's men. Large columns of ice stuck out of the floor, and in the far corner of the room, one of the Duke's men was trapped in a cage made of icy spikes. Hearing a shout, Hans looked over and saw that an icy wall was pushing the other man closer to the edge of the balcony.

Standing behind the wall, pushing it forward with her magic, was Elsa. But this was not the nervous, timid Elsa that Hans had seen at the coronation. This Elsa was wild and unrestrained. And while her power was terrifying, she herself was dazzling. *Dazzling and deadly,* Hans reminded himself. If she wasn't stopped, there was no telling what damage she would inflict. Hans knew, without a doubt, that he had to play this next part perfectly. One wrong move and Elsa would likely bring down her whole palace just to escape him and his men.

He watched Elsa for a long, tense moment, as though he were a lion stalking its prey. And then it hit him. She was terrified. Her rage was fueled by fear. He could work with that. He just needed to show Elsa what she was . . . and then he would show her just how *he* could help her.

"Queen Elsa!" he shouted, startling her. "Don't be the monster they fear you are!"

Hans's voice seemed to snap Elsa out of the fear-fueled rage she was in. She looked around, her eyes wide. As he watched, she lowered her hands, and the wall that had been pushing the Duke's man backward began to retract. The spikes keeping the other man captive began to lower. Within moments, they were both free.

But Erik and Francis were no less determined to do what they had started out to do—kill Elsa. Before he could shout a warning, Hans saw Francis grab his bow and arrows off the floor.

Hans's breath hitched in his throat and his shoulders tensed as time seemed to slow.

Francis notched the arrow.

Hans's head moved back and forth between Francis and Elsa. Elsa and Francis.

The Duke's man pulled back the bow . . .

Instinctively, Hans's feet began to move until he was just inches away from Francis. He could hear the other man's labored breathing, see the tension in the string holding the arrow back. As soon as Francis let that thing fly, it would be propelled forward—right at Elsa.

Francis narrowed his eyes and aimed.

Hans stepped closer. He was now almost atop the smaller man. Hans looked around the room, desperate for a plan, and noticed the giant chandelier directly above Elsa. That could work, if he could just arrange for Elsa to be hit by the chandelier instead of the arrow. True, it might kill her, but would that be so bad? One less obstacle to the throne. And if it didn't? Well, he'd told his men they were coming to capture the queen alive. Saving her from the Duke's men would only serve to make him appear true to his word. Either way, he came out on top.

And then, Francis released the arrow . . .

In that instant, time began to speed up again. Hans felt as though he were watching the events from afar. The moment felt foggy and crystal clear at the same time.

He saw himself nudge Francis. He saw his elbow hit Francis's. He saw the small movement send the arrow flying out of the bow. But instead of shooting straight out, it shot straight up. Hans watched as the arrow whizzed through the air and broke the icicle holding the large chandelier.

For one long, tense moment, the fixture hung, suspended by nothing. It stayed that way just long enough for Elsa to look up and see what was happening. Then it came crashing down. Elsa tried to dive out of the way, but she wasn't fast enough. The chandelier smashed to the ground, pinning Elsa beneath it and knocking her unconscious.

Hans spun around on the Duke's men. "What did I say about killing her?" Hans said, his jaw clenched. "You blatantly ignored my orders."

"But, but . . ." Francis stammered.

"She was going to kill us," Erik finished.

"That is not my concern," Hans replied. "My concern is stopping this winter. Which, if Elsa had been killed, might have been impossible." He paused as the men shuffled on their feet. "Oh, and about that reward? You can forget it. But I will be sure to let the Duke know how very *helpful* you've been."

Turning, Hans called to one of his more loyal men, still below in the entryway. The man held out a bag. Reaching into it, Hans pulled out a pair of thick iron manacles. "Put those on the queen. I want to make sure that when she wakes up, she doesn't hurt anyone, including herself." *Or worse,* he added silently, *stop me from getting everything I deserve.*

CHAPTER 25

ANNA HAD SEEN SOME pretty crazy things over the past few days. The castle gates being opened. A weaselish little man who danced like a rabid peacock. Her sister turning everything into ice and snow. *But this,* Anna thought now, *this might take the cake.*

In this particular case, "this" was Kristoff. Who, as Anna watched with growing concern, appeared to be talking to a bunch of rocks. They were rather lovely rocks. Some were smooth and others a little more jagged. Some had moss growing on them, others did not. But nevertheless, they were rocks. Which were, last time Anna checked, inanimate objects.

After hearing Kristoff talk about his family, Anna had been more than eager to meet them. She had pictured sitting around a cozy little kitchen, holding a warm cup of tea while listening to

Kristoff's adopted family share stories about him as a boy. Then they would let Anna see Kristoff's first ice sled and Sven's first little harness which, of course, would be adorable. It would be the picture of family bliss, and Anna, for the first time, would feel right at home in the middle of it all.

What she did *not* picture in this fantasy scenario was standing in the middle of a field of rocks. Nor did she imagine that Kristoff would insist on talking to them. But he was, quite cheerfully in fact. As though it were the most normal thing in the history of normal things.

"Meet my family!" he called over to Anna and Olaf, who were standing at the edge of the rocks.

"They're rocks," Anna said, voicing her thoughts out loud.

Beside her, Olaf looked as perplexed—and worried—as she felt. "He's crazy," the snowman said. Then, lowering his voice and talking out of the side of his mouth, he said, "I'll distract him while you run."

Anna didn't move.

"Hi, Sven's family! It's nice to meet you," Olaf said in an overly enthusiastic, singsong sort of way.

Beside him, Anna still didn't move. She couldn't. Her feet felt glued to the ground. She couldn't have been that wrong about Kristoff, could she? She had really begun to think of him as a friend. Someone she could trust and count on. Now she was worried that her sister was right—she *was* too quick to embrace strangers.

"Because I love you, Anna, I insist you run," Olaf said under his breath. "Why aren't you running?" He gave her a gentle shove.

"Okaaaay," Anna said, backing away from Kristoff. Maybe Olaf was right. Maybe she should get away from Kristoff and whatever episode he was having as soon as—

Just then, the rocks began to roll. They started off slowly, but picked up speed as they headed straight toward Kristoff. And then, in front of Anna's startled eyes, the rocks stopped and began to transform—into trolls!

"Kristoff's home!" they shouted.

Kristoff laughed as the trolls all tried to greet him at once. One troll yanked down his arm, trying to get a look at him, while another attempted to take off his clothes to wash them. Kristoff put a stop to that just as another troll, this one smaller than the rest, proudly showed Kristoff a mushroom growing on its back.

Throughout the reunion, Anna was silent. Her head was spinning. True, this was nothing like the image of Kristoff's family that she'd had in her head, but there was something rather . . . charming about the whole thing. While not human, the trolls clearly loved Kristoff—a lot. And he wasn't even one of them, technically.

"Trolls," she finally said. "They're trolls."

At the sound of her voice, the trolls turned around. Silence descended. They stared up at her, their eyes blinking in unison. Anna took a nervous step back. *Maybe I should have run when Olaf told me to,* she thought as the trolls continued to stare at her. But just as she was mustering up the courage to flee, the trolls all let out a huge, happy shout.

"He's brought a girl!"

All at once, the trolls left Kristoff and swarmed to Anna. Before she could protest, they had picked her up and carried her over toward Kristoff. "What's going on?" she said, laughing as the trolls threw her into Kristoff's arms.

"I've learned to just roll with it," he said, winking at her before gently putting her down.

Not a second later, Anna found herself face-to-face with a female troll whose name, she thought she had heard someone say, was Bulda. By the way Bulda had greeted Kristoff when he first arrived, Anna had guessed she was his adoptive mother. And by the way she was now examining Anna, she *knew* this was his mom.

"Let me see," Bulda was saying. She used her fingers to open Anna's eyes wide. Then she pried her mouth open. "Working nose. Strong teeth. Yes, yes, yes. She'll do nicely for our Kristoff."

"Wait!" Anna said, pulling her face out of Bulda's hands. "Um . . . no." The words came out harsher than she had planned, and she shot Kristoff an apologetic look.

He nodded understandingly before turning back to Bulda. "You've got the wrong idea. That's not why I brought her here," he explained.

"Right," Anna agreed. "We're not. I'm not—" She stammered awkwardly and let out a nervous laugh. Then she shook her head. What did she have to be nervous about? Or awkward?

Bulda, however, was not taking no for an answer. "What's the issue, dear?" she asked. "Why are you holding back from such a man?"

As Bulda began to list all of his qualities—good and bad—her question echoed through Anna's brain. Why *was* she holding back?

She knew the immediate answer. She was in love with Hans. They were going to get married and grow old together. But the more Bulda talked, and as others from Kristoff's adopted family joined in, the harder it became to remember exactly why she had agreed to marry Hans in the first place. Yes, she loved him. But did she *know* him? The way she knew Kristoff? When Bulda mentioned the way Kristoff walked, Anna laughed because she had seen it—a lot. He clumped more than walked. And when Bulda pointed out that he was a little too attached to his reindeer, Anna grinned because she had thought the very same thing. Even the things Bulda admitted to as faults in her adopted son—his fondness for being alone, his wild, shaggy hair, and his need for hugs (which, Anna had to admit, she had yet to see)—Anna already knew and found endearing.

What do I know about Hans? Anna asked herself as the trolls tried to convince her that Kristoff was the one for her. *I know that he has a lot of brothers. And he comes from the Southern Isles. But what else?*

"Enough!" Kristoff finally shouted, cutting off Bulda and interrupting Anna's thoughts. "She's engaged to someone else. Okay?"

Bulda's eyes narrowed and she leaned in closer to Anna. They stood that way for a long moment, their eyes locked. Finally, Bulda sighed and placed a hand gently on Anna's heart. "Love is a powerful emotion. First love. Young love. But remember, you are young and your heart is just opening. Take some advice from an old troll who knows a little something about love. You must always remember that love is a gift given to all of us. It should be cherished, yes. It should be cherished and it should be reciprocated. Always. Because love is special, and anyone who gives you their heart is giving you a part of them. . . ."

Bulda turned her gaze from Anna to Kristoff and a warmth infused her gray face. "But don't forget that love comes in so many forms. The love I have for Kristoff goes deeper than the roots of the oldest tree. It is special because it is my love for my son. And so is the love you feel for your sister. Or that your parents felt for you or that Kristoff feels for Sven. Love is a beautiful thing. It has the ability to render you senseless. It can take over your head and alter your vision so that you can't see what's in front of you. Sometimes, that can be a fantastic thing. But other times it can end up hurting you."

Bulda stopped and let out a breath. Taking Anna's hand, she led her over so she was standing underneath an arch covered in flowers. "Remember, whatever it does, love should always, always be respected. It is the most magical thing in the world. But that's just one old troll's opinion."

Anna was so focused on Bulda's words that she barely noticed when a few of the younger trolls covered her in moss and hung crystals from her hair. As another chill overcame her, Anna shivered and hugged herself harder. She couldn't tell if the chill was from the cold that now seemed to have invaded every part of her body or from the sudden doubt she felt about her own views on love.

She *did* feel better when she was around Hans, didn't she? He had comforted her when Elsa's magic had been revealed. And he had made her problems *his* problems when he agreed to watch the kingdom. *No,* she thought, her vision going blurry as her body was once again racked by a spasm of cold, *Hans is a good person, whom*

I love. So why did the trolls seem so intent on matching her with Kristoff?

But I don't love your son, Anna wanted to shout. *I mean, I admit he's a totally great guy, and when you get past the grumpy pout he can be kind of cute, but he's Kristoff. And sure, he does bring out some good things in me. I didn't realize I was brave enough to face that snow creature or attempt to hike a mountain before him. But so what? He's my friend. I'm sure if I spent more time with Hans, he would totally make me into a better person. . . .*

"Do you, Anna, take Kristoff to be your trollfully wedded—"

"WAIT!" Anna shouted, snapping back to reality. Bulda's talking and the other trolls' attention had woven some sort of trance over her. "What?"

"You're getting married," a troll dressed in a priest's robe explained.

"Oh," Anna said, surprised she didn't instantly say no. And then, before she could process what that might even mean, her ears began to ring, her vision grew blurry, and she collapsed in Kristoff's arms.

"Anna, your life is in danger."

Anna heard the words but didn't process them. She couldn't. She felt like she was sinking through thick, murky water. Everything was blurry and, try as she might, she couldn't open her eyes. Voices spoke over and around her, but they sounded as though they were coming from miles away. It was as though she were stuck in some dream, just on the verge of waking.

But even in her semiconscious state, Anna knew it wasn't a dream. She had been taken to Kristoff's troll family, almost ended up marrying the ice harvester, and now she was being told she was in danger. *No,* she thought as she finally opened her eyes, *this is no dream. Possibly a nightmare, but definitely not a dream.*

Kristoff, she realized, was the only reason she was still on her feet. He had one arm wrapped around her waist and a steady, reassuring hand on her arm. He was looking down at her, worry lines creasing his face. She gave him a thankful smile and then weakly turned to the sound of the voice. A troll with a mane of hair around his head and a string of crystals hanging from his neck was staring at her intently. While his expression was serious and a bit intimidating, his voice was kind and gentle and, for some reason, familiar to Anna. She remembered Kristoff asking Bulda to get Grand Pabbie—mentioning the wisest of the trolls. This, she figured, must be him.

"There is ice in your heart," Grand Pabbie went on, seeing that Anna was now listening. "Put there by your sister. If not removed, to solid ice will you freeze, *forever.*"

Anna could feel her heart beating and knew the blood still pumped through her veins, but just hearing Grand Pabbie's words made her feel colder and less alive. "What? No," she said, struggling weakly to stand up straighter. But the effort was too great, and she leaned back against Kristoff's strong chest. She could feel his heart beating through his thick jacket.

"But you can remove it, right?" Kristoff asked, his voice strained. He squeezed Anna's arm.

The troll sighed. "I cannot," he said softly. "If it was her head, that would be easy. But only an act of true love can thaw a frozen heart."

Anna shivered. "An act of true love?" she repeated, confused.

"A true love's kiss, perhaps?" Bulda said, turning to her husband and puckering her lips.

All around them, the trolls began to give each other kisses. If Anna hadn't been so cold, confused, and downright scared, she would have found it adorable. Instead, she shivered again.

"Anna," Kristoff said. "We've got to get you back to Hans."

"Hans," Anna said, nodding.

She knew why Kristoff had said that—Hans was her fiancé. He was her true love. His kiss *would* save her. It *had* to save her. But she could not stop thinking about what Bulda had said about love. What it did to a person—changed them for the better. How it made them feel warm and comforted. Her heart, which was so fragile already, felt as if it were going to shatter as it began to pound against her chest.

Anna thought back to the questions Kristoff had asked her about Hans when they first met. *Hans hasn't had a chance to see anything but the good, fun side of me,* she thought. *What if he doesn't like me when he gets to know me better?*

As Kristoff put her onto Sven's back and jumped up behind her, Anna shivered violently. She barely registered the movement as Sven's gait went from a brisk walk to an all-out gallop. She was losing feeling throughout her body, and she knew it was only a matter of time before things got much worse. With the last of her energy, she looked up at Kristoff. His eyes were narrowed with concentration as he steered Sven through the trees, and his cheeks were rosier than usual. *He's doing this for me,* Anna thought. *He's leaving his family behind and risking his safety to bring me back to Hans. And for what? For me? Because I've been such a good friend to him?* She let out a sad moan. She had done nothing to warrant his loyalty. Nothing at all.

Mistaking her sad moan for a groan of pain, Kristoff looked down, worried. Under his kind gaze, she shivered. "We'll be back soon, Anna," he said gently. "I promise. I'll get you home." Reaching up, he took the hat off his head and slipped it over hers. "Just hang in there. It's going to be okay. Hans is going to make it all okay."

Anna opened her mouth to say thank you, but before she could, her vision began to blur and she felt herself slipping into unconsciousness. As the darkness swallowed her up, she had one last thought. Kristoff had said it was going to be okay. But what if it wasn't? All this time, she had been sure that Hans was what she wanted. That he would be the one who could save her. But for the first time since this whole thing had started, Anna wasn't sure anymore.

CHAPTER 26

THE CHANDELIER HAD certainly done its job. Elsa remained unconscious for the entire trip back down the mountain. Hans had managed to get Elsa safely locked in a tower where, with luck, she could do no more harm. The palace servants had been annoyingly persistent in asking after the welfare of their queen. He brushed them off as quickly as possible, assuring them that they would hear the full story of what had happened on the mountain in due time. *As soon as I figure out exactly what that story is,* Hans thought. The next few hours were crucial for Arendelle's future—and his.

Hans made his way to the tower in which he had locked Elsa. Arriving at a large, heavy wooden door, he peered through a window into Elsa's cell. It wasn't exactly a dungeon, as the peaceful kingdom of Arendelle had no need for such things, but it was isolated with minimal ways in and out. Inside, Hans saw Elsa staring sadly out the lone window to the outside. She was watching as the snow continued to fall and the world became whiter and whiter. Her face was full of sorrow, and Hans couldn't help wondering how terrible it must feel to know you had lost control of a situation so completely.

He *never* lost control.

Hans's hands clenched as he continued to stare in at the queen. This was all her doing. This was all *her* fault. If Elsa had just kept it together and not lost her cool—literally—he and Anna would probably have been knee-deep in wedding planning. He would have been setting his ultimate plan in motion, figuring out how to overthrow Elsa, and proving that he, the loyal prince Hans, would be able to help Anna rule Arendelle well.

Instead, he was stuck trying to pick up the pieces of the mess Elsa had left in her wake. He had a kingdom full of very cold people, dignitaries breathing down his neck to fix the winter, a missing fiancée, and now Elsa, in chains but still powerful. For any other man, it might have been too much. *But not me,* Hans thought. *I've already taken this and molded it to my advantage. I just need to keep doing that until everything is back on track.*

Pushing open the door, he entered the room. He hung his lantern on the wall, and then he waited. It was best, he had learned, to let the enemy speak first. It gave him time to measure his emotions and properly respond.

"Why did you bring me here?" Elsa asked, when she saw Hans standing there.

"I couldn't just let them kill you," he said, forcing his face into an expression of concern.

Elsa lowered her head and stared down at her hands. "But I'm a danger to Arendelle," she said sadly. "Get Anna."

"Anna has not returned," Hans stated harshly. Elsa recoiled and looked out the window again. Softening his voice, he went on. "If you would just stop the winter, bring back summer . . . please?"

Elsa raised her eyes until their gazes met. "Don't you see . . . I can't," she said sincerely. "You have to tell them to let me go."

Hans narrowed his eyes, trying to see if Elsa was being genuine, privately hoping that she wasn't. But Hans could read people, and he knew Elsa wasn't lying. She couldn't stop the winter she had so recklessly started. And now she wanted to flee back to her mountains and leave her sister to clean up the mess. Her sister, who had not yet returned and was lost god knew where up on the mountain. The sister whom he was supposed to marry after he had helped save Arendelle. The princess who would then make him king and let him rule happily ever after . . . if she was alive.

"I will do what I can," Hans promised her.

As he left the cell, part of him wanted to scream at Elsa, to reveal his true colors and end things right then and there. Forget caution and well-calculated moves. Elsa was useless to him now. She wasn't going to help him with Anna, and she couldn't stop the winter. Why not destroy her and be done with it once and for all? That would be one fewer obstacle in his way.

No, he thought, collecting himself. He had not made it this far to throw it all away in a moment of rage. There would come a time to kill Elsa. He had come to realize that there was no other way. But that time was not now. It would serve his purposes better to eliminate the monster with an audience. It would solidify his power, and he would be able to show everyone that he had tried to end winter. For now, he needed to get to Arendelle's advisers and tell them the bad news—winter wasn't going anywhere.

Hans's footsteps echoed loudly as he made his way quickly back through the winding halls of Arendelle's castle. He pushed past a servant, brushing off her attempt to ask him a question, and didn't even look into the Great Hall to see how the people were faring. He barely registered the icy wind that was now seeping through the cracks in the windows or the snow that continued to fall wildly outside. Hans knew he had only one course of action. If he wanted to salvage anything of his original plan, he needed to get his fiancée back to Arendelle. He could deal with Elsa and her powers later—*after* he became king. Which could only happen if he married Anna. So despite the fact that the last thing he wanted to do was head back out into the cold, Hans knew he had no choice.

At last Hans arrived at the doorway to the library. "I'm going back out to look for Princess Anna," he said, addressing the dignitaries and guards that had gathered there to await his news.

"You cannot risk going out there again," the dignitary from Eldora protested, fiddling with his mustache.

Hans shook his head. "If anything happens to her . . ."

The Blavenian dignitary cut him off. "If anything happens to the princess, you are all Arendelle has left."

All Arendelle has left? The words sang in Hans's ears, and for a glorious moment it felt as though the snow had stopped and he was bathed in the warm glow of the sun's rays. This was a gift. A box wrapped in gold paper and tied with a silver bow. He looked around the room, struggling not to smile despite how badly he wanted to do so. He, Prince Hans Westergaard of the Southern Isles, was *All. Arendelle. Had. Left.*

And then it hit him. What that *really* meant. What he had not been able to see because he was so focused on his current plan. This whole time he had been thinking he needed one of the sisters to make him king, but he had set himself up perfectly to need *no one*. If what the Blavenian dignitary said really was true, he would actually be better off if Queen Elsa fled or died and Princess Anna never returned. It was perfect. And given the fact that Anna was still missing, it didn't seem like he would have to wait long to announce his new role.

Or . . . maybe not.

Just as it looked like Hans was in the clear, the door to the library flung open. Standing there, held up by Kai and Gerda, was Princess Anna. She seemed terribly weak, and her hair was now more white than bronze, but she was alive. And, from the way she was looking at him now, still very much under the impression that they were betrothed.

"Anna!" Hans cried, rushing to her side and catching her just as she collapsed into his arms. He wasn't sure what Anna seeming so weak meant for him, but he did know that he had to play the part of the doting fiancé. "You're so cold."

"Hans," Anna said, "you have to kiss me."

Had he just heard her correctly? Her teeth *were* chattering pretty loudly and she was barely speaking above a whisper, but it had sounded a lot like she had told him to kiss her. "What?" he asked.

"Now," Anna answered. Closing her eyes and puckering her lips, she tried to bring her mouth to his. But she was too weak. With a cry, she fell back.

From somewhere nearby, Hans heard one of the men clear his throat. In the excitement of Anna's return, he had forgotten they had an audience. Tearing his gaze from Anna's pained face, he saw that Gerda was waiting to speak. "We'll give you two some privacy," she said.

As Gerda began to usher everyone out the door, Hans pulled Anna closer to him. She was so cold, he could feel the chill even through his thick jacket. Her skin was like ice, and with every passing moment, her lips were turning bluer. She seemed to be freezing from the inside out, if that was even possible. Which, given what he had seen today, it definitely was.

Hans began to lead Anna over to the couch in front of the library's roaring fireplace. "What happened out there?" he asked as they walked.

"Elsa struck me with her powers," Anna replied sadly.

"You said she'd never hurt you."

Anna shrugged, defeated. "I was wrong." She could barely keep her head up to meet his gaze, but when she did, Hans was taken aback by the emotion he saw in her eyes.

No one, Hans realized, had ever looked at him the way Anna

was looking at him now—with simple love and need. She needed him. For the kiss, yes, but it seemed like there was more there. It was as though she needed him to fill the hole left by her sister's rejection.

Hans shook his head. He wasn't there to fill a hole in Anna's heart. He was there to win a throne. He had heard what the Blavenian dignitary had said—without Anna, he would be all Arendelle had left. If Anna died now, everything would fall into place for him. *That* was the far simpler, cleaner, less emotionally messy plan. The Westergaards didn't do emotion—that was the one legacy he had been given.

Gently, Hans lowered Anna onto the couch and wrapped her in a blanket. Her shivering, despite the new warmth, only increased. She was getting worse by the minute. Was this the result of Elsa's magic? Hans knew it was powerful and strong, but he had yet to see it be this deadly.

"She froze my heart, and only an act of true love can save me," Anna added, as if reading Hans's mind. With effort, she raised her eyes until she was looking right at him.

Her expression said it all. She expected him to be the one to save her. "A true love's kiss," he said, knowing without being told that it was the act Anna was referring to. He was no fool. He had read his fair share of fairy tales with their perfect happy endings. Did she honestly think this was one such tale?

Hans couldn't help himself. After years of bullying by his brothers, after years of taking the joke but never making the joke, after years of being the thirteenth son, he was going to get the last laugh. And he wanted to make it count.

He leaned closer to Anna, putting his hands gently on her shoulders. Through his gloves, he could feel the chill pouring from her body. He could feel her soft, nervous breath as he came closer and closer. He could feel, and hear, the sharp intake of breath as she waited, anticipating the moment his lips would touch hers. He saw her eyes flutter closed. He drew closer . . . and closer . . .

And then he pulled back.

Wiping the simpering expression off his face, he removed his hands from her shoulders. The sudden removal of support caused Anna to fall back against the couch. She looked up at him, confusion racing across her face. At one time, he might have pretended to care. But he was done playing games.

"Oh, Anna," he said, his voice dripping with condescension. "If only there was someone out there who loved you."

CHAPTER 27

ANNA HADN'T THOUGHT it possible to feel any colder. Until now. Wave after wave of ice seemed to attack her heart anew as Hans's chilly words echoed through her mind. If she had heard him correctly, and there was no doubt she had, he had just told her in no uncertain terms that he didn't love her. The realization hit her harder and more painfully than even the bolt of Elsa's magic.

As Anna watched helplessly, Hans stood up and moved away from the small couch. The absence of his warmth deepened the chill in her body, and she began to shiver uncontrollably. What had happened? How could the man who was now standing there looking at her with empty eyes be the same man who only a day before had asked her to marry him? It didn't make sense. None of this made any sense.

Images of the past two days flashed before her as though her mind was coming to grips with Hans's words before her heart could process them. She was, it seemed, watching their love play out before her very eyes. Their first meeting and how happy Hans had seemed to have run into her. The way he had waved shyly at her during Elsa's coronation and saved her on the dance floor. Running through the castle halls and sharing stories of their families up on the roof. The moment Hans had asked her to marry him, as water rushed past and stars twinkled in the sky above. It had all been so perfect and felt so real. She couldn't have imagined his love, could she?

"You said you did," Anna finally managed to stutter. Her voice sounded weak and desperate, even to her own ears.

Hans looked over at her and shook his head. "As thirteenth in line in my own kingdom, I didn't stand a chance," he said as he began to move around the room, pulling all the curtains closed. "I knew I'd have to marry into the throne somewhere . . ."

"What are you talking about?" Anna asked. What he was saying was so preposterous, it was as though he were speaking a foreign language.

Hans walked back toward her, and her treacherous heart thudded hopefully in her chest. But he simply leaned over and blew out the candles on the nearby table. "As heir," he went on, detailing his awfulness to Anna, "Elsa was preferable, of course. But no one was getting anywhere with her. But you . . . You were so desperate for love that you were willing to marry me, just like that."

Anna sucked in her breath. She had been so terribly, *terribly* naive. She had blindly opened her heart to Hans without once questioning his motives. If she only had thought to look past his dreamy eyes and charming smile, she might have figured out that, to him, she was nothing but a political pawn in a nasty game of chess.

Crossing the room, Hans grabbed a pitcher of water and approached the fireplace. He looked back at Anna, a wicked gleam in his eyes. "I figured, after we'd married, I'd have to stage a little accident for Elsa," he said, revealing his ultimate plan piece by piece. Slowly, he began to pour the water over the flames, dousing them.

"Hans!" Anna cried out desperately, feeling the temperature in the room drop instantly. "Stop!"

He didn't. In fact, Anna saw that he simply poured the water faster, as though relishing the way the dying flames made her shiver more violently. This was not the man Anna thought she knew. This was a monster. Someone so full of evil that he didn't even care about the pain he was causing her with every word he spoke. Had he truly had such a miserable life to have no heart? Anna wondered. Was his father that cold? His brothers that terrible? Something *had* to have happened to make Hans into this creature.

Or maybe not, Anna realized sadly. Maybe he was just a terrible excuse for a human being.

"But then she doomed herself, and you were dumb enough to go after her," Hans added with a nasty chuckle. "All that's left now is to kill Elsa and bring back summer."

Anna raised her chin. Hans might have made a fool of her, but if his plan was to get rid of her sister, he was in for a nasty surprise. "You're no match for Elsa," she hissed through clenched teeth. *You try and go up against her and she'll show everyone in Arendelle the weak, horrible man you are.*

Squatting down next to her, Hans put a finger under her chin just as he had done not so long ago. But this time, when he lifted her head, there was a violence to his actions that made Anna recoil. "No," he sneered. "*You're* no match for Elsa. I, on the other hand, am the hero who is going to save Arendelle from destruction."

"You won't get away with this," Anna said, wrenching her face free of his slimy hands. How could she have ever longed for his touch? It repulsed her now.

Hans got to his feet and walked to the door. Putting a hand on the doorknob, he gave her one last look over his shoulder. "Oh, I already have," he said darkly. He turned and walked out the door, gently shutting it behind him.

Inside the dark room that was growing colder by the second, Anna pushed herself off the couch and struggled to the door. Weakly, she turned the knob. But it was no use. It was locked. Hans was now somewhere on the other side, about to take over her kingdom—and she had never seen it coming.

Anna didn't know how long she had been lying on the cold floor. All she knew was that it was becoming harder to breathe. It felt as though Elsa's snow giant were sitting on her chest, like her hands were trapped in blocks of ice.

But that pain paled in comparison to the shame and anger she felt at having been duped—at having *allowed* herself to be duped.

For a while after Hans left, Anna had lain in front of the door, trying to shout for help. Her voice, though, was weak and growing weaker, and the door was thick. It was futile to try, and eventually Anna stopped, desperate to conserve what little energy she had left. She had leaned back against the door and let her head sink to her chest.

At some point, the rest of her hair had turned white, and now she stared at the tip of her braid, both horrified and fascinated by the transformation. *Seems like everything is changing fast around here,* she thought sadly. *First Elsa, then my hair and my heart. And if Hans gets his way, the whole kingdom is going to be in for one huge change.*

The thought of Hans sitting on the throne sent a fresh wave of anger coursing through Anna. He had left her there to die. The man she had wanted to marry—the man who had ultimately driven the final wedge between her and Elsa—had left her to die.

What was wrong with her? Why did things like this keep happening to her? Love wasn't supposed to hurt, yet it felt like all she knew when it came to love was pain. Every time she opened her heart, she just got burned. Or, in this case, frozen. And she was getting sick and tired of it.

Looking back on the loves of her life, Anna saw the pattern clear as day. She had loved her parents. So very much. And then they had been ripped away from her. Anna still mourned for all the days they would never share.

And then there was Elsa. Her big sister had been her world

when they were younger. Even now, surrounded by cold and shivering to death *because* of her sister, Anna could remember the fun they had had. The adventures they had gone on and the way Elsa used to drop everything to play games around the castle. And then that all stopped. *Elsa pulled her love away from me.*

Finally, there was Hans. The man of her dreams. A man she had been convinced would never pull away from her. Hans, who had known how much Anna's family had hurt her, and who had been equally hurt by his own family. It hadn't seemed possible that someone with whom she had shared such intimate details of her life would be able to just turn from her. But Hans had—and he had done so with such ease.

A fresh wave of tears—ones born of frustration now—welled up in Anna's eyes as she began to see the injustice of it all. Here she was blaming herself for believing in Hans, but how was she supposed to have learned how to give and receive love when she had so little experience with it? No wonder she had fallen for Hans's act. It was the first time in a long time that someone had cared for her—or at least, had pretended to care about her. *What a fool I've been,* she thought sadly.

Raising her head, Anna saw that the last of the embers in the fireplace had flickered out. Through the one window Hans had not covered, Anna could just make out the gray sky and knew that while she had been locked away, more snow had fallen over Arendelle. The wind had picked up still more, and occasional gusts of snow fell through the open flue into the fireplace. A thin layer of ice now covered the pitcher Hans had used to douse the fire, and even the candles' wax looked frozen mid-drip. Soon the room's temperature would be well below freezing.

"Well, I guess that's that," Anna said aloud. Her energy was fading, but she felt the need to get the words out, even though she knew there was no one to hear her. "Tell my sister, if she ever comes back, that I didn't mean for any of this to happen. Tell her I didn't know that Hans was just using me to get the throne. Tell her I never meant to hurt her. I just wanted my sister back. I wanted the doors to stop slamming in my face. I just wanted her to love me. That's all I ever wanted. For someone to love me." She stopped, a sob catching in her throat. Saying the words aloud made them so much sadder to her own ears. Raising her eyes toward the ceiling, with the last of her fading strength, she added, "And tell the people of Arendelle that I love them and not to listen to Hans because he's awful. Please let them know I had no idea, and that if I had been given the chance, next time I would get to know the guy I was going to marry first . . ."

Suddenly, Anna stopped herself. She pictured Hans standing in front of the people of Arendelle with his smarmy smile and his secret agendas. She imagined Elsa, still hiding on the North Mountain, unaware of her kingdom's fate. And it made her mad. It made her so mad that for the first time since Hans had left the room, she forgot to be sad. She felt the cold recede ever so slightly.

So Hans had made a fool of her, so what? She had made a fool of herself on plenty of occasions and always bounced back. She was practically a champion at rebounding from rejection. She couldn't let Hans ruin everything. If she did, then he would have won and gotten the best of her. And she was too strong to let that happen. She had spent too many years alone, surviving on her own company, to be taken down by one awful man's actions.

No, she resolved, *I am not going to let Hans win. I'm not going to give him the satisfaction of finding me in this dark room with tears frozen on my face. He doesn't deserve that victory. He doesn't deserve to go on living thinking he finished me and broke my heart. I am stronger than that. I made it up the North Mountain without him. I fought wolves and huge snow creatures. I made friends and met a whole valley of trolls. I did that. Not Hans. And if he thinks he is going to take that from me by not kissing me and leaving me here to die, well, then he's got another thing coming. Because I know the truth. I know that I'm a better person despite him, not because of him. I'll never let him take that from me. Ever.*

CHAPTER 28

HANS STOOD IN THE shadowed hallway just outside the council chamber and watched. Inside, the dignitaries, representatives, and various other royalty had gathered to await his return. But he wasn't quite ready to make his entrance. Not yet at least.

After leaving Anna to freeze, Hans had walked through the castle, gathering his thoughts. Much hinged on how the next few moments played out. After acting the part of the loving, doting fiancé for the past forty-eight hours, he knew it would not be difficult to feign sadness when he announced Anna's tragic death. What *would* be difficult was not appearing too eager to step up and take over the throne. He would need to seem distraught, angry, and of course, a little bit frightened. Otherwise, the others might find him suspicious. And that was the last thing he needed.

What he needed now was to make his story believable. When everyone was convinced of him, he would make sure Anna was gone and deal with Elsa. With both sisters out of the way, his path would be clear. He would be king of Arendelle and he would never, ever have to return to the Southern Isles. He would never again have to suffer humiliation at the hands of his brothers or his father.

Now, as he stood outside the chamber, biding his time before his grand entrance, he was amazed at how well everything had come together. Given the fact that he'd had only the barest of plans upon arriving in Arendelle, the end result was something of a miracle. True, he'd had to lie, manipulate, and con his way to this point, but that was just part of the game. And it turned out he played the game very, very well.

He could see that the men inside were growing restless. It was almost time. Pacing back and forth in front of the blazing fire, the Eldoran dignitary wrung his hands nervously. "It has been too long," he said. "Why has Prince Hans not returned?"

"I imagine he and the princess have much to discuss. And she was in no condition to speak when we saw her," the lord of Kongsberg pointed out. Compared to the others, he seemed untouched by the cold. He sat, legs crossed, on a large wingback chair. A book lay open in his lap. But, Hans noticed as he observed the goings-on, the lord hadn't turned the page once. It was the only indication of his nerves. Looking over at the Eldoran dignitary, he added, "The prince has everything in hand, I'm sure. We just need to be patient."

"But it's getting colder by the minute," the Duke of Weselton pointed out. "If we don't do something soon, we'll all freeze to death."

Leave it to the weasel to stir the pot, Hans thought. It was time to step inside, before the Duke could start trouble. Straightening his shoulders and lifting his head, Hans wiped the smug smile off his face and replaced it with a look of distress. Time to start the final act.

Pushing the door open wider, Hans stepped into the council chamber. All heads swiveled at his arrival.

"Prince Hans," the Blavenian dignitary said, taking a step forward.

Hans held up a hand, as though the thought of human contact were too painful for him at that moment. Sighing dramatically, he placed his own hand on his heart. "Princess Anna is . . ." He pretended to struggle to get the words out. "Dead," he finally said. For effect, he stumbled, as if overcome with grief.

As several of the men helped him to a chair, Hans did his best to appear the heartbroken fiancé. Biting the inside of his cheek brought tears to his eyes, and a well-timed shudder made him look like he was holding back sobs.

"What happened to her?" the Duke asked.

Hans was surprised to hear no suspicion in the Duke's voice. His confidence growing, Hans paused before answering, building the tension. Everything hinged on what he was about to say and how it would be received. "She was killed . . . by Queen Elsa." He paused again as the chamber filled with gasps. He nodded sadly, letting the tears well up even more. The inside of his cheek was going to be a mess later, but it would be worth it. Especially when he added the next little gem. This one he had come up with even before leaving Anna. It was, he realized then, the only way to ensure his success. "At least," he said, laying the emotion on thick, "we got to say our marriage vows . . . before she died in my arms." As if the announcement were too much, he hung his head in his hands and let the tears fall.

"There can be no doubt now," the Duke of Weselton said, his voice serious. "Queen Elsa is a monster and we are all in grave danger."

Beside him, the Blavenian dignitary nodded. "Prince Hans, Arendelle looks to you."

Hans stifled the smile that threatened to spread across his face. His brilliant display of grief had worked! Raising his head slowly, Hans looked around the room. Prince Wils's usually cheerful expression had been replaced by a look of abject worry. The Eldoran dignitary was wringing his hands so hard that it seemed he might rip them off altogether. Even the lord of Kongsberg was finally showing some emotion. While apparently not as distressed as the others, his face had turned distinctly paler. A few of the younger representatives looked almost sick with fear, and Hans heard one of them mumble to the man next to him, "What is he going to do now?"

Pushing himself off his chair, Hans wiped his cheek dramatically. This was his moment. "With a heavy heart," he said in his most somber of voices, "I charge Queen Elsa of Arendelle with treason and sentence her—to death."

Despite his bold words earlier, as Hans led the others toward Elsa's cell, he felt a nagging doubt at the back of his mind. He was reluctant to kill the queen. He was sure Anna would be happy to call him many things—a cad, a scoundrel, and a liar, to name a few—but he was not, and had never been, a murderer. Murdering painted you into a corner. It took away your options and made you a brute. He *hated* not having options, and he *refused* to be a brute. His brothers were brutes, and he didn't respect them in the least. He wanted respect, and he wanted to know that he always, *always* had a way out of whatever situation presented itself.

But, he thought now as he peered around at the men looking to him for definitive action, *sometimes exceptions had to be made.* A declaration of treason and an execution, while a bold course of action, seemed to be the move he had to make. *Besides,* Hans reasoned, *how else are we going to stop this winter if not by putting an end to its source?*

No. It was clear he had no choice. There was no other way for Hans to get what he wanted. When the time came, he would do what had to be done.

Turning a corner, Hans saw the two guards he had posted outside Elsa's cell. He had picked the strongest of the castle guards and equipped them with sharp swords and, more importantly, fire. Large torches stood in metal holders on either side of the guards.

It seemed to him that the only thing an ice queen might fear was heat. While not a tested theory, Hans had figured it wouldn't hurt.

Hearing Hans's approach, the guards came to attention and bowed. "Your Highness," they said in unison.

"Men," Hans acknowledged. "How's our prisoner doing?"

The larger of the two guards stepped forward. "She has been crying, sir," he reported. "And she was pulling at her chains, but that stopped a short while ago."

Looking over his shoulder at the men who had joined him, he saw a few disturbed looks at the news that Elsa had been chained. "It was for her own protection," he explained. "And yours. You were not with me on the North Mountain. I cannot stress enough how powerful and—"

As if on cue, the floor beneath their feet shuddered violently. Thrown off-balance, Hans reached out and clung to the wall beside him, trying to steady himself. There was another shudder, this time followed by a loud groaning noise. Then, through the small window in the cell door, wind began to blow, carrying snowflakes into the hall.

Instantly, the guards grabbed their weapons. Shouting to the others to stay back, Hans moved in right behind them. He needed to get in that cell before the others had a chance to see what had happened. He had a feeling it was going to be nothing good.

"She's dangerous," one of the guards said, pausing with his hand on the doorknob. "Move quickly and with resolve."

Oh, good god, man, Hans fumed silently. *As if I need to be told that. I know exactly what Elsa is capable of when angry.*

Pushing open the door, the guards stepped inside. Hans followed hesitantly. Instantly, he wished he hadn't. Where there had once been a solid wall of stone, now nothing remained but a few broken rocks. The whole wall was gone—as though blasted from the inside out. Snow had already begun to cover the floor, but where it hadn't, Hans saw that the tiles had been frozen solid. In the middle of the room, shattered to pieces, was all that remained of the manacles Hans had placed on Elsa's hands.

Hans's vision went red as fury flooded through him. She had escaped. Despite his guards and despite her shackles, the queen had gotten away. Now she was out there somewhere, ready to do who knew what to the kingdom and—Hans gulped—him.

Walking over to the edge of the room, Hans looked out into the blinding snow. Almost nothing was visible through the storm, which seemed to be growing stronger by the second. Soon any tracks Elsa might have left would be swallowed up.

Hans shivered—both with cold and anger. Elsa had ruined everything. He had just been about to tie his plan up in a neat and tidy bow and then she had gone and messed it all up. Now he was going to have to go after her or risk looking weak, and then he was going to have to kill her. She had given him no choice. Despite his best efforts to keep the blood off his hands, he saw no alternative. It was her or him. And he hadn't gone through the past few days to not come out the winner. He was going to kill her, put an end to winter, and get himself on that throne.

CHAPTER 29

WITH THE LAST of her strength, Anna rubbed her hands up and down her arms, hoping the motion would make her feel warmer. It didn't. The energy required was too much, and her hands were basically just bricks of ice at that point anyway. As her body was racked with another spasm of shivers, Anna let out a pained cry. The spasms were coming harder and faster now.

Anna knew it was futile to think about the future. It was only a matter of time now before her body, like the room around her, froze over completely. After Hans's sudden revelation and subsequent departure, anger had fueled a small fire in Anna's belly. Fantasies of finding the slimy beast and calling him out in front of everybody warmed her heart.

And then there had been the fantasy where Elsa returned to Arendelle to avenge her sister's death. In a billow of snow and ice, she came down from the North Mountain and found Hans, shivering and quivering in the corner of the courtyard. His hands would be held up in front of his face, tears falling down his cheeks and snot pouring from his nose as he realized just how much trouble he was in. Elsa would stare down at him, no sympathy on her beautiful face. "You are a sad, sad excuse for a man, Hans," she would say. "Do you honestly think you are special? That Anna didn't see through your act? My sister was amazing. She was wonderful and kind and I loved her. I loved her so much. And you destroyed her. So now I'm going to destroy you."

Her favorite fantasy, though, was far less vengeful. In that one, Anna made it out of the room and found her way back to the North Mountain. There, she found Elsa waiting, arms outstretched. "I've missed you so much," her sister would say, pulling her close. They would stay that way for a long, long time, and when they finally drew apart, Elsa would vow to return. "Together," she would say. "We will save Arendelle together." Then Elsa would end the winter, and the sisters would open the door to the rest of their lives—together.

Overcome by the sudden emotion, Anna closed her eyes. Her breath slowed. She just needed to sleep for a few minutes. Then she would feel better. "Just for a minute," she said softly. "Just need to rest my eyes . . ."

Above her, the door handle jiggled.

Anna's eyes flew open. Had she imagined it?

The door jiggled again. No! This was real! "Help," she said, her voice barely a whisper.

The handle jiggled one last time and then—with a loud groan—the door swung open. From her prone position on the floor, the first thing Anna saw was a carrot sticking out of the lock. A moment later, Olaf, minus his nose, wobbled into view. Seeing Anna, the little snowman let out a cry.

"Anna!" he said happily, grabbing his nose and shoving it back in place. Then he saw the state she was in. "Oh, no!"

Anna tried to smile, but a fresh wave of shivering made it impossible. She could only watch helplessly as Olaf tried to figure out what to do. She had no idea how he had gotten inside the castle, but she didn't care. Just seeing him made her feel better. Unfortunately, it didn't make her feel any warmer.

But Olaf was on it. Spotting the fireplace, the snowman wobbled over as fast as his little snow legs would let him and began to put fresh wood in the hearth. When there was a rather significant pile in place, Olaf grabbed a match, lit it, and then tossed it into the kindling underneath. Instantly, the fire roared to life.

Even from her spot by the door, Anna could feel the first fingers of heat flickering across her face. It felt better than eating chocolate fondue or dancing in her slippers. It felt better than the first time she had jumped Kjekk over a fence or when she had seen her first shooting star.

Unfortunately, Olaf seemed to think the fire was pretty

amazing, too, and was standing directly in front of it. "Whoa!" he said, watching the flames flickering higher and higher. "So this is heat. . . . I love it!"

Anna watched in horror as the snowman reached for the fire—with his twig finger. "Oooh! But don't touch it!" he added, as his finger caught on fire. Laughing, he shook out the flame and then focused his attention back on Anna. "So, where's Hans?" he asked, wobbling over and helping Anna to her feet. "What happened to your kiss?"

"I was wrong about him," Anna said sadly. "It wasn't true love." Gingerly, she lowered herself down on the couch. Letting out a sigh, she closed her eyes and let the fire warm her. But even with the flames roaring, she still felt chilled to the bone.

"But . . . we ran all the way here!"

Anna's eyes opened, and she looked down at the little snowman. He had not left her side and was now staring at her with big, confused eyes. Anna sighed. He was right. Olaf, Kristoff, and Sven *had* raced her back to the castle. The three had done everything in their power to get her safely home to Hans. But it had been for nothing.

"Please, Olaf," Anna pleaded, gently maneuvering the snowman away from the fire. "You can't stay here; you'll melt."

Olaf crossed his stick arms and shook his head. "I am not leaving here until we find some other act of true love to save you," he said stubbornly. He did, however, move away from the heat slightly. Taking a seat on the ground behind her, he put a twig finger to his mouth, thinking. "Do you happen to have any ideas?" he asked after a minute.

Anna didn't respond right away. All this time, she *thought* she had known what love was. She had been sure she knew better than Bulda back in Troll Valley. She had been convinced what she felt for Hans the moment she first saw him was true love. She had even laughed when Kristoff had questioned her ability to recognize love, choosing instead to believe her foolish heart. Yet as it turned out, she really hadn't had a clue. Looking over at the sweet snowman, she couldn't even pretend anymore. What was the point? "I don't even know what love is," she said to Olaf.

"That's okay. I do," Olaf said, standing up and putting a hand on her shoulder. "Love is . . ." he began, oddly confident. "Love is putting someone else's needs before yours, like, you know, how Kristoff brought you back here to Hans and left you forever."

Anna raised an eyebrow. "Kristoff *loves* me?" she asked, bewildered.

"Wow," Olaf said. "You really *don't* know anything about love, do you?" As he had been talking, Olaf had once again moved closer to the fire. Now he was practically right on top of it, and the heat from the flames had begun to melt his face.

"Olaf!" Anna cried, watching in horror as his eyes began to sink toward his mouth. "You're melting!"

"Some people are worth melting for," the snowman said. He tried to smile at Anna, but his mouth had begun to drip and so it came out crooked. Realizing what was happening, he panicked and moved away from the fire. "Just maybe not right this second," he added.

As Olaf began to push his face back into place, Anna stared at him, her mind racing and her heart pounding. Olaf was a genius. This, she realized, watching the snowman struggle, was love. Olaf had been willing to put himself in danger because he didn't want to see her get hurt. Love wasn't the canned romantic declarations. That was nothing but fluff. That was what Hans had thrown at her and what she had mistaken for love. Pure, *true* love was what Olaf was showing her right now—sacrifice. And, she realized, that was exactly what Kristoff had been showing her all along. She had just been too blind to see it.

Love was telling someone the truth even when they didn't want to hear it, like Kristoff had done when he pointed out that she didn't know Hans as well as she thought she did. It was putting others before yourself, like Olaf had just done, or like she had done when she went up the North Mountain to find Elsa. It was Kristoff racing back to the castle because he thought that what Anna needed was Hans. When, all along, she just needed Kristoff!

Kristoff loves me! The thought burst inside her like a volcano. She smiled, warmth flooding her body and filling up her heart. How had she not seen it? *Kristoff,* she thought again. *Kristoff loves me. And I . . .*

Just then, a gust of wind blew open one of the windows. Instantly, the flames began to flicker, and the small bit of warmth Anna had felt returning to her fingers and toes vanished.

"Don't worry, I've got it!" Olaf shouted, weaving and wobbling his way over to the window. He managed to pull one panel shut, but when he tried to close the second one, it wouldn't budge. "We're going to get through . . ."

The snowman's voice trailed off, and Anna craned her neck to see what had gotten his attention. All she could make out was snow. Breaking off an icicle hanging from the window, Olaf held it up to his eye. Then he gave a shout. "It's Kristoff! And Sven! They're coming back this way!"

"They . . . they are?" Anna asked. She was shaking even harder now, but she wasn't sure if it was the cold or the fact that Kristoff was coming back. To her! At least she hoped that was why he was coming back.

Olaf nodded. "He's really moving fast. I guess I was wrong," he said over his shoulder. "I guess Kristoff doesn't love you enough to leave you behind."

But she knew that wasn't true. Kristoff loved her enough to *risk* coming back even if it meant facing Hans or being rejected by her. She struggled, trying to get to her feet. "Help me up, Olaf," she said when she couldn't do it on her own. "Please."

"No, no, no, no, no!" Olaf said, wobbling back over and pushing her down on the couch. "You need to stay by the fire and keep warm."

She shook her head. "I need to get to Kristoff."

"Why?" Olaf asked, unaware of the impact his words had had on Anna.

She smiled and shrugged sheepishly.

Olaf's eyes lit up and he clasped his hands together. "Oh! I know why!" he cried happily. He began to hop around the room excitedly. Then he pointed out the window. "There's your act of true love! Right there! Riding across the fjords like a valiant, pungent reindeer king!"

Anna looked over at Olaf and smiled. She hoped the little snowman was right and that Kristoff's kiss would be the one to save her. But she wouldn't know that until she got to him. *Which I need to do*—she shivered again, more violently this time—*before it's too late.*

Chapter 30

THERE WAS NO denying it—the weather, which he hadn't thought could get worse—was definitely getting much, *much* worse. If the increasing winds and blinding snow were any indication, Elsa was running scared. Hans knew enough about her strange powers to know they were tied to her emotions, and ever since she had broken free of her cell, her emotions had been in overdrive.

And I had to go and make a big show of going after her, Hans thought as he ducked his head against another blast of arctic air. *And so here I am, out in this godforsaken storm, blind and freezing and with no clue where I'm going.*

Hans let out a groan. This was not what he had envisioned happening when he led the men to Elsa's cell. His plan had been so simple, and with Anna taken care of, it had been far less complicated as well. Now he didn't know what he was doing or what he would do when, or if, he found Elsa.

Stopping to catch his breath, Hans tried to get a sense of his surroundings. It wasn't easy. The whiteout conditions made everything look the same. The ground right in front of him was no easier to discern than the mountain he knew loomed miles in the distance. Through the howling wind he could hear the occasional groan of wood being pressed by ice, so he knew that he hadn't made it past the harbor. Occasionally, when the wind relented slightly, Hans could even see small patches of blue in the sky above.

Suddenly, he saw the faintest of shadows flash a short distance ahead. The shadow flitted in and out among the snow, but as the day grew brighter, the shadow began to take on a clearer form. To Hans's delight, he saw that it was Elsa. Opening his mouth to let out a shout of victory, he quickly clamped it shut. It would do no good to give away his presence. Not yet, at least.

As quietly as possible, which luckily wasn't hard on the soft, snow-covered ground, Hans began to close the distance between him and Elsa. When he was only a few feet away, he slowed his pace. Observing the queen, he saw that she was struggling as much as he was against the weather. The flight from the cell must have exhausted her, and she no longer seemed as in control of the storm as she had been before. That was just what Hans wanted to see. In her weakened state, Elsa would be far easier to kill.

"Elsa!" he shouted, pleased when he saw her startle. "You can't run from this!" Taking a few steps forward, he stepped right in front of the queen.

Seeing Hans, Elsa stepped back nervously. "Just take care of my sister," she begged as another gust of wind violently whipped the bottom of her dress around her ankles.

Hans bit back a cruel laugh. Did Elsa honestly think she was in any position to ask *him* for favors? He was the one in control. He alone knew all that had transpired. The queen had no idea. She didn't know that he had locked Anna in a room and left her to die. She didn't know that he wasn't the lovesick prince he had made himself out to be or that he had plotted and planned his way to her throne. He could pretend, for just a few minutes longer, that he cared about Anna. He could use that to bring Elsa down. "Your sister?" he said, trying to sound distraught. "She returned from the mountain weak and cold. She said you froze her heart."

"What?" Elsa said, shaking her head. "No."

Hans watched in delight as Elsa's face crumpled. *Love,* he thought bitterly. *It only serves to make one weak—even one as powerful as Elsa.*

As he readied himself to deliver his final blow, Hans put a hand on the hilt of his sword. "I tried to save her, but it was too late," he said. "Her skin was ice. Her hair turned white . . ." As he detailed Anna's physical deterioration, Elsa sunk to her knees. Each word seemed to stab at her more painfully than the sword he held at his side ever could. "Your sister is dead," Hans finished. "Because of *you.*"

As the words left his mouth, Elsa let out a moan and dropped her head into her hands. Watching her, Hans felt a surge of pride. Once again, he had taken a situation that seemed out of his control and molded it until he came out the victor.

I honestly couldn't have made that turn out any better. Unless, of course, I figured out a way to make the snow . . .

. . . stop?

The snow, he realized suddenly, *had* stopped. Hans corrected himself. It hadn't stopped—it had frozen.

All around him, the snow hung suspended in midair. The wind had ceased to blow. Elsa, the epicenter of it all, sat motionless. If Hans hadn't known better, he would have thought he was looking at a still life. Despite himself, Hans was awed by the beauty and power of the moment, and he took his hand off his sword.

He was witnessing something as foreign and unbelievable to him as magic—the grief that came from the loss of true love. *Does she regret it all? Does she wish she had the chance to say good-bye?*

Shaking his head, Hans pulled out his sword and stepped toward Elsa. There was no point in trying to get inside Elsa's head. Love was an emotion for the weak, and he needed to strike while Elsa was at her weakest. Raising his sword, he took a step closer. It was time to put an end to this winter, and to Elsa, once and for all.

CHAPTER 31

WHITE AND BLUE. That's all Anna could see and all she could feel. The world around her was blindingly white, snow blasting at her from every direction. Looking down, she saw that her hands were now an icy blue.

Grand Pabbie had been right. She was turning to ice.

Bowing her head, Anna struggled to take another step forward. But the howling wind pushed back against her like a brick wall. Even in her healthiest state, Anna would not have been able to make it far in these conditions. Now, weakened by the ice in her heart, it was almost impossible. When she breathed, it felt like she was inhaling sharp knives that ripped at her lungs. Her eyes stung and teared, leaving trails of ice on her reddened cheeks. Her toes had gone numb long ago, and she was sure that even her hair was frozen by now. Still, she knew she needed to reach Kristoff.

"Kristoff!" she shouted as loudly as she could. But the wind whipped her words away almost before they left her mouth. "Kristoff!"

The pit in her stomach grew. She wasn't sure how much longer she was going to be able to hold out. It felt as though she were pulling her legs through quicksand, the limbs heavy and cumbersome. Still, she would not give up. She was going to find Kristoff. She *had* to find Kristoff. If for nothing else than to see him one last time. To tell him that she cared for him, too.

Pain seared through Anna. Pain worse than any she had felt yet and pain that seemed to now linger in her heart. Clutching her chest, she closed her eyes. Spots flashed behind her eyelids, pulsing in time to her slowing heart. With her eyes squeezed shut, she felt rather than saw a ray of sun break through the clouds above and then, to her surprise and relief, the wind faded.

Anna opened her eyes.

The storm had stopped—completely. Snowflakes hung in midair, their unique patterns twinkling in the weak light. The wind was gone and with it the persistent howling and biting chill. It was as if they were suspended in some sort of giant snow globe.

Slowly, things that had been rendered invisible by the storm began to take shape. The ships that had been trapped in the frozen fjord began to reappear, their snow-covered decks warped and their sails torn and beaten. Turning her head, Anna could see the walls of Arendelle and the castle beyond. She could just make out the silhouettes of people clustered together atop the wall, their tiny arms waving.

In the silence of the stilled storm, new noises were amplified. The creaking of the ice under her feet sounded like gunshots and the wooden hulls let out loud moans. Even Anna's own body sounded loud to her ears. Her jagged, sharp breaths rattled, and her bones seemed to crack with the slightest of movements. The horrifying sounds of her failing body were too much for Anna and, with effort, she started to lift her hands to her ears to block it all out when she heard a noise that was anything but horrifying.

"Anna!" Kristoff's warm, booming voice echoed across the fjord.

Looking up, Anna saw him running toward her. His hair was falling in his eyes and his cheeks were bright red. He was breathing hard, but he showed no signs of slowing. In fact, when he saw Anna, his pace increased.

"Kristoff!" she tried to shout back to him. But her voice was nearly gone, and all that came out was a whisper. It didn't matter, though. Because Kristoff had found her! He was going to be able to save her! All she had to do was make it a few more—

Before she could finish that thought, the unmistakable sound of a sword being pulled from its scabbard came from somewhere close by. As if in slow motion, Anna turned around. Elsa sat on the ground not ten feet away. Her sister's head was bowed and her shoulders hunched, as though she were carrying the weight of the world. A sob of relief started to form in Anna's throat. Elsa was here! Right here! And so was Kristoff! Everything was going to work out.

Kristoff would save her with his kiss, and Anna could tell Elsa how sorry she was for everything.

But Anna had forgotten the sound of the sword. And now, instantly, she saw exactly where it had come from. Standing behind the despondent Elsa was Hans. His sword was drawn, and he was poised to strike.

This couldn't be happening. Elsa wasn't even supposed to be here. She was supposed to be up in her castle, and Hans was supposed to be back in Arendelle pretending to be a good guy. Yet here they were, both out on the fjord, and from the murderous look in Hans's eye, he was eager to put an end to Elsa once and for all.

Some people, Anna thought, remembering Olaf's sweet words, *are worth melting for.* That was true love. Anna loved her sister. And, she realized now as Hans raised his sword for the final blow, she needed to keep Elsa safe.

Looking back over her shoulder, she saw that Kristoff, unaware of what was unfolding in front of him, was still racing across the fjord. She gave him a small, sad smile, and his gait slowed, confusion flickering across his face followed by fear as he caught sight of Hans. *I'm sorry, Kristoff,* she said silently. With the last of her remaining strength, she turned around. Then, letting out a cry, she flung herself in front of her sister. She had only a moment to raise her arm in a feeble attempt to protect Elsa and then, with a *whoosh*, she felt Hans's sword swing down at her . . .

Am I dead? Anna wondered. *Is this what it feels like?*

In the moment before she had flung herself in front of Elsa, her body had felt like it weighed a thousand pounds. Her limbs had finally gone completely numb with cold, and she had been unable to draw a breath. Yet her mind had been alert, and she found herself observing everything as though from a great distance. In slow motion, she had seen Hans's sword swing through the air and registered the look of shock on his face as the sword collided with her hand and he was thrown back into the air.

She had heard Elsa's frightened shout and sensed Kristoff as, too late, he reached her side. In the distance, she thought she had even heard the collective gasps of those watching from the walls of Arendelle.

Then everything had gone silent.

For one long moment, Anna felt as though she were wrapped in a cocoon. The light grew dim, and it seemed like her body was suspended in midair. She seemed to be neither here nor there, but trapped somewhere in between.

She struggled, trying to surface as though coming up for air after a long dive. But she kept getting sucked back down into the murky depths.

Suddenly, the pressure in her lungs began to relax, and her body was infused with a warmth that made her toes and fingers tingle. She felt her sister's arms wrap around her and squeeze tightly. Shadowy figures began to appear in the periphery of her vision, and the muffled voices became clearer. Her heart began to pound against her chest and, finally, she felt movement return to her limbs. Opening her eyes, the first thing Anna saw was the top of her sister's head, nestled against her shoulder. Elsa's body shook with violent sobs.

For a moment, Anna didn't move. She knew she could, but she wanted to make this hug last. She had waited for so long to feel her sister's arms around her, and she wasn't going to waste a minute of it. Finally, ever so slowly, she lowered her own arm, wrapping it around Elsa.

"Oh, *Elsa*."

In her arms, Anna felt Elsa stiffen in shock and then, with a cry of joy, Elsa hugged her tighter. The sisters stood there, clinging to each other.

"You sacrificed yourself for me?" Elsa said, finally pulling back.

"I love you," Anna replied simply. She wanted to tell her sister what she had learned about love, but she was still weak, and she found herself unable to go on.

Luckily, Olaf didn't have the same problem. The little snowman was dancing excitedly back and forth in front of the sisters, his twig hands clasped together. Finally, unable to contain himself any longer, he popped his head off his body and raised it so his face was level to the sisters'. "An act of true love will thaw a frozen heart!" he announced happily.

Anna cocked her head. Did Olaf mean what she thought he meant? Whose heart had been thawed? Hers or Elsa's? She hadn't jumped in front of the sword to save herself. The thought hadn't even crossed her mind. She had done it because she wanted to save her sister. She had done it because . . . And then it hit her. What the trolls had said, what Olaf had known all along, what she had been too blind to see. She *did* know how to love. She loved Elsa. More than anything in the world. And she would have done anything to protect her. Climbed a mountain, faced off against Hans, even jumped in front of a sword being swung by her evil ex-fiancé. Her act of love toward Elsa had broken through the magic. Smiling, she turned and looked at her sister.

"Love . . . will thaw," Elsa said softly. Then, meeting her gaze, louder. "Love . . . of course!"

"Elsa?" Anna asked. Had her sister figured out what she herself had discovered only a moment before—that Anna's was not the only heart that needed thawing?

As if she could hear Anna's thoughts, Elsa nodded. "Love," she repeated.

And then she raised her hands into the air. In one glorious, elated swoop of her fingers, she shot magic up high into the sky.

As the torrent shot into the air, the clouds above Arendelle seemed to burst apart, revealing a brilliant blue sky. The air began to warm, and the snow all over the kingdom started to melt and disappear. Just like Anna and Elsa, Arendelle was getting a fresh start. Flowers and plants snapped to life, more beautiful and fragrant than before, eager to soak up the sun. Squinting, Anna could make out children running around the docks of the kingdom, playing in the small puddles that had only moments before been snowbanks.

Love. All along that had been the key. Love for Anna had kept Elsa isolated and alone, scared to hurt the person she cared the most about. Frightened to live a life absent of love, Anna had flung herself into the arms of the first man she met. Consequently, seeing the power of true love in the eyes of Olaf and Kristoff had pulled her free and opened her eyes to Hans's real nature. And ultimately, love, it seemed now as Anna watched her sister put an end to winter, had proven more powerful than even the greatest magic. The bond of sisterhood and the sacrifices they had both made had been able to thaw everything that day. *Now,* Anna thought, *Elsa and I can begin again. We can have the life we were denied for so long.*

Out on the fjord, the ground beneath Anna's feet began to shake. The ice started to crack and, for one terrifying moment, she wondered if they would all find themselves swimming. But then, to her delight, the ice gave way completely, and she felt herself lifted into the air. Looking down, she saw they were standing on the deck of a ship that had been obscured beneath snow. Now the wood glistened and gleamed in the returning sun, making everything sparkle.

With one last wave of her hands, Elsa drew all the remaining snow together. Anna watched in disbelief as the snow rose into the air, its shape shifting and changing until it formed the most beautiful, perfect snowflake she had ever seen—and then, with a burst, it exploded like a firework. As it faded from view, all that was left was a perfect, sunny, warm July day.

"I knew you could do it," Anna said, looking over at her sister and smiling proudly.

Elsa smiled back and opened her mouth to say something. But she was stopped by Olaf's happy-go-lucky voice.

"Hands down," he said, "this is the best day of my life . . . and quite possibly the last."

Looking over at the little snowman, Anna let out a gasp. In the warm sunshine, he had begun to melt. But he didn't seem to care. A blissful smile was spread wide across his face, and he had his head raised toward the sun, feeling, for the first time, what he had always dreamed about—summer.

Anna swung her gaze back at her sister. *Do something,* she implored silently. She was glad that the winter was over, but she couldn't imagine Arendelle without her new friend. Elsa seemed to feel the same way. "Hang on, little guy," she said gently.

Once more, Elsa waved her hands. A swirl of cold air shot out of her fingertips and wrapped itself around Olaf, instantly refreezing him. Then, just to be safe, she created a small cloud from which a soft snow fell constantly.

"Hey!" Olaf shouted happily, wobbling this way and that and laughing as the cloud followed him. "My own personal flurry!'

Anna laughed joyously. *I have a feeling having a sister with ice powers is going to be amazing,* she thought. *We'll be able to go skiing in August if we want. We will never need to hire an ice sculptor for events. We could throw a skating party every summer! And,* she thought, once again amazed by the turn of events, *we can do it all together. Everything really has turned out perfectly.*

Then she heard a groan.

Well, *almost* everything.

There was still the teeny tiny issue of Prince Hans.

Looking over, Anna saw that he was lying on the ground, holding his head and moaning. *Oh, right,* Anna thought. She vaguely remembered hearing his cry as his sword shattered against her frozen body. He must have been knocked out, she realized. Which was fine by her.

Unfortunately, Anna was not the only one who had seen him. Kristoff, who up until then had been standing quietly and patiently to the side, took one look at Hans and his fists clenched. Raising his hands, he began to stalk toward Hans.

Actually, Anna thought, *I think I'd like to handle this personally.* Reaching out, she put a hand on Kristoff's arm as he passed by her. Gently, she shook her head. "Uh, uh," she said, giving him a long look. *I can take care of this myself,* she told him with her eyes. Then, turning, she made her way over to Hans.

Seeing his ex-fiancée approaching, Hans struggled to his feet. He looked around, confused by the suddenly warm weather, not to mention a moving, living Anna. "But . . . but . . . she froze your heart," he stuttered.

"The only frozen heart around here is yours," she said, her voice ice-cold.

Turning to leave, Anna paused. She looked over at her sister, who had suffered so much because of Hans. Then she met Kristoff's eyes and saw the anger he was barely containing. Hans had hurt him, too. Not as deliberately, but he had hurt him nonetheless. And then she looked down at her own two hands. They had returned to their normal color, but she would never forget how cold they had been and how scared she had felt when Hans left her to die. She took a deep breath. She knew she was a princess, and princesses were supposed to be ladylike, but she couldn't just walk away from him. There was one thing she had to do.

Swiveling on her heels, she turned so she was once again facing Prince Hans of the Southern Isles. And then she pulled back her arm and punched his smug face with all her might. Her fist landed on his cheek with a resounding *thunk*, and he fell backward, flipping right over the ship's railing. A moment later there was a satisfying splash as he landed in the water below.

Now, Anna thought, as Elsa gave her a hug and Kristoff shot her a proud look, *everything is definitely perfect.*

CHAPTER 32

HOW DID EVERYTHING go so terribly wrong? Hans thought miserably. One minute, the crown and all the power it brought with it had been within reach and then, just like that, it had been snatched away from him.

Sitting inside the same room where he had imprisoned Elsa not even a day ago, Hans stared out at Arendelle. The wall, which had been ripped away by Elsa, was still missing. But it didn't matter. There was no snow to blow in, no cold to keep out. Instead, bright beams of sunlight swept across the stone floor, and a gentle breeze carried in the soft scent of salt water. In the distance, he could make out the top of the North Mountain and—closer to the kingdom—he saw the green of the trees and the bright colors of the blooming flowers. From the courtyard below, the sound of children's laughter filtered up, and Hans could make out the distinct slap of sailcloth as boats in the harbor prepared to depart.

It was idyllic.

And it made Hans sick.

Ever since he had been brought to this room, he had been replaying his last moments of freedom over and over in his head. And no matter how many different ways he looked at it, no matter how many times he tried to see where it all went wrong, he could not wrap his head around any of it. One moment he was standing over Elsa, his sword raised, ready to put an end to her once and for all and take the crown, and then . . .

. . . Anna was there, standing before his falling sword on the frozen fjord. He could still feel her blue eyes on him, judging him silently. He felt the shock that reverberated through his arm as the iron struck not Elsa, but Anna's frozen body. The instant after, he was thrown to the ground, knocked unconscious.

When he awoke moments later, everything had changed.

The snow had stopped. The clouds had disappeared and the temperature had warmed. And it was not just the weather that had thawed, Hans saw instantly. Anna and Elsa had thawed, too. The distance between them had vanished the second Anna had sacrificed herself for her sister. Then they stood, laughing and giving each other spontaneous hugs, making up for the years they had lost.

That, too, had made Hans sick.

If only I had acted just a moment sooner, Hans had thought. *Then they would never have known forgiveness. Never felt the love of a sibling again. Just like me. Just like my entire life. Elsa would have been dead. Anna would have followed soon after, and I would have taken what I deserve.*

Instead of the crown, all he had gotten was a punch in the face.

Hearing the jingling of keys outside the door, Hans looked up. "Prince Hans," a voice said from the other side of the door, startling him. "It's time to go."

"Go where?" he asked, his voice cracking.

"Home," the voice replied.

Slowly, the door creaked open. The breath hitched in Hans's chest. Two guards stood on the other side, their hands on the swords at their sides, their expressions serious.

"Stand up," one of them ordered.

Hans did as he was told. His hands shook ever so slightly as he held them out so that the other guard could tighten the manacles around his wrists. "Any way you might want to, I don't know, take them off for our little walk?" he asked hopefully.

The guard did not respond.

"It's just that, well, I am sure the queen and princess would rather I'm not paraded around town in shackles. It isn't good for political relationships and all that."

"Princess Anna said you might say something like that," the other guard said. "She told us to ignore you. She said not to believe a word that comes out of your mouth. We are to bring you straight to the harbor."

Why am I surprised? Hans thought as the two men began to escort him from the room. *Did I honestly think that Anna would overlook the fact that I tried to kill her and her sister? Or the fact that*

I tricked her into thinking I loved her? He shrugged. A part of him had, sort of. He had been so sure of himself and his plan, he had never factored in failure.

Yet he *had* failed. Completely. And if what the guards said was true and he was going home, he was never going to live that failure down.

As the reality of what was happening began to set in, Hans started to drag his feet. He struggled against the guards and tried to pull away, but the guards held on, ignoring his protests.

I can't go back. Please, I can't go back home, Hans thought desperately. But as far as the Arendelle guards were concerned, that was exactly where he was going!

CHAPTER 33

ONCE AGAIN, the Arendelle port was open. The castle gates were thrown wide, and the market was bustling. The air, rich with the warmth of a summer day, had a celebratory feeling as people hustled to and fro, happy to once again be outside.

Inside the castle, the celebratory feeling continued. The windows let in every delightful breeze, and not one door was shut. The abundance of dinner plates that Anna had found so incredible only a few days before remained out, ready for the next party or ball. The Great Hall no longer resembled a relief station. The floors had been repolished and the candles replaced, while the blankets taken from storage had been put back. Even the firewood had been recycled, used to replace fences that had been knocked down in the storm. Servants made their way down the halls, talking and giggling among themselves, amazed at their good fortune to have such a wonderful, loving queen and kind princess. All in all, the castle felt alive and rejuvenated.

And it was not just the castle that had changed. Inside her room, Anna sat at her vanity, staring at her reflection. The girl who looked back at her appeared the same as the one who had stared out just a few days before. *Yet I'm not the same at all,* Anna thought, twisting her hair. The physical differences were subtle: the white had vanished from her hair; her eyes, which had once looked so sad and lonely, were now full of hope and life; her smile now came quickly and happily. Small, subtle shifts, Anna thought, that reflected so many huge changes.

The emotional changes, Anna mused, now *those* were far less subtle. No longer did she tiptoe around the halls of her home, expecting rejection at every turn. For the past few mornings, she had burst from her bed before the sun had even risen to race to Elsa's room. They would sit for hours, catching each other up on all the things they had missed as the sun's rays lengthened across the floor. And then, together, they would start their day. Anna had shown Elsa all her favorite spots on the grounds and introduced her to Kjekk. She had shown her where Cook now hid the chocolate and, just as they had when they were young, they had tried—and failed—to take some without getting caught.

They had also adventured outside the gates. Both knew so little about life beyond the walls of the castle. Every moment brought with it a new experience: going fishing, watching a chorus of children singing in front of the small school, walking out in the fields beyond the kingdom's gates and running their hands through the now green fields of grass.

"I never thought I could be this happy," Anna had told her sister the night before as they sat in the cozy library.

"Me neither," Elsa had said softly. "I can't believe how much time I wasted hiding. I'm sorry."

Anna had shook her head. Her sister had told her all about what happened the night everything changed. Knowing the truth—that Elsa had struck her in the head by accident—had lifted a weight off both sisters' shoulders.

"You were so young when you hit me," Anna had said. "I was so young. We didn't know any better. And Mama and Papa should never have told you to hide who you are, Elsa. Who you are is beautiful and amazing. I'm the one who's sorry. Sorry that I couldn't see you were just trying to protect me."

"Oh, Anna," Elsa had said, smiling. "I love you and I have always loved you. And I always will. Let's never make the mistake of hiding things from each other—ever again."

Anna had laughed and held out a hand. "Deal," she'd said happily.

Sighing, Anna stood up from her vanity and crossed over to the window. She and Elsa had made their peace and gotten closer. But there was still one thing Anna needed to do before she could fully move on.

Out in the harbor, the ships rocked gently back and forth on their moorings while those tied to the docks pressed back and forth on their bumpers. Most of them were empty, the captains and crews delaying their departures to take advantage of the fine weather and enjoy their time in Arendelle. But several were a hive of activity. And one of them was the boat that was going to take Hans home—as soon as Anna stopped stalling and went downstairs.

The decision to send Hans back to the Southern Isles had, much to Anna's chagrin, been a group decision. Elsa, Kristoff, and Olaf had *all* wanted to weigh in. She had just wanted to get him on the boat and gone as soon as possible. Elsa, on the other hand, had wanted him to stand trial for his actions and for his attempted murder of both sisters.

"He would have put me on trial," Elsa pointed out when the group had gathered in the council chambers. "So why should I not do the same?"

"Because there would be no point," Anna had said. "Trust me, I thought long and hard about it when I was stuck in that freezing room. I came up with so many ways I would have punished him. But the best way to punish him is to make him come face-to-face with the one thing he is most scared of—going home. Let his father and brothers deal with him. If they are truly as terrible as Hans says they are . . ."

"I bet they are wonderful!" Olaf had interrupted, always seeing the positive. "Imagine! Twelve brothers! You would always have someone to play with."

Anna had smiled at Olaf's innocence. But he was probably right. All she had heard was Hans's version of his family. For all she knew, they could be the most wonderful people in the world and Hans was just the black sheep.

"Well, I, for one," Kristoff had piped up, "agree with Elsa. Hans hurt you, Anna, and he deserves to pay." He had looked over at her and given her such a warm look that Anna had blushed. They still had yet to discuss the fact that he had raced back for her. But she had learned her lesson from Hans—no use rushing into anything. Having him there was good enough—for now.

"You are all wonderful and I appreciate your advice," Anna had finally said, putting an end to the conversation. "But this is my decision. And I want him sent home."

Shaking her head to clear her thoughts, Anna turned from the window. So what was she waiting for? It was time to send that prince packing—once and for all.

Anna stood on a bluff overlooking the dock. From her vantage point, she could see the guards dragging Hans back to his ship. The last time she had seen him, he had been splashing around in the water, looking fittingly like a drowning rat. Now he was back on dry land and he once again looked like the handsome prince that had so cleverly fooled her. It stung a bit to see him so composed, but not as much as Anna had feared.

She had written a detailed account of Hans's crimes to be sent back home with him. Southern Isles justice would surely be more terrible than any punishment that might befall him in Arendelle. Any time Anna started to pity Hans for being sent home to his father, she reminded herself that Hans was a grown man—he was responsible for his actions, no matter how miserable his home had been.

She heard a horn blow on the deck of Hans's ship. It was time for them to set sail. Grabbing Hans by the arms, the guards threw him onto the brig.

"Good-bye, Hans," Anna said softly, knowing he wouldn't hear her voice over the waves lapping against the boat. But she didn't care. Saying good-bye was more for her than for him. It was the closure *she* needed. Turning, she made her way down the long path toward the stairs that led back to the palace. She would never forget Hans, even if she wanted to. But she was not going to allow him to hurt her any longer. She wasn't going to let him turn her heart cold or ruin her outlook on life or love. No. Prince Hans had hurt her. That would never change. But she wasn't going to let him win by taking away another moment of her happiness. She wasn't going to let him be a mistake she couldn't overcome.

Reaching the top of the steps, Anna paused. Her shoulders already felt lighter, her heart already fuller. Looking up, a smile spread across her face. *And speaking of fixing mistakes . . .* she thought. There—tucked behind one of the fishermen's stalls—stood a shiny new sleigh. *Kristoff's* shiny new sleigh, to be exact. The wood gleamed in the bright sun, and the leather harness creaked, ready to be broken in. Anna clapped her hands together. Kristoff was going to love it. *I can't wait to see his face,* she thought as she resumed walking. *I bet he turns all red and starts tugging at his hair and gets all embarrassed. He'll probably want to show Sven right away. Or he'll start talking like Sven. . . .* The thought made her smile even broader. Getting the sleigh made had been her secret ever since Elsa had ended winter. She didn't even know if Kristoff remembered her promise—to get him a new sleigh—but it didn't matter. She *had* made the promise, and she couldn't wait to deliver.

Letting out a happy little laugh, Anna increased her pace. Until this moment, she had wondered if she would have any regrets about all the events that had transpired. But now she was sure: what-ifs were pointless when the here and now was so much more fantastic. She had three wonderful new friends, the castle had come back to life and, most importantly, she had a life full of countless possibilities now that love had opened the door between her and her sister. And the sooner she got away from the dock—the sooner Hans was nothing but a memory—the sooner she could start living that amazing life.

And that is just what she did.